ADMIT YOU WANT ME

TAYLOR HOLLOWAY

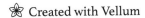

TAYLOR HOLLOWAY
ROMANCE

'Former All-American Quarterback Ward Williams' is absurdly hot and charming.
He's also infuriatingly cocky, a notorious player, my best friend's brother, and my brand-new boss.

Ward loves to tease me.
His favorite topics include what an innocent little bookworm I am and our unbelievably hot one-night stand in college. Oops.
Did I mention we'll be working side by side in his bar all summer long?

I can't stand how he makes me blush and squirm, but I also can't deny the feeling I get when he's protecting me from handsy drunks and evil ex-boyfriends.
His penetrating gaze, easy smile, and alpha attitude are testing my resolve.
My defenses are already starting to crumble.

I can't let him know how incredible he was that night.
How much it hurt to lose him.

Or how much I want to be back in his strong, steady arms.

But I just don't know if I can look into his arrogant, knowing eyes and admit how much I want him...

Admit You Want Me is a sweet and sexy second chance romance featuring a bold alpha hero who's about to meet his match in a feisty, smart-mouthed heroine.

All the books in the Lone Star Lovers series share characters, locations, and events but can also be read as standalone stories. This is the first book in the series.

PROLOGUE

EMMA

"COME ON, EMMA!" Kate cried, banging on my bedroom door for the fifth or sixth time. "You can't hide in there forever. I'm sure you look fine. People are going to be here soon."

I glanced at the clock. She was right. It was almost go time. I slid into my green, marabou trimmed boudoir slippers and straightened my sheer tights. I had a bad feeling that I looked more than a little bit like a stripper.

"Just a second," I yelled. "I'm almost ready."

I frowned at my reflection in the mirror, poked at my fake eyelashes, and adjusted the mesh and wire wings strapped to my back. The wings were already annoying me, but not as much as the length of my dress.

My Tinkerbell costume was much sexier and more revealing than I'd thought it would be when I bought it online. My boobs were threatening to spill out of the bright green satin bustier, and the nearly transparent matching skirt barely made it halfway down my thighs. This is what I got for trusting the photos on eBay. It would just have to do. The only other option at this point was cutting a couple of eye holes in a sheet and going to our Halloween party as a ghost.

"Wow," Kate stammered when I opened the door a second later. "You look *amazing!*"

I smiled nervously. "It's not too slutty?"

Kate shook her head. "It's the exactly right amount of slutty. The fact that it's your real hair up there in that silly bun is what makes it."

Kate was blonde for Halloween too, but her flowing, gold Rapunzel hair was a wig. Our Halloween party was Disney themed and our apartment looked a bit like a five-year-old's birthday party (but with way more booze). I grabbed myself a cup of the pink punch and tried to work myself up for being social.

My current pair of wings notwithstanding, I was not a natural social butterfly like Kate. If it wasn't for her, I probably wouldn't have many friends. Moving in with my best friend at the beginning of my sophomore year was the best decision I could have made for my social life, even if it meant living inside a kegger one night a week. This Halloween party promised to be no exception.

Costumed people began to trickle into our apartment,

armed with beer, smiles, and excitement. I struggled to fit in. After the disaster that was my freshman year at a school back east, coming to the University of Texas had been a case of serious culture shock. They don't call it a party school for nothing, and I'm a natural introvert and a bit of a nerd. Before coming here, I'd never had a drop to drink.

Unluckily for my liver, I was also a quick study. I'd determined that I hated most beer, most wine, and anything with a harsh liquor taste, but I loved anything sweet and fruity.

"Are fairies your age supposed to be drinking, Tinker-bell?" someone asked me when I went to grab another hard apple cider from the fridge. I spun around, surprised.

Kate's brother, Ward, was leaning against the door. I hadn't realized that he'd followed me. I straightened abruptly, hoping my ass hadn't been totally exposed by my tiny skirt when I bent over.

My breathing sped up and I felt myself biting down on my bottom lip nervously. The hand not clutching a bottle sent fingertips to my hemline and found that my skirt had ridden up a bit. Yeah, he'd definitely just seen my ass. His cocked eyebrow and even cockier smile told me that he had appreciated it, too. I felt a hot flush burn my cheeks.

It didn't help that he seemed to know exactly what he did to me every time he came around, although this was only the third time I'd met him since Kate and I moved in together in August. I couldn't hide my attraction to him at all. He teased me mercilessly at every opportunity, and it felt like he did it just to see me blush. He clearly found how bookish, quiet, and prone to embarrassment I was simply hilarious.

I wasn't shy for his entertainment. I *wished* I could be different. But I would never be an extrovert like Ward, or his sister. Even dressed up like Tinkerbell and pumped full of alcohol, I was still just doomed to be a wallflower.

Ward and I stared across the kitchen at each other. Usually, I turned into a stammering mess whenever he was around. Thanks to the magic of alcohol, that wouldn't be happening tonight.

I flicked my gaze up and down his figure and then did my best to tear my eyes away again. It was all I could do not to sigh dreamily. Broad shoulders and an obviously muscled chest narrowed to a slim waist and long legs. Powerful, sinuous arms ended in large, strong-looking hands. But it was his classically handsome face, with fair skin, dark blue eyes, an aquiline nose, and dark curly hair, that made my heart pound against my ribs.

"Who are you, the morality police?" I smiled at him confidently and floated across the kitchen floor toward him. I was buzzed and feeling good. Brave. For once I was brave. "I might be underage, but at least I follow directions. You're not even wearing a costume." I leveled a finger at his chest and pushed him back an inch. He laughed lightly.

Ward was dressed up as a football player, which was

not a costume, because he *was* a football player for the Texas Longhorns. He'd actually graduated last May, but was in town for Kate's birthday, which was two days after Halloween.

"Sure, I am," he replied, grabbing my hand and tracing the logo with my finger. "This is the wrong team."

I thought that red color looked unusual. I shrugged and smiled up at him. "You can't expect me to know that. I don't have much interest in sports." We were still almost holding hands. His enveloped mine completely. I liked the feeling.

"Hmm. What do you have an interest in, Tinkerbell?" His voice was soft, and there was something hot and heavy in his gaze.

"Emma," I corrected automatically, still not pulling my hand away. I didn't want him to get in the habit of calling me Tinkerbell.

Ward laughed at my answer. "Oh, so you're self-obsessed?" He shrugged. "At least you're honest. Most girls really try to hide that, at least at first."

I giggled at him and my tone turned teasing. "*Don't call me Tinkerbell*. And I have lots of interests. But what about you? Do you have any outside of football or is it all just visions of sweaty men with balls in your head?"

He smirked and set the beer he was holding down on the counter with a decisive clink. His response was slow and suggestive. "Well now, I just have all sorts of interests beyond that." His native, Texas drawl gave the words a few extra syllables we didn't have in Connecticut. I smiled shyly up at him and listened as he continued. "For one, I'm finding myself very interested in you, Emma."

My lips parted in surprise. Ward was *interested* in me? As in, *romantically* interested? Interested in sexy-fun-times with me? The fact that we were standing alone, basically holding hands in the darkened kitchen, suddenly percolated through my alcohol-soaked brain. He seemed to realize it too and straightened. He blinked like he'd just been awoken from a trance, releasing my hand, which I pressed to his chest. I could hardly believe I was touching him. I stared at the hand like it belonged to someone else, and then looked up at him.

The look in his eyes suggested that he was thinking us through, just like me. He was Kate's brother, no longer a student, and definitely not going to stick around. I was on the rebound from the world's worst relationship, painfully shy, semi-drunk, and essentially wearing lingerie in public. We'd spent almost all of our time at this party until this point trading pointed jabs. But now I had a very different sort of exchange in mind.

Before I could overthink anything, I leaned up and up —he was much taller than my five-two—and kissed him. He wrapped his arms around my waist, crushing my stupid wings and then mumbling an apology against my lips. I could hear his heart beating hard as he pressed me closer into his chest, and he teased my tongue mercilessly with his until I was breathless. A dull, throbbing ache was starting in my core, and any silly things like consequences receded in importance. I only needed to fix that needy ache. The sound of someone laughing in the room beyond pulled us back to the moment. We needed to get out of this kitchen.

"Come on," I told him, pulling him towards the hall. "My room is this way."

He hesitated. "Emma, in three days I have to go back to —" he started to say. I shook my head and cut him off with another kiss.

"I know," I told him when I pulled away. I leaned up to play with the soft tendrils of dark hair that curved around his ear, and then leaned up to whisper, "I'm not asking you to go steady." He shivered and squeezed my waist.

"Are you sure?" he asked again. Distantly, I admired his willingness to be honest about what he was offering me and to obtain my consent. He wasn't offering love, or friendship, or even companionship. Just... right now. Just tonight. Impulsively, I decided it could be enough.

In that moment, I didn't care that this would be very, very temporary. I was taking a risk and part of me knew I'd pay for it later, but at that second... I wanted to be the sort of girl who did fun and spontaneous things. I wanted to be brave. I wanted to be the girl who could recover from the last asshole I'd been with and come out swinging. I'd never done anything remotely like this before, but I found myself more excited than scared. Maybe I was channeling my inner, plucky Tinkerbell. Or maybe I was just dumb, drunk, and horny.

Whatever the reason was, my desire was simple. My answer was simple too.

"I know when to admit what I want, Ward. Do you?"

He smiled a slow, crooked smile, and then followed me back to my room.

1

EMMA

THREE YEARS LATER...

I'd gone to twelve years of primary and secondary school. Four more years of undergraduate university. One year of graduate school. Almost two solid decades of formal education and what was I doing on a sunny afternoon in September? Mopping the filthy floor of a bar. All because my landlord wouldn't let me pay my rent in poems and essays. Such was the life of a starving artist and student.

My new boss and old friend, Kate, was easing me into my first day at the Lone Star Lounge with a little light manual labor. We'd been roommates a few years ago when we were both undergrads and had been friends ever since. I was lucky she could hook me up with this waitressing gig when I really needed it, even if it wasn't exactly my dream job.

Coming back from my extended study abroad in the UK to find my grad school advisor on maternity leave had meant a sudden lack of stipend for me. I was planning on working as a teaching assistant this semester and had to scramble to find something last minute to make ends meet. I may have been a bit over-educated for bar work, but I could still mop and scrub with the best of them. I've secretly always found cleaning to be very satisfying.

"The early afternoons are usually super dead during the school year," Kate told me from her position behind the register. She wasn't kidding. There were only a few patrons, all nursing drinks or happily ensconced in their laptops. "I'm going to go work on some stuff in the office for a few minutes. Will you be okay by yourself for a while?"

I resisted the urge to be sarcastic or snippy and put a pleasant smile on my face. "Sure. I got this."

It wasn't Kate's fault that I was sulking and irritable. She was a great friend. She'd also been a great teacher so far, instructing me in the little particulars of serving patrons and tending bar here. No. It was something else that had me all worked up. With Kate in the other room, and Willie —the other employee—distracted by his newspaper, I couldn't resist the masochistic impulse to tune the TV behind the bar into the source of my foul, irrational mood.

I was probably one of only a handful of people in the

world that knew that CSPAN was playing the award ceremony for the United States Poet Laureate today. It's also probable that I was one of only a handful of people who cared. But there I was, caring so deeply about who would be selected as this year's national poet that my blood pressure was high, and my face was flushed.

Up on the screen above the bar, the camera found the man I was looking for: Adam Barnstead, PhD. Brilliant writer. Gifted scholar. Consummate liar. Total asshole. And finalist for today's prize. An esteemed professor of literature and my former mentor. My former lover.

Everything in my life seemed to keep drawing me back into his destructive orbit like a comet around a black hole. His gravity well was too deep, and my inertia was too weak to escape. Even watching him now felt like a personal failure of will. Like an aching, open wound or a burst blister, seeing him caused me physical pain. All these years later and my heart was still raw and bleeding over Adam.

If he wins Poet Laureate while I'm working as a glorified janitor, I'm going to fucking scream.

As I watched, the announcer smiled and congratulated all the finalists. He extended his handshake and the award, however, to an older woman with graying hair. She beamed and cried as she accepted, fanning her hands elatedly like she'd just won an Oscar. I could hardly believe my eyes. Another writer had just won the position Adam coveted. He lost. The bastard lost. Today was Adam's turn to stand on the sidelines while his hopes and dreams burned up and compressed into a singularity of empty nothingness. His turn to feel his pride get ripped in two. It was clear from his face that he'd been sure he would win.

Adam's almost-handsome and ever-smiling face turned shocked. Then anxious, confused, and ashen. Then, at last, utterly blank. Although his smile returned after a beat, it now looked painted on. Mine, however, had never been more genuine. He would have to start his new job at the University of Texas without this feather in his cap.

His expression made me remember when he made me feel like that: small and insignificant, weak, and fragile. Stretched so thin by shame, failure, and mortification that I might tear apart. Adam ran his hands through the salt-and-pepper chestnut hair at his temples and looked, for once, his age: forty-three.

Behind his horn rim glasses, his eyes were focused murderously on the winner as disappointment gave way to something more malignant. Dark, envious energy glittered in his hazel eyes. In answer, pure schadenfreude suffused through me like a drug, electrifying every synapse with vicarious, uncharitable pleasure. There wasn't a thing he could do.

He deserved to lose. In fact, he deserved to lose everything. At least this was a decent start.

I'd been a *freshman* in college when he used me. Just nineteen years old. I thought I'd been in love with him, and he said he was in love with me. I was really just a toy. Another pretty coed who was too naïve, too proud, and too dumb to listen when a grad student tried to tell me what Adam really was. Like a fool, I'd told her she was just jealous.

My humiliation was a distant and unimportant memory as I watched Adam squirm on the podium.

While I was basking in the glow of heartfelt revenge, I heard the door behind me swing open. What started as a slight turn of my head became a fully-fledged three-hundred-and-sixty-degree rotation of my body when I realized who had just walked in the door. My battered little heart did a somersault.

Ward Williams. Kate's brother. I knew this was coming —*he owned this bar*—but I was still unprepared. He hadn't noticed me yet. I prayed it would stay that way for a while longer. I hadn't seen him since our one-night stand several years back, and still felt awkward and ashamed about the whole thing. I'd known what I was getting myself into, but I'd still cried the next day when I woke up and he was gone.

I wished it had never happened. The night I spent with Ward was the night I'd learned that I wasn't the type of girl who could do 'no strings.' It might work for some girls, but it just made me feel empty and unwanted, especially after the earth-shattering sex we'd had. I hated feeling like I was disposable. I'd promised Kate I could handle seeing Ward again, but now that I was seeing him, I wasn't so sure.

Kate had told me all about Ward's early retirement from the NFL and the collapse of his relationship with his fiancée. She told me that these days he drifted from hookup to hookup, never dating or getting attached. Just for a second, I fantasized he was going to walk right over to me and strike up a conversation and things would pick up right where they left off.

Ward joined a group of guys at a table to my left, poured himself a beer from their pitcher and settled in with fist bumps and friendly teasing. I didn't even attempt not to stare. He was attracting my focus like a sailor looking for a lighthouse in a hurricane, even though I had been so intensely interested in the Poet Laureate ceremony a moment before.

He deserved to be stared at.

Those deep blue eyes finally flicked my way a moment later. I suddenly became extremely interested in the patch of floor I was mopping. I pretended not to notice that he elbowed one of his friends and inclined his head in my direction. Whatever the question was, the other men at the table shook their heads. I struggled to avoid tripping over my own two feet. Ward was watching me. They all were.

Ward continued to stare at me as I mopped, long after his friends had lost interest. He was drinking me in above the rim of his beer, and I felt a hot blush creep across my face. I stole furtive glances at him, and in between, I could almost feel the weight of his gaze on my body as I moved.

Was he drawn to me like I was to him? Did I make his pulse race? Did I make his breath burn?

Why does this guy who I haven't seen in years command my attention?

The frustration reminded me of the spectacle of revenge I now sought to enjoy.

I glanced back at the television and Adam still looked miserable on the live feed of the awards ceremony. His face was still deliciously pained. I hardly got to relish it, however, because one of Ward's buddies crossed the room, reached up over the bar and changed the channel to football.

I was sure he didn't realize I was the one who turned on the ceremony. I weighed my desire to bask in my ex's misery with the possibility of coming into conflict with a customer.

"Excuse me," I said, forcing my voice to be as honey-sweet and friendly as I could when I wanted to get back to watching Adam's misery as quickly as possible. "I was actually watching that."

The guy shrugged. "Really?"

I nodded seriously. "Yes."

"Well, can you watch it later on YouTube?" He seemed mystified by the idea that I might not want to watch football.

I bit my lip and said nothing. I didn't need to get into an altercation with a customer, but I really wanted to watch the ceremony. Ward arrived next to his friend a second later. He cast his glittering sapphire eyes over me curiously. He was even better looking up close.

"Hello there, Emma," he drawled, grinning. "It's been ages. What have you been up to?"

He did remember me. Should I be flattered?

"I just got back from studying in Europe." The way he was looking at me made me feel feverish and lightheaded. I looked at Ward's dumb friend who turned off my show. "Could you please turn the channel back?"

Ignoring the issue at hand, Ward was smiling at me. "So, you haven't been avoiding me these past few years?" His tone was teasing.

Of course, I've been avoiding you.

"Don't flatter yourself." I said with a nervous grin. I turned to his friend, "Could you change it back to CSPAN, please?" I pointed up at the screen.

Ward looked up at it in fake-looking surprise and then down at me, shaking his head. "You can't be serious. I didn't know anyone actually watched that channel." Ward looked over to his friend and must have telepathically communicated with him, because the guy returned to his chair, leaving us alone. Ward was wearing that teasing look that he'd worn at that Halloween party four years ago. I got the feeling he was *trying* to get a rise out of me, to test me or mess with me. He must enjoy seeing me blush and struggle to stick up for myself. I could only imagine that I was as red as a lobster now, but I wasn't going to let myself melt in front of him. Not this time.

What makes you think I'll just give up on what I want? I didn't say it. There was no point in arguing with Ward. He was as stubborn as his sister. I simply smiled, leaned my mop against the bucket, and climbed atop the bar to turn my program right back on. I wasn't going to give Ward what he wanted.

Behind the bar, Willie looked up from his newspaper and raised his eyebrows at me. I shrugged and scrambled back down. Ward could stick his condescending attitude right up his hot, amazingly toned butt. Willie frowned and returned his attention to the paper. A wise choice.

"Emma, sweetheart, please turn that back to the channel it was on. My friend wants to watch the game." Ward was now back at my elbow. His voice was a bit less teasing than it had been. All across the room, patrons were beginning to tune into our little clash. Ward was now grinning from ear to ear. He was definitely enjoying seeing me get flustered.

Sweetheart?

I forced my clenched teeth open to smile at him again. "Ward, *sweetheart*, I don't really care for football. I want to watch the poet laureate ceremony." I affected an innocent face and played with the end of my ponytail.

"Why the hell would you want to watch that? It sounds incredibly boring, even by CSPAN standards." He said

'CSPAN' like I might say 'hardcore furry pornography' or 'the Miss America swimsuit competition.' I resisted the temptation to roll my eyes at him.

"What's wrong with CSPAN?" I asked. My voice, unlike his, was reasonable and pleasant, although slightly more tart than it had been. I just wanted to watch my program and was starting to lose my patience. "I was watching it. *It's educational.* No one else was paying any attention to it. Why can't you just go drink your beer with your buddies and let me work?" I truly didn't understand some men's attachment to watching grown men in tight pants throwing themselves into one another's arms. For being such a popular pastime amongst straight men, it seemed like a deeply homoerotic game. The players even swatted one another on the ass.

Ward didn't answer my question. He simply reached up again and turned off my program.

"No one wants to watch anything *educational* in a bar but you," he told me. His voice was light and teasing. "Watching some football will do you good, anyway. Think of it this way, it'll be *educational for you.*" He paused. "Unless there's an actual reason you want to watch CSPAN. Or are you just being stubborn to mess with me?"

Don't let him fool you. He's the one messing with you, I reminded myself. *Don't let him see you get annoyed. It'll only encourage him. And don't tell him why you want to watch it so badly.*

I smiled and nodded, and then, once he walked off and sat down, I clambered up on a barstool to hoist myself atop the bar. I tuned the channel back to CSPAN. I wasn't even off the barstool before I heard him clearing his throat directly behind me.

"Really?!" he asked loudly, right behind my ear.

I heard a sharp, unladylike squeak escape me. Surprise made me gasp and slip, and I turned and nearly fell backwards off the barstool. Ward's strong hands shot out to grab me, gripping my shoulders and under my knees and then setting me on my feet and pinning me to the bar before I could regain my footing.

He'd caught me. Damn, he was fast.

We were now only inches apart. My heart thudded against my ribs. His lips parted in surprise, and I remembered kissing them. My mind was a thousand miles away...

Ward was tall. At least a full foot taller than my five-one-and-three-quarter-inches. I had to look up and up to see his eyes, which looked surprised, and then confused. We stared at one another for a long, long moment.

Suddenly, he released my shoulders like I was on fire and stepped back. His face went blank as if remembering something. I was too shocked to speak, so I just stared instead.

But it was his fault I'd fallen in the first place. Belatedly, I felt myself scowling. I drew myself up to my full height—all five foot two inches—and glared.

"Come on, Emma. You've lost this round. Give it up," he ordered me before I recovered the powers of speech. With his height, there was no need for him to climb up on a barstool precariously. He just reached up around me and returned the channel to football. "Also, you really shouldn't stand on the barstools or the bar. They aren't meant to be climbed on. Perhaps you're used to dancing atop bars, but this isn't that kind of place."

He let out a small chuckle and looked me up and down appreciatively.

"Excuse you?" I hissed. He might own the bar, but Kate managed it. I dropped the sugary tone from my voice. He no longer deserved sweet Emma.

"Nobody here likes CSPAN."

"I do. Please turn it back on."

His eyebrows lifted in apparent amusement and he laughed at me while shaking his head. "Yeah, I don't think so." Perhaps being so ridiculously sexy meant women just did whatever he ordered them to do. Likely so. It was time someone knocked him down a peg. And these days, I was just the woman to do it.

"Listen Ward, you need to—" I started.

At the same time, he said, "Last time I checked, this is still my bar."

I made a dismissive, huffy little noise that silenced him —at least temporarily, because he chuckled. It wasn't exactly a dignified noise and his reaction seemed to indicate he found it cute rather than intimidating, but I used the moment to explain,

"Your bar or not, I'm a human being who doesn't appreciate being talked down to! I don't put up with jerks ordering me around for no reason and being condescending, sexist, and high-handed."

He laughed. "I'm hardly a sexist because I want to watch football. By that logic, all men are sexists." He looked down at me like he was having the time of his life. He was definitely getting off on this little spat, and it was infuriating me. Another part of me—a small but vocal part—was enjoying his attention and our fight *way too much*. I shifted from foot to foot as my brain pinged between anger and attraction. Anger won. Nobody calls me sweetheart.

"Not everyone likes football. There's no reason I shouldn't be able to mop in peace and have the TV tuned to something that isn't boring sports."

"Boring?!" He looked horrified. You'd have thought I'd just personally insulted him or blasphemed against the lord himself.

"Boring?!" I repeated Ward's previous words, complete with a rude exaggeration of his slight southern accent.

My impression only made him laugh. When he spoke, he was still grinning, "*Woman, you are in a bar. My bar. TVs in bars play sports. What the hell is going on here?*" he asked the air around him rhetorically. "Is this the twilight zone?" Clearly, he was not used to being challenged.

Willie pulled his newspaper up higher around his face, insulating himself from the conversation despite being only two feet away. I thought I could hear him sniggering behind it. Coward.

"Is it really so surreal for you that someone might stand up to you? You're a walking stereotype." I shook my head at him.

He smirked. "Says you. I bet you live entirely off a diet of quinoa, kale smoothies, and smug superiority."

I happen to like quinoa and kale smoothies.

"While I suppose you like to spend your time drooling in front of the latest Sharknado sequel when you aren't reliving your glory days on tape. I've seen your silly truck, too. Are you compensating for anything?" A couple of his buddies laughed.

He leaned in close to whisper in my ear, "You know there's absolutely nothing I need to compensate for, now don't you, Emma?" When I felt my blush burning my cheeks, his smile was knowing. His voice was soft and amused when he added, "You have no idea what's going on here right now, do you?" His utter confidence was sexy as hell. It was also obnoxious as hell. Being turned on *and* angry wasn't something that I was used to.

"Clearly, we need Kate to come and talk some sense into you. I'm going to go get her."

He nodded and sunk down on a barstool. A frustrating smile was still on his face. "Yeah, you do that, Tinkerbell."

Tinkerbell?! I stormed off toward the office, practically quivering with anger, attraction, confusion, and embarrassment. I was so stuffed full of emotion I worried I was going to spontaneously combust, and I definitely didn't want Ward to see it.

2

WARD

"Yep, there he is. Right there," Emma said, pointing at me from the doorway. Even her annoyed expression was adorable. Good to her threat, my sister was reluctantly in tow. Kate pinched the bridge of her nose in frustration like she always did when she had a headache. Kate grabbed Emma by the elbow and pulled her toward me. Emma shot me a shit-eating grin. Her look of smug superiority made me want to put her over my knee.

A thrill shot through me. She thought she was going to get *me* thrown out of my own bar? *Bring it, Tinkerbell. I remember what you look like naked.*

Kate imposed herself between us. "Ward, Emma is one of our waitresses now, so please try not to bully her into quitting during her first shift," Kate said tiredly as she approached. "Emma, as annoying as he is, I can't throw out my brother. He owns this place. I know it's going to be tough for both of you, but y'all are just going to have to figure out a way to get along."

My sister, Kate, had been telling me we needed help. She'd been prodding me for months about it, and as usual, she was right. I'd just been dragging my feet. Apparently, Kate had finally decided to stop asking and solve the problem herself. Perfectly, I might add.

Emma might be hotter than sin, and now she was here, in my bar. I had thought I'd never see her again and was happily surprised to be wrong. She was also ten pounds of opinion and attitude in a five-pound bag and was no longer hiding it under her natural shyness. The memory of our drunken one-night stand jolted through me like lightning. I was still massively attracted to her, even if she was one of Kate's best friends and, therefore, ought to be off-limits according to Kate.

Emma blinked her wide green eyes in shock. Her full, pink lips parted in disbelief and I felt a satisfied smile replacing any remaining annoyance.

"S-so, he just gets to bully me?" She asked. Her cheeks were pink, and I could tell that she couldn't believe Kate wasn't taking her side.

Kate smiled at Emma. "I've had to deal with it my whole life. Don't worry. He's mostly harmless."

Emma smirked. She clearly didn't need to be drunk to work up the courage to speak her mind anymore. Part of me was proud of her. The other part just wanted to tease her some more. How brave had Emma become?

"Were you planning on telling me you were hiring someone?" I asked my sister. "I would have liked to have been involved in the interview process. As adorable as Emma is, finding the right fit is important."

A cute pink blush spread across her face. Tinkerbell. That's precisely who she looked like to me. Right down to the bright golden hair and upturned little nose. She looked just like Tinkerbell, only dressed casually in black jeans and a white t-shirt instead of wings and a minidress this time. Pity.

"Emma, don't worry about him," Kate said, "go do what you need to do." She patted Emma comfortingly on the arm. Emma dashed off. I felt unexpectedly guilty for giving her a hard time. Had I been a jerk? Kate frowned at me. "Why did you have to rile her up on her first day?"

"I swear, I didn't start it," I protested. Kate's blue eyes, which were identical to mine in shape and color, looked completely unconvinced. She sighed at me and took a few deep breaths before speaking again. I would put money on the idea that she was counting to ten in her head to avoid yelling at me.

"Are you going to make it hard for her here? I know you two hooked up back in the day, but I thought you could both handle a professional situation. Please don't tell me I was wrong."

"Oh, for God's sake, I didn't even do anything!" I told her. "I'm not the one you need to worry about, either." I was a big boy. I didn't exactly go around making women uncomfortable for fun, especially ones as pretty as Emma; I would much rather have her like me.

"So, you'll be nice to her?" I smirked and looked over at Emma fondly while I nodded, and my sister's eyes narrowed and she instantly backpedaled. "Not *that kind of nice*. No touching."

"I'll be nice to her." I shook my head. "*I like her. I've always liked her.*" My personal feelings aside, I thought Emma had been an excellent influence on Kate. Her GPA went up considerably when they were living together. "She might be a bit snobby, but she's secretly pretty fun." Memories of our night together pinged through me like a ball hitting a combo in a pinball machine.

Kate grimaced at the look on my face. "To be honest, that's sort of what I'm worried about, too." She looked over at Emma with concern.

"Why? You think she can't keep her hands off me? I take no responsibility if she comes *on to me*." Even now, Emma was stealing glances at me that said she was interested in more than fighting. "I'm only human."

Kate's reply was a low hiss. "If you end up costing me my friend, I'll never forgive you."

We'd had this same conversation in the kitchen the morning after the Halloween party three years ago. I'd taken off before Emma woke up, promising Kate that I wouldn't touch her roommate again. It was the right decision for everyone involved. I had just started my first season in the NFL and couldn't exactly stick around, anyway. Still, I'd thought about Emma more than I wanted to admit.

"I have no intention of making your friend hate you," I replied honestly. Kate didn't look entirely satisfied by my answer, but she probably knew that was the best she was going to get. I wasn't going to promise not to touch Emma. It just wasn't going to happen. Things were different now, and we were all adults. If Emma wanted to sleep with me, I was more than game.

"Emma doesn't sleep around," Kate told me after a moment. "She's a committed relationship type of girl."

We'd had this discussion once before, too. My protestations that Emma had been okay with a casual hookup had fallen on deaf ears. Kate was convinced that I'd led Emma on or somehow tricked her. To be honest, it had been somewhat offensive then, and it was still offensive now. I might be promiscuous, but I've always been honest about it.

I shrugged. "Well then, neither of you have anything to worry about, since I'm not a committed relationship type of guy. You know that."

Kate nodded. "And don't antagonize her, either."

"I really didn't start it."

"Oh yes, you did," Emma interjected. She'd come back up to the bar to grab something and heard me defending myself. "Willie," she pleaded, "tell Kate what happened. Tell her what a jerk he was." Her irritation was back in a flash. The woman clearly wanted to win.

Predictably, Willie shook his head. "Who me? Oh, I wasn't listening." I looked over to my buddies at the table behind me, but they were also pretending not to be paying attention while attempting not to laugh. Disloyal jerks. Then again, seeing Emma again and getting her all hot and bothered was a rare treat.

"Yes, you were," Emma insisted to Willie. She was determined to win our argument. "You were definitely listening. Tell her that Ward was trying to get a rise out of me."

"Oh no, I can't Emma. I really wasn't listening. That's just my bartender face," he said sagely. "I always look like I'm listening. That's how I get such good tips."

Emma glared at him, but Willie was immune to negativity. He'd been doing this longer than we'd both been alive, combined. When I bought this bar from him four years ago, he'd taught me everything. The fact that he was silent meant a great deal more than Emma realized. He was, in his way, defending her.

When I purchased the bar from Willie, it had been an investment and an impulse buy. The Lone Star Lounge had been operating out of a converted bungalow in Austin for more than forty years and was as popular among students as it was with the Yuppie crowd. Austin had become a tech and culture Mecca, a city that more than a hundred people moved to *a day,* and I felt like I had a responsibility to preserve a piece of original Austin culture. Owning a bar had *seemed* like a cool idea as well as a solid business move. When the local institution came up for sale, I pounced.

Even so, I hadn't necessarily thought it would ever be my livelihood. But after my NFL career came to a screeching halt, my dumbass approach to money and lifestyle inflation came back to bite me in the ass. This bar rapidly became one of my only sources of income. If not for the business acumen of my sister and a heck of a lot of time and effort from the both of us, I'd have lost everything. I'd learned to respect her opinions. And occasionally, her orders. Still, I wasn't sure I would be able to obey her request of professionalism.

Oblivious to my inner conflict, Emma flicked her long gold hair at me and marched back toward her tables with a satisfied spring in her step. I had never expected her to walk back into my life and suddenly couldn't stomach the idea of her walking back out of it.

3

WARD

EMMA, who looked just like Tinkerbell whether she wanted to admit it or not, was watching me. She'd been keeping an eye on me all evening, even before we got into our little re-introductory fight. She wasn't exactly subtle about her interest. Every time my eyes slid her direction, which I found them doing often, she was suddenly looking away and blushing that adorable bright pink color. She was still very cute, I'd give her that. Better than cute. Stunningly beautiful.

I liked being stared at by a beautiful woman. Loved it. There is no better drug for the male brain than basking in the glow of an attractive female's attention. I preferred it over any legal or illegal drug I'd ever tried. I found myself daydreaming about Emma all night long.

"You know," Willie said to me about halfway through

the evening crowd, "having some more help around here isn't so bad. We're usually running on fumes by this time of night."

He'd been quieter than usual tonight. Watching me and Emma. Watching me watching Emma. Watching Emma watch me. I rolled my eyes at him. He probably thought he had us both figured out. Heck, he probably did. The man was far too good at reading people's faces.

"I take it you like her," I told him. He shrugged as if totally uninterested.

"You don't?"

I didn't reply, focusing instead on pulling the four beers that Emma needed for table three. She returned after a moment and scooped them off the bar without so much as a 'thank you.' I watched her round ass twitch back and forth as she carried them to their destination. She had a fantastic body, shaped like a perfect, petite hourglass—especially when she bent forward over a table to wipe it off, as she was doing right then. I was momentarily distracted by Emma's incredible, heart-shaped ass. Willie cleared his throat to get my attention. I looked at him in embarrassment. He'd seen me looking Emma's way while she was bent over. Willie knew I'd been staring and why. Admiring. Whatever.

"I'm not sure it's a good idea for her to be here."

"What's not to like?" Willie asked.

"That's the problem. I'm not sure if she belongs here."

"Why not?"

I busied myself with cutting some citrus for garnishes. "I would think that would be obvious to you. She's clearly just doing this because she couldn't find something better. She thinks she's too good for this place, and she's probably right." I punctuated my words with little chops of the knife.

"*Oh, do tell,*" came Emma's voice from behind me. Willie tottered off to check on the patrons at the other end of the bar, leaving me alone with my foot in my mouth. He'd set me up.

Emma looked up at me expectantly. Embarrassed, I shook my head at her after a moment.

"When will you get your PhD?" I asked her instead. "You're working on it, right? Surely you're too busy for this job."

She shook her head. "Look, you don't know a thing about me," she sighed. "I need two Cosmos and a Bud Light." Emma turned and walked away before I could say another thing, grabbing a water pitcher to make the rounds.

Part of me admired the fact that she hadn't quit on the spot earlier when I'd pushed her buttons. She was doing well tonight, if I was being totally honest. It was a busy Friday night and she'd managed to ride the rush without getting flustered. Her customers seemed happy enough, not that we ever attracted a particularly rough or demanding crowd.

"How long have you been a cocktail waitress?" I asked her the next time she arrived at the bar to grab drinks. Despite having spent the night together once, I barely knew anything about Emma. Kate was too protective of their friendship to ever feed my desire to know more.

She looked at her watch. "Four hours, thirty-six minutes, and twenty seconds."

I blinked at her in disbelief. "This is your first time waiting tables?"

"It's not exactly rocket science." She took the drinks off the bar and disappeared again.

That wasn't an answer. There's no way she'd never waited tables before, and no way Kate would hire her if she hadn't. Emma was using the register, pulling drinks off the taps, and moving with the grace of someone used to carrying a heavy tray of drinks. I must have been too specific.

"How long have you been working in restaurants?" I asked her during her next visit to the bar.

"Since I was fifteen in one way or another," she replied. She looked annoyed at either the question or her time in the restaurant industry. Maybe both. "Any more questions about my qualifications?"

"Am I bothering you?"

"Yes, you are. I'm trying to work. Kate has my resume if you want to check my references or something. I need two pitchers of Bud Light, a glass of the red house wine, and another pair of margaritas no salt." Emma walked off again without further comment. I found myself getting annoyed with the way she was doing that, even though I knew it was her job to be on her feet and circulating around to her tables. I was trapped here behind the bar.

Speaking of the devil, my sister chose that moment to check in on me.

"Everything going okay now?" she asked, watching Emma settle a new table in with satisfaction. The eyes of the male patrons followed her around the room longingly, myself included.

"She's an alright waitress," I conceded, "but I really wish you hadn't hired someone without telling me. Especially not someone that I'd...well, you know." This part, at least, was true. Call me a control freak, but I do like to be involved in the decisions that affect my everyday life.

"Sorry about that," she said, softening. "I really was desperate. I just couldn't do another Friday night like last week. It was insane." Kate touched my arm, making me look at her and imploring me with her eyes to believe her.

I sighed. "Yeah. I know." We'd both gotten blisters on our heels that night from all the running around.

"Plus, she really needed this job. But wouldn't you have picked Emma? If you put aside your history, she's exactly what you said you wanted. See, I even wrote it down." Kate pulled out her notebook, where she'd recorded the attributes that I'd told her we should look for when we inevitably hired someone. Of course, she'd written it down. She read it out loud, "Organized, diligent, reliable, and sexy." The last one had been a joke, but Kate was very literal.

"I don't think I would have hired someone who hates sports, bars, and sports bars." My voice was dry.

"This isn't a sports bar." Kate went straight for the obvious, ignoring my other points. "Half the people coming in here have no idea who you are," she pointed out.

"Gee, thanks sis."

"You know what I mean! They're hipsters, musicians, computer nerds. Everyone that knows who you are is hanging out down the street at the wing bar. I told you we should fill this place up with TV's and start serving 100 different flavors of wings, but you told me it's important that we keep this place *authentic*. So, it's still the divey coffee shop-bar-event venue it's always been."

"Fine. Fine."

"So what if working as a cocktail waitress isn't Emma's ultimate dream job? So what if she hates football? She's doing a good job isn't she? She already organized both supply closets, mopped all the floors. She even cleaned out all the garbage disposal traps—and you know how much I hate doing that."

"She's just going to quit as soon as she gets a better opportunity."

"So am I. By the way, I need one margarita no salt, three

Miller Lites, one Fat Tire, one Guinness, and an extra dirty martini."

"You didn't think she might be a bit too snobby and intellectual for this crowd."

"Snobby?" Emma was back, and she'd heard me again. Damn. It was extremely difficult to shit-talk a coworker in this environment. She pursed her pink lips at me in apparent disappointment. "Hmm. You really do like calling me names, don't you, *sweetheart*? I need a bloody mary, a vodka tonic, one jack and coke with a lime, two Dr. Peppers, one margarita no salt."

Kate snickered.

"Oh fine. Whatever. Maybe the place could use a touch of sophistication," I said to Emma. She grinned at me triumphantly. It was her first real smile of the night. It made me feel weirdly tingly and lightheaded. I'd totally lost my train of thought. "What was I making again?"

Kate and Emma shook their heads. Down the bar, Willie chuckled.

I turned my head towards him, "Glad I'm amusing you."

4
———

EMMA

"ALL THOSE CONCUSSIONS have really done a number on your memory, huh Ward?" Kate seemed to take every opportunity to tease her brother.

Concussions?

"My memory is just fine, thanks." Ward rolled his blue eyes at her as he made the drinks. His voice was less defensive than amused. "I remember more stuff than you've forgotten," he mumbled.

"Why would you get concussions? Do you get in a lot of bar fights or something?" I asked. Looking at Ward's size and imposing build, I'd doubt many men would pick a fight with him. He was practically a giant. He could probably punch someone through a wall. Then again, drunks were stupid. Maybe it was an occupational hazard. My words had an unintended reaction. Willie's jaw dropped open. He looked utterly *horrified*.

"No, I was talking about football," Kate said.

I shook my head, remembering. "Oh, right. You played football." I shrugged. I'd done everything I could to avoid Ward and news about him. That meant avoiding football, which wasn't exactly hard since I hated watching sports.

Willie pointed at Ward, looking offended on Ward's behalf that I wasn't an expert on his career. "That man is a legend. His first two seasons in the NFL were art." Willie's voice was full of second-hand pride. He slapped Ward on the shoulder affectionately, causing the later to laugh uncomfortably.

"Huh," I managed. "So, I guess you got tackled a lot?" He didn't answer, but now his face looked simply mystified by my ignorance.

I looked him up and down, trying not to linger too much on the good parts (which was pretty much all of him). Ward looked physically intact, at the very least. I knew that Ward had retired due to a catastrophic injury early in his career, but he looked just *fine*.

Ward looked at me like I was speaking another language. He pushed the glasses at me across the bar. "Here are your drinks."

Suspecting that was the best I was going to get, I shrugged and headed off. My tables were waiting and

Google would tell me all I needed to know later. I wasn't going to give Ward the satisfaction of knowing how curious I was about him. "Thanks," I said over my shoulder to Ward, which earned me the world's tiniest, least-sincere smile.

Ego. That's what Ward had--too much damn ego. Obviously, Ward had developed an inflated sense of self-importance because he was slightly better at feats of strength and agility than the average man. As if being born with a physical advantage was some sort of character recommendation.

Our societal feedback loop rewards guys like Ward far beyond what they objectively deserve. People like to think we've progressed over the animals, but we're just the same. Ward's sports career was the human equivalent of resplendent plumage on a bird. Like any peacock during mating season, all a guy like Ward would need to do is shake his tail feathers and screech the loudest to find a mate. Now he thought that all us peahens wanted him to put an egg in us.

The next time I stopped by the bar to grab the water pitcher, Ward was still talking about football and traumatic brain injuries. Only now, he was talking to a customer who I vaguely recognized as one of Ward's buddies from earlier in the afternoon. He was a lanky, sandy-haired guy about my age.

"They don't wear helmets in rugby," the guy was arguing, "and they don't seem to have the same sort of issues with brain injuries later on. Maybe the league should just get rid of helmets altogether."

"Rugby matches are much more like wrestling than football though," Ward countered. "They don't run nearly as much, so they don't have as much force when they hit slam into each other."

"All I'm saying is that I hear that bare-knuckle boxers have a lot fewer concussions than gloved boxers."

"Sure. They have to protect their hands as well as their faces. But the sports are wildly different. Football isn't about hitting the other team repeatedly in the face until they fall over. At least usually." Ward grinned like the idea of a match devolving into a brawl was exciting, rather than disgraceful.

"But maybe the sport needs to change," the man argued. "You don't want to end up with Parkinson's disease just because you have a nostalgic attachment to the starting line configuration, do you?"

"I think I'm safe at this point," Ward said. He sounded annoyed. Did I detect some bitterness there? Was Ward disappointed that he *was safe from Parkinson's disease?* What a strange man.

"Are you sure?" His buddy pushed. "You wouldn't know if you had memory loss. That's kind of the point."

"Oh, for Christ's sake. My mind is like a steel trap." He tapped his temple with a long, thick finger. Ward noticed me staring and smirked down at me. "For instance," he continued to his friend all the while maintaining eye contact with me, "I remember the name of every girl I've ever slept with."

I ground my teeth, suddenly regretting my eavesdropping. *Yuck. What a complete and total asshole! Who says shit like that in a public place?*

"I stand corrected," Ward's buddy said with a laugh. "I can't even remember the number of girls I've watched you go home with in the time I've known you." He sounded genuinely impressed with the number of his buddy's conquests. Their subsequent fist bump made me feel positively ill.

I *knew* Ward was just trying to get a rise out of me. I *knew* responding with some sharp comment was what he wanted. This was all entirely childish, and frankly, I'm above this sort of talk. I wasn't going to take the bait.

"Gee, you're such a gentleman, Ward." My sarcastic voice wasn't obeying my brain. It almost never did.

Ward and his friend looked over at me. Ward's surprise was obviously, and poorly faked. "What? Would you rather I didn't remember the names of all the girls I've slept with?" Ward laughed. "Jealous already, Emma?" He smiled a slow, smoldering smile, revealing perfect, white teeth. Like a shark. "A name like Emma isn't hard to remember. Just two syllables: Em-ma."

I sucked in my breath and squeezed the water pitcher

with a white-knuckled grip. *Don't dump it on his head, Emma*, I reminded myself. *You really, really need this job.*

"I'm hardly jealous." I wanted to storm off, but I needed something first. "I'm feeling nothing but pity for you, Ward. You may know my name, but I bet you can't spell it."

The last word.

5

EMMA

THE CROWD finally thinned out and became more manage-
able around one a.m. My knees hurt from walking, my
arms hurt from lifting trays, my face hurt from fake-smiling
at the customers, and my brain was exhausted. At least I'd
been bright enough to wear proper shoes. That's the first
rule of waitressing, learned long ago at home in Connecticut: buy the best shoes you can afford or pay the price in
blisters. But my feet were just about the only part of my
body that didn't ache. After being unemployed during the
spring semester, I was out of practice.

I stole away for a quick bathroom break and was
returning to check on table two when one of the drunks—a
guy Ward had cut off half an hour ago—decided it would
be a great idea to turn around and pinch my ass. Hard.

I squealed in surprise, loudly enough to cause everyone

to stop what they were doing and stare.

"What the—" managed to slip out before I got ahold of myself. I'd learned from hard won experience that it was generally best to de-escalate these situations. Exploding only makes things worse, even if it's more satisfying in the moment.

"Hey Angel," the fifty-something, balding cretin slurred, "when does your shift end?" He smelled like a drunk ashtray.

Not being able to slap drunk and stupid people was my absolute least favorite thing about working in hospitality. I'm generally not a violent person, but I'd be willing to make an exception at the moment. I rubbed my rear end, embarrassed and sullen. The creep really got a big old handful of my ass.

"Whoa there," I said in lieu of something vile. I was using my drunk-people voice: loud, clear, and unambiguous. "I'm not interested in you. You need to keep your hands to yourself. Do. Not. Touch. Me. Got it?"

"But darlin," he whined, reaching out to try and grab at... something. Hopefully my hand, but he wasn't even going to get that. I twisted away and danced out of his range, getting angrier by the second. Now that he no longer had the element of surprise, he wouldn't be touching me again. I'm not athletic in any traditional sense, but I'm quick enough when I need to be. More than quick enough to avoid drunk guys with wandering hands.

"—but nothing, Carl." Ward appeared out of nowhere at my side. If I thought I was angry, Ward looked *livid*. Murderous, actually. The man hadn't even been in the room ten seconds before. He was really, really fast. Especially for such a big guy. Ward loomed over the drunk. "She's not your darlin'. You heard the lady. No touching. Being drunk is okay but getting handsy is not. Period. Christ, you're supposed to be a *doctor*, man." His voice was sharp.

Carl looked up at Ward, swaying slightly on his barstool and looking extremely put out. He was pouting and petulant, which was never a good look on a grown man.

"I'm gonna need you to tell me you understand the rules, Carl. And I need you to apologize to Emma," Ward told him, not giving Carl any time to complain. Willie ambled up from around the bar to provide backup. Everyone in the room was now watching our exchange with interest. You could have heard a pin drop. I shifted uncomfortably from foot to foot. Having so many pairs of eyes on me made me feel lightheaded. I could feel myself blushing.

"Er, yeah whatever," Carl grumbled. He tried to turn around. He must be feeling the pressure of being center-stage too.

I shrugged and was ready to let the matter drop, but evidently Ward was not. He still looked *majorly pissed*. He set a heavy-looking hand on the guy's shoulder and spun him back around to face us.

"Not good enough, Carl." His voice dropped an octave, dipping dangerously into the growly-range. I was stunned and dumbstruck.

Carl rocked on his barstool, but his long-suffering sigh cut off in a little hiss when he saw Ward's expression. Ward's anger had begun to permeate the thick membrane of Carl's drunkenness (or perhaps just his thick skull). His sense of self-preservation kicked in and the blood drained out of his big, pink face.

"Now Carl. This is your last chance." Ward had Carl by the shoulders. He gave him a good shake and then aimed him my direction. He had lifted the smaller man up off the barstool, literally dragging him about like a ragdoll.

"I'm so sorry, Miss," Carl said instantly, not meeting my eyes. "I shouldn't've touched you. It was very out of line and won't ever happen again." The words rushed out of him like Ward was chasing them.

"As long as it doesn't happen again, I accept your apology," I said stiffly. I turned to go back to work, just wanting to forget the whole thing. Ward, however, wasn't finished. He let go of Carl, who instantly fell to the ground with a loud thump.

"You're going home now," he told Carl. "And I don't mean that you're driving yourself there. I don't need that on my conscience. Willie's going to call someone right now to come get you. And don't show your face around here again unless you can behave yourself and show my bar and everyone in it some respect."

The man seemed to fold into himself, shrinking away from Ward's anger and into the ground. For his part, Ward stared around at the shocked faces of his customers as if daring them to step out of line or question him. No one did. Ward yanked Carl back up and then stood next to him while he paid his bill and then walked with him outside, presumably to wait. I slunk away from action, shocked at Ward's reaction.

Never in my many years waitressing had anyone stood up for me like that. Ever. Even 'good' managers in the restaurant business don't go out of their way to confront bad customers, when they were even around, that is. Ward hadn't just stood up for me, either. He'd thrown the guy out and announced to the entire bar that no one was allowed to treat me poorly. In a perfect world that would be a given, *but in the real world*? The world where Carl, who was apparently a doctor (cue vomit), had learned it was okay to behave that way and then had thirty years to practice his waitress-ass-pinching skills? It meant a lot to me.

About five minutes later, Ward intercepted me on my way to grab more glasses and set a gentle hand on my forearm. I froze at the physical contact, suddenly paralyzed. *He touched me.* For the second time tonight (not that I was counting). My heartbeat surged as my body betrayed me. I might rationally know that he was an egotistical philanderer, but my body just wanted him. All of him.

"Are you okay?" he asked, looking surprisingly concerned. He was close enough I could smell his cologne. The rational side of my brain turned off when the alchemy of his smell, woodsy, clean, and masculine, hit my senses.

No, I'm not alright. Kiss me. Right now. Make me feel all better.

I didn't say it, but I thought it, against my much better judgement. It was all I could do not to stare at him open-mouthed.

His eyes, so strikingly bright blue against his dark hair, transfixed me. He shouldn't be allowed to have such beautiful eyes. On top of everything else, it was just unfair. I shook my head to clear it.

"Sure," I finally stuttered. I'm not sure why, but I felt strangely like I needed to reassure him, all of a sudden. He looked so *worried about me*. The change in his demeanor was shocking. "Grabby drunks come with the territory, right?" I patted his hand.

"Not in my territory, no they don't." He clearly didn't appreciate that someone had touched me. Or more likely, he didn't appreciate that someone misbehaved in his domain. "I'm sorry this happened on your first day."

"Well, don't worry about me, I'm just fine," I told him, shaking my head again, and slinking out from under his arm. I gave him my practiced customer-service smile. "I've got lots of practice with drunk creeps trying to grab my ass."

My answer didn't seem to please him. If anything, he looked unhappier. "Just let me know if it happens again and I'm not around. I'll take care of it. Willie and Kate will look out for you too."

I nodded. "Okay, I... thanks." There were plenty of places that didn't really care if the drunks touched the staff so long as they paid their tabs. This place might have some drawbacks, but this attitude about sexual harassment was a serious recommendation. I reached out and touched his arm back, earning me a wide-eyed look. "I really appreciate that."

Ward's sandy-haired, lanky friend chose that moment to chime in. "Hey Ward, if you really wanted to keep the patron's hands off your staff, you should probably change your hiring practices." His voice was too loud. He was obviously a bit inebriated at this point.

Ward made a dismissive gesture with his hands, but I must have looked confused and weirded out because the guy clarified his statement. "I heard what Kate said earlier," he added, looking at me square in the eye. "You wanted someone that was... what was it again, Ward?"

"Lucas, cut it out," Ward tried, but his buddy clearly thought I ought to hear this.

"Oh right. Wasn't it organized, hard-working, and hot? I definitely know that hot was in there somewhere. Sounded like an advertisement for a wife, not a waitress!" He laughed.

I blinked. The tips of Ward's ears were pink, either in embarrassment or annoyance. Otherwise he didn't react except to give his friend a 'seriously bro?' type of look. The guy shrugged and chuckled.

"Is that true?" I asked Ward, instantly on edge. It was probably true, given Ward's obvious irritation. "You think you can insist that your employees be physically attractive enough to be in your presence?" What a pig. At the same time, a tiny voice in me wondered whether Ward still thought I was hot. Had I passed his attractiveness litmus test? I had once. The tiny voice was hopeful. I squashed it.

Ward rolled his eyes at my question. He laughed. "Hell yes. Haven't you seen Willie? People come in just to bask in his glory." His sarcasm was not an answer, even though I felt a smile tugging at my lips when Ward jerked his thumb in the older man's direction.

"Well, that's just sexual harassment right there," Willie joked, patting his 'curves.' "You're creating a hostile work environment for me. I shouldn't have to be objectified for your base, animal pleasures." He put one hand on his hips and pretended to flip his non-existent hair dramatically. I couldn't help my giggle.

"If anyone pinches your ass, Willie, you let me know," I told him seriously. I winked. "I'll take care of it right away. Hot commodities like us have to stick together."

6
———

EMMA

I WENT HOME, crashed instantly, slept like the dead, got up at noon, and knew I had to repeat yesterday's long, grueling schedule all over again. My shower felt positively transcendental, despite the fact that my roommate Rae had obviously used my shower pouf and conditioner again. Ugh. I loved Rae, but I was an only child and didn't like to share. One of these days I was going to make enough money to live alone, and then my coconut lime conditioner would be mine all mine. One day.

The Lone Star Lounge was more of a coffee house during the days, complete with an extensive selection of coffee drinks and all the laptop loners they attracted. The rooms were full of quiet people poking away at their computers and a few study groups discussing things in low voices. The place had a totally different vibe during the day, and it looked like it was a popular destination for remote workers. Luckily for me, I was actually here early for a staff meeting, not to work.

Kate, Willie, Ward, and I were supposed to be discussing the private party that was going to take place this afternoon, but they were nowhere to be found. I circulated through the old converted house looking for them, but they must all be running late. Frustrated that I was the only one to show up on time, I circled back to the office and pushed the door wide open.

Ward, who was in the midst of changing, stared at me in shirtless surprise. I froze like a deer in the headlights.

Oh. My. God.

The man looked like he belonged in one of those black-and-white underwear ads on a billboard, or better yet, sculpted out of marble in a museum where he could be appreciated for centuries. I'd never seen anything remotely like him in person, except for that one night. Every inch of his fair skin was smooth and stretched over long, lean muscles. If I were asked to come up with an ideal male body, I wouldn't have even dreamed up Ward. He was beyond my memories. And I have a very good, incredibly specific, extremely detailed memory.

My body reacted to his forcefully, tugging me forward an involuntary two steps into the room and making my heart flutter.

"Hi." I'm not sure why I said it, probably just to fill the silence. It came out in a breathy whisper.

"Hello, Emma." His voice was low and obviously amused. "How are you?"

The question echoed in my brain, but I couldn't come up with a response. We stared at one another for a long, extremely charged moment. I could almost smell the pheromones in the air, and arousal made my limbs and eyelids feel heavy and sluggish. In the silent office, I could almost pretend that we were alone. My eyes dipped to his belt buckle when his eyes became too much. Staring there probably wasn't any better.

"Earth to Emma? Um... See something you like?" Ward finally asked me, reaching toward me. I backtracked out of his reach like a frightened animal, cringing when I realized he was just grabbing a button down off the back of his chair. He shrugged it on and grinned. He knew precisely what he'd done to me. And I was speechless again. I backed out of the office without another word. His laughter rang in my ears as I ran away to wait at the bar until my heart stopped pounding.

It was not my finest moment. I was daydreaming on a barstool and staring into space when Kate found me fifteen minutes later. In my fantasy, Ward reached for me instead of his stupid shirt. We stole away into the alleyway behind the bar and got *properly* reacquainted right there against the wall.

"There you are," she said cheerfully. Her appearance snapped me out of my reluctant, but extraordinarily graphic fantasy about Ward. I smiled at her in embarrassment.

"Hi Kate." *I was just thinking about fucking your brother's brains out in the alley behind the bar.* I could only imagine I was blushing like I had a third-degree sunburn.

"You came back!" She sounded somewhat surprised.

"Of course, I came back." *My bank account has four hundred dollars in it. Even if your brother wasn't surface-of-the-sun hot, I'd be here.*

"And right on time as always, unlike me. Come on, we're meeting outside on the patio. That's where the party is going to be."

Yay, a party. I wanted nothing more than to run away, but it wasn't an option.

I followed along behind her, feeling numb and totally mortified. Ward and Willie were waiting outside, and I avoided Ward's eyes like they might turn me to stone. Kate started rolling napkins on a table and I joined her. It was easier not to look at Ward if I was staring at forks instead. Thankfully, he didn't decide to tease me in front of the others. Instead, he launched straight into business.

"Okay, so the College of Liberal Arts rented out the space this evening," he explained. My ears perked up. "They've got some kind of reception tonight for the English

Literature Department faculty. They're welcoming a new professor or something."

I dropped the fork I was holding, causing it to bounce noisily on the stone pavers. Ward looked at me in suspicion, but I dove under the table to get the fork to avoid him seeing my face. *All* the English professors were going to be here tonight? *Shit.*

"Oh, sorry Emma. That's your department, isn't it?" Kate asked me, filling the silence as I scrambled under the table to recapture the fork. I nodded on my way back up. "So, I guess you know them all, huh?"

"Yeah. This should be *interesting.*" My voice probably betrayed my concern, because Kate looked at me with worry.

Oh God. Adam would be here. I'd read the email about the new faculty member just like every other grad student, but I didn't think I'd be seeing him anytime soon.

"Anyway," Ward continued before his sister could ask me any follow-up questions, "they're going to be here from three to seven. It's a long-ass party, and we're serving champagne and doing an open bar for the whole thing. They're bringing in some food as well, specifically a couple of appetizers and a cake. It should be a fairly tame affair. Apparently, they're doing a poetry reading for part of the time or some shit. Some new professor? I didn't really read the contract that closely."

Poetry reading or some shit? Typical.

"Sounds exciting," Kate said. Her voice was dripping with sarcasm. "No offense, Emma," she added a moment later. She at least had the graciousness to look embarrassed.

I shrugged. I was fairly used to people being less enthusiastic about poetry than me. Ninety-nine percent of the world seemed to think that poetry was dumb. Which was probably why it didn't pay as well as waitressing.

"Do you know who's reading at the party?" I asked in spite of myself. Even as a graduate student, there was no way I'd be invited to a faculty-only party if I wasn't serving champagne, and I had a bad feeling that I knew exactly who was going to be reading. A certain professor who was new to the University, having just transferred here as a tenure-track prospect from my Alma Mater. Someone who very nearly became Poet Laureate yesterday. Someone the other professors probably wanted to welcome onboard. Christ, what were the chances? This could only happen to me.

Ward shook his head at my question. "No. I don't. Hopefully it isn't too boring. I hate poetry." He didn't apologize for his opinion.

If I wasn't so shocked and nervous, I could have smirked at that. People always think they know what poetry is, and most of the time they're wrong. Good poetry is never boring. Adam's work was a lot of things—not all of them positive—but *boring* wasn't one of them. Unfortunately, the thought of being in the same room with Adam again made me feel slightly ill. I couldn't even manage a snappy comeback.

"Are you okay, Emma?" Willie looked genuinely concerned. "You look kind of pale all of a sudden."

I really wanted to say that I didn't feel well and beg off, but today was my second day. I couldn't afford a sick day. If I didn't earn my rent money this month, I'd be couch surfing and living off ramen by next month.

"Of course," I replied. My voice was too high, and too thin to sound convincing, so I added a big, bright smile. I was not about to spill my guts to two total strangers. Especially not to Ward. I still had my pride. "Why wouldn't I be?"

A FEW HOURS LATER, and I was cursing my hubris. I should have pretended to get violently ill in the bathroom, cut myself on some glass, tripped down the stairs—anything to weasel out of this. The party was even worse than I thought it would be, and the 'guest of honor' hadn't even arrived yet.

"Yes, I'm working here for the semester," I explained to Dr. Lieu, one of the professors who would one day decide whether I graduated with a PhD. He looked down his nose at me with obvious, obnoxious pity and shook his head.

"It must be tough with your advisor on maternity leave," he replied. His tone indicated that Dr. Abernathy's timing for her pregnancy could be something I might find personally annoying. He clearly did. "Taking a leave from your research can't be fun, and it's too bad we couldn't find you a TA position in the department. It's bad timing. But I suppose Melissa's biological clock was ticking."

"I'm very happy for her," I said, trying to be diplomatic. While mildly inconvenient to me, as it would delay my graduation until at least next year, I wasn't willing to judge another woman's choice about when to start a family. Privately, I knew that Melissa's pregnancy was hard won, much prayed for, and a near miracle. She was on bed rest at the moment, and I was not going to interrupt her just because I wanted to graduate a little bit quicker. Particularly when I had no idea what I'd do afterward.

"Hmm, yes, of course. We are all thrilled for her and her wife." Dr. Lieu, the department head, resisted rolling his eyes. *Barely.* He was such a freakin' tool. "Well, hopefully you'll get out of this *service job* soon enough." You would have thought I was scrubbing toilets, not distributing champagne. Then again, for Dr. Lieu and those like him, anything that wasn't a life wholly devoted to writing and reflection was hardly worth living.

I'd been repeating versions of this conversation with every partygoer who caught sight of me, although only Dr. Lieu was quite so transparently patronizing and misogynistic. The faculty inevitably recognized me as I circulated with champagne flutes. I'd worked as a teaching assistant for most of them over the years, so I tried to keep my head down and my presence to an absolute minimum.

Kate had picked up on my uneasiness and offered to put me on dishes, but I knew it would mean she'd need to work twice as hard. We exchanged a look when I returned to switch out my tray.

"How's it going out there?" she asked, popping another bottle of bubbly.

"I think they're all having fun. We might need to cut off a couple of them soon though. Or start pushing water on them."

"I meant you. It must be weird to serve your teachers and watch them get slowly drunk, huh?"

I almost giggled. "Very weird. I've taken their classes at both the undergrad and graduate level, and I've also worked for most of them as an assistant—teaching undergrad classes, grading papers, emailing with students." I shrugged. "They all pity me for working here, that's what's really annoying."

Willie, who was standing nearby, made a grossed-out face.

"Why would they pity you?" Kate asked innocently.

"Because they're career academics." It wouldn't be possible to explain the bizarre mindset of these ivory tower dwellers in a thirty second conversation. They were so insulated from the real world that they barely acknowledged its existence. "They see regular jobs and the people who do them as inferior. They clawed their way up the ladder of academia just so they wouldn't have to do anything else but write and think. The intellectual class can't be dirtying themselves with labor, you know. Working at a *bar* is anathema for them."

Kate shook her head at me. "I won't pretend that I understand that at all, but hang in there. We've only got forty-five minutes left."

Forty-five minutes to go and Adam still hadn't shown up yet. The thought that I might escape this debacle without seeing him was beginning to look more and more probable. Of course, the instant I really started to think I should be so lucky, a light touch on my shoulder and a familiar voice pulled me back down to earth.

"Emma, is it really you?"

I took a deep breath to steel myself and turned around.

7

EMMA

"CHAMPAGNE?" I asked. My voice was neutral and emotion-less, a true achievement given the circumstances. I stared at Adam like he was no one special at all. Just another customer in a long line of faceless customers. Inside I was a churning ball of emotion (mostly hate), but externally I was a fucking glacier: placid, serene, immovable. My smile was thin, but I forced myself to keep it on my face with herculean effort.

Nothing to see here, dirt bag. You can't make me feel a god damn thing. Not anymore. I'm a glacier now. In the past five years, I've frozen solid.

"I didn't know you were even in town. It's really great to see you!" He appeared dumbfounded and pleasantly surprised, but I knew it was at least partially an act. He knew I was in town. Not only was he a terrible liar who squinted when he was making shit up (something I'd learned too late), but he'd looked at my LinkedIn page at least three times in the past year. The cyberstalking bastard knew precisely where I lived and what I was up to.

He tried to hug me, but I brandished the tray in front of me, effectively blocking his approach. His lips parted in surprise, and possibly hurt.

My reply was bland. "Hmm. Well, here I am. Do you want some champagne?"

Glaciers like me don't give a shit about you.

He blinked at me, noticing the tray for perhaps the first time.

"Are you still waitressing?" There was definite pity in his tone, and it irked me.

"What does it look like to you?" My voice was droll.

I may still be waitressing, but I was not the same. I'd grown up considerably since we broke up. Adam, however, seemed to be exactly the same. He had the same tall, spare figure, the same wide hazel eyes, the same long-fingered hands. He dressed like he always had in black pants and a white Oxford shirt. As far as I knew, he had no other clothes, just endless versions of this one outfit. He'd even worn it to the Poet Laureate ceremony the day before.

"Emma, I—" He reached out and touched my shoulder. At the contact, my defenses shuddered. My mental walls, the ones I'd spent three long years rebuilding and reinforcing, shook to their foundations. But they held. I flinched away from him.

"I've got work to do, Adam." I took another step back from him, pulling out from his grasp. "See you around."

"Wait." His voice was sharp, but barely above a whisper. I paused reluctantly and raised an eyebrow at him inquiringly. He took the tray from my hands and set it down before pulling me by the elbow away from the crowd. Resisting would cause a scene, so I let him do it. As I was pulled away, I saw Ward and Willie watching. I hated that this conversation was on display, but more, I hated that it was happening at all.

What do you want Adam? What could you possibly want from me now? Surely, you've got a whole class full of nineteen-year-old girls to chase. I'm sure you can find some dumb blonde just like me in there.

"Emma," he whispered, "It really is good to see you. I've been thinking about you for a long time. I owe you an apology."

I blinked. My lips parted in shock. Seeing the change in my expression, a possible softening in my blankness, Adam kept talking.

"I never—we never should have—it was all wrong. Being with you, our relationship, it was wrong. It was all my fault. You were my student. You were too young, and I abused the power I had over you back then. It was an inappropriate dynamic."

I stared up into his eyes in disbelief. Of all the things he could have said, this was the most surprising. I never thought he would *apologize*. Not that I didn't deserve it, or that he was some sort of sociopath who couldn't feel remorse. It was just odd. He'd seemed perfectly willing to use and abandon me three years ago. Unable to reply in any coherent fashion, I just nodded at him. I tried to pull away and get back to the party, but he grabbed both my shoulders to hold me in place. I stared up at him, frozen and unsure.

"Say something, please," he asked. His voice was thick with emotion. It sounded real. "*This guilt has been eating at me for years.*" His hands on my shoulders felt warm and familiar.

I looked at him, at the man who'd stripped me of my innocence atop a desk after class one afternoon, a man who regularly fucked me during office hours and then gave me an A- in his class, and I felt shame. He swore me to secrecy about our relationship because of the damage I could have done to his reputation, like I was a dirty secret. At the time, I'd thought it was exciting to have a secret. I thought it was romantic. I sighed. How could I have fallen for him? I was such an idiot.

"What do you want me to say?" I finally managed.

"What are you thinking?" His hazel eyes searched my face. For forgiveness? Regret? Anger? Surely, he found some of all three. He wasn't the only one who'd made bad decisions.

"I... I'm thinking that I need to get back to work." I pulled away from his grasp. There was no way I'd let him know one iota of the pain he'd caused me. No way I'd let him know how terribly depressed I'd been when he broke it off with me after finals, telling me he needed to focus on his writing. Not a week later, he announced his engagement to a doctoral candidate in the history department. He'd been cheating on me the whole time, or rather, he'd been cheating on her *with me*. I'd been the other woman, and I hadn't even known.

A little curious part of me noted the absence of a ring on his finger. There was no wife with him at this party. Either their engagement was unusually long, and she just hadn't moved down yet, or it hadn't worked out. Good. Hopefully the poor woman wised up before her heart got crushed like mine had.

"Enjoy your welcome party, Adam."

Walking away from Adam felt a million times better than when he walked away from me, but it still didn't feel good. I felt exhausted. Ward saw my face as I reentered the patio and paused mid-shake with the martini shaker to stare. Was it that bad? I forced myself to smile again and make the rounds like I wasn't wishing I were anywhere else. At that moment I would gladly have accepted the offer for a free root canal to get away, but no alternative was forthcoming, so I continued to serve champagne.

Adam didn't do his poetry reading. Instead, he spent the next twenty minutes staring at me from across the room in between congratulatory handshakes. Awkward didn't even begin to describe how that felt. Every time I turned his way, he was staring intently at me. I tried to ignore it, but it was useless. I was keenly aware I was being watched. And not just by Adam. Kate, Willie, and Ward were all keeping an eye on me. Ward zeroed in instantly when I had to go to the bar to switch out my drink selection.

"Do you know that guy?" Ward asked, nodding toward the patio. I knew which guy he meant.

"Yeah." Denying it seemed pointless. I filled the tray of fresh flutes as quickly as I could. My hands were shaking a bit, but there was nothing I could do about it.

"Is he bothering you? Do you want me to get rid of him?"

I looked up at Ward in surprise. He was staring across the room with an expression on his face that I'd not seen him wearing before. It wasn't a look I ever wanted to be the recipient of; that was certain. It wasn't quite as frightening as the look he gave Carl the night before, but it was close.

"Oh, no," I said, swallowing and trying to regain my composure. "It's fine. He didn't do anything."

Ward looked at me doubtfully. "Are you sure?" His concern looked real. I didn't think I could handle a caring, sincere version of Ward at the moment, even if it was a pleasant departure from teasing Ward.

"Yeah, it's no big deal." I smiled at Ward, attempting to look professional and collected. I was about to walk away when he spoke again, almost like he couldn't help himself from asking.

"He's your ex-boyfriend, isn't he?"

I nodded, and my pleasant expression faltered. Boyfriend felt like the wrong term given the circumstances, but saying I was his 'fuck toy' wasn't very polite. Or flattering to me. My head hurt. I must be totally transparent. So much for being an emotionless glacier. Ward frowned at my admission.

"Are you sure you don't want me to get rid of him? If he's being shitty to you or making you uncomfortable..." Ward seemed oddly eager to throw Adam out.

I shook my head and squirmed. "No. I'm fine. Really."

"You don't really look fine." He frowned.

Gee thanks, boss. Because I feel like shit.

"Sorry about that. I'll try to do better." I smiled brightly and stood a bit straighter.

"That's not what I meant at all." Ward looked frustrated. He shook his head in apparent irritation.

"It's really fine. This whole party is for Adam. To welcome him to the department. Even if I really wanted you to, you can't throw him out of his own party."

"I can do whatever I want," Ward replied. "We're on my

property." He seemed perfectly sure there would be no adverse consequences.

I sighed. I'm not sure a testosterone rush would do anything to make me feel better at this point, even if it would be objectively fascinating to see the two men interact. They were so different in most ways and so similar in others. "It's really not necessary," I said. "It's all just fine. A little awkward, sure, but you know how it is. It's almost over anyway."

"Hmm. Well if you want me to rescue you, just wink at me and I'll come help. He looks skinny. I could probably toss him a good fifteen feet."

I smiled at the suggestion, and my spirits lifted a bit. "Okay, I will. Thanks."

"DRIVE SAFELY EVERYONE! BE RESPONSIBLE!" Dr. Lieu cried as I led him off by the shirt sleeve. He toddled along behind me with a shambling gait. He had gotten a bit tipsy over the course of the party and would be taking an Uber home. Given that he'd consumed at least three bottles of champagne alone, it was impressive he was even standing. Leave it to a bunch of writers to drink their weight in free alcohol. I led him away from the party and out the back way to where his car was waiting.

After double checking the address with the driver, I

deposited the man who would one day sign my diploma into the back of the car, and then I took a moment alone in the alley. I chewed a mint to get the vile taste of defeat out of my mouth, but it didn't do the job. This had been one terrible party. I hadn't even received very good tips. It seemed that my fellow academics had forgotten that while the drinks were free, my service was not.

Back on the patio, things were finally winding down. There were only a few people left. Predictably, Adam cornered me again as I was picking up.

"Emma, can we talk?" He was persistent. I'd give him that.

"I'm working, Adam." At the moment I was, in fact, picking up trash. Very important and pressing trash. It required my full concentration.

"I know, but... Your advisor is on maternity leave, isn't she?"

I nodded warily. "Yes, she is." Adam wanted something from me, and by the way he was looking at me, I suspected that I knew what it was. His eyes traveled over my body liberally.

"Why don't you let me take over?"

I froze. "What?"

"I know your work and your interests," he said, smiling at me excitedly. "I know what you enjoy writing about, what topics make you excited to learn. We've always worked well together."

He had a point. I had loved working with Adam and talking with him about the topics we both enjoyed. We'd spent hours, half-dressed, talking about writing. It had been beautiful. But now I wondered if it was because of the attention he was paying me more than anything else. Still...

Adam must have read the indecision on my face because he pushed on. His voice became more confident.

"I learned from some of the other faculty that you've almost finished your research and are already drafting your dissertation. You could graduate much more quickly if you didn't wait for your adviser to return. Plus, I really could use a good teacher's assistant. I've got a full course load this summer."

So, there was something in it for him. I should have known. He had no graduate students right now to do all his menial grunt work. But if I were his teaching assistant, I'd get a stipend, too. I wouldn't have to work at the bar. I bit my lip, feeling totally confused and out of my body.

"Besides," Adam said, reaching out to touch me, "we could pick up where we left off." He dragged his fingers along the soft, delicate skin of my forearm and stepped closer. "But better this time."

My indecision cut off like a light switch in my brain.

I'm not a toy.

"No," I told him firmly. "I don't think that would be a good idea. For a lot of reasons."

Adam stepped closer to me, stupidly deciding to press

his physical advantage. "Come on, Emma," he said softly, stepping closer still and brushing his lips along the skin where my neck met my shoulder. It felt pleasurable, and nostalgic, to be touched like that. But also, very wrong. And I hated myself for even considering Adam's proposition.

I pulled away from Adam, but he grabbed my hand before I could escape. I felt trapped, although he had only lightly grasped my wrist. In a panic, I looked around, trying to find a way out that would be polite and effective. It was then I realized that there was no one else left on the patio. I was alone. With Adam.

"There you are, Emma." Ward's low voice, so often obnoxious, was welcome. He'd arrived at my rescue without me even requesting it. He pulled me smoothly out of Adam's grasp with a huge hand around my waist. "I've been looking all over for you."

As Adam watched, Ward slipped an arm around my waist, pulled me close, and kissed me.

8

WARD

EMMA'S LIPS WERE WARM, and she tasted sweet and minty like she'd been chewing gum. She folded into my arms like she'd been the missing piece all my life. I hadn't intended to deliver much more than a peck, just to discourage her unwelcome ex, but I couldn't resist a bit more.

Before I considered the consequences, I was kissing her. And then I was really kissing her. Passionately, seriously, and deliberately kissing her. *Properly* kissing her. Like she was mine. My tongue sought hers fiercely, and I pinned her against me, gripping her narrow waist tightly enough that I could feel her heart beating against my chest. Or maybe that was my racing heart, brought to a crazed gallop by the feel of her soft body against mine.

Someone—probably the creepy old dude that Emma had the misfortune of dating at some point—cleared his throat to our left. Distantly, I was aware of how loud it was, but I wasn't really paying attention. All my focus was on the woman in front of me.

I was totally overcome by her. Her little gasp when I pulled her in. The smell of her. The feel of her skin against mine. Her tongue twisted and danced against mine, seeking, probing, and exploring. I could have gone on kissing her for hours.

When we finally broke away from each other's embrace, more because we needed to breathe than anything else, we were alone. Creepy old dude had disappeared, likely to lick his wounds in disappointment. He was clearly barking up the wrong tree. Emma was obviously not interested in rekindling anything with him. She'd been avoiding him like a frightened rabbit while he leered at her all evening.

Now, however, it looked like it was me she wanted to avoid. She looked around and then stared up at me in disbelief. In a fraction of a second, her disbelief melted into anger.

"What. The. Fuck." She hissed. "How dare you?"

I had no good explanation for why I'd kissed her. But I wouldn't apologize for it. It was too good of a kiss to apologize. It was worth her irritation.

"Well, you wanted him gone, didn't you?" I asked her, fighting back a laugh.

"I didn't want... that," she stuttered. Her eyes were huge

in her face, and her cheeks were flushed. She pushed her hair back from her face and glared balefully.

"Are you sure? You didn't seem to mind a moment ago. You were kissing me back." The more annoyed she looked and sounded, the better I felt. Her annoyance had quickly become familiar territory for me. Safe territory.

"I mind very much that you think *that* was a rescue."

"You don't consider yourself to be rescued? Look, he's nowhere to be found." I gestured around to the now-empty patio. All the other guests had already departed when creepy dude chose to make his move on Emma. I followed him out here, suspecting trouble, and finding it. "I got rid of him."

Emma frowned at me like I was the one who she needed rescuing from. "That wasn't what I thought you meant."

"Beggars can't be choosers."

She made a dismissive little noise. "I didn't beg you to rescue me from Adam. I certainly didn't beg you to kiss me."

Adam. So, the creepy old dude had a name. I very much disliked *Adam*.

"No. But if you keep this attitude up, I won't kiss you again *unless* you beg me to."

Her little hands balled up into tiny, adorable fists. It was so easy to push Emma's buttons, but that didn't make it any less amusing. She continued to glare up at me with a furious expression on her face, perhaps too angry to speak.

"Speechless again?" I taunted. "And I didn't have to take my clothes off this time or anything."

Her voice returned enough to insult me. "You are such an asshole." She sounded astonished at the depths of my awfulness. I couldn't help chuckling a bit at that.

"You might want to wash your mouth out then. You know, since you just stuck your tongue so far down my throat." I winked at her and headed back inside, smiling.

Part of me wondered if she would follow me in or disappear forever into the dusk, but a few minutes later, she appeared. She started making the rounds with the evening crowd, looking no worse for wear. I'd have been disappointed if she ran off, I realized, although maybe it would have been for the best. Kissing waitresses—waitresses who worked for me and who happened to be my sister's friends—was a bad idea. A tremendously bad idea.

Yet, there I was, imagining something even worse for my human resources record than merely kissing an employee or a past hookup. Imagining it in vivid, lurid, explicit detail. In fact, I'd been imagining it on and off since Emma walked in on me in the office. When she'd looked at me with fuck-me eyes and walked toward me with that sexy sway in her step before remembering herself and fleeing.

My fantasies about Emma were getting wildly out of hand. Before this went any further, I needed to put a stop to it. Emma might be playing hard to get now, but she'd been kissing me back like she wanted me. This was a bad situation all around. Kate wouldn't let me fire Emma, and she wouldn't let me sleep with her, but a plan for something entirely different had begun to reveal itself to me.

"I need two margaritas no salt," Emma requested a few minutes into my introspection. She frowned at me no differently than she had last night.

"Coming right up," I replied, smiling pleasantly at her while she scowled. I had an idea of how to get Emma to spend time with me outside of the bar. The only problem was that she was going to absolutely hate it.

"Say, Emma," when she came around to retrieve her drinks, "you know, you owe me for my valiant rescue back there."

Emma rolled her eyes and collected the drinks without taking my bait. "Yeah whatever." She got her next few rounds from Willie instead of me, so it was more than an hour before I got to talk to her again. I cornered her on her break.

"Emma, my dear, if I didn't know better, I'd think you were avoiding me."

She looked at me like she was wishing she could shoot laser beams out of her eyes. "No, no, you're right. I am avoiding you. And don't call me 'dear.'"

Emma was very honest, I was realizing. To a fault. It was a quality I liked, despite its likelihood to get her in trouble.

"Well, I can understand that, I suppose." I watched her as she poked about on her phone and tried her best to ignore me. "I'm sure you don't want to pay your debt."

That got her attention. She looked up at me in confusion. "I'm not indebted to you."

"Of course, you are," I replied. "You owe me a proper thank you. I rescued you from that creepy old dude."

"Oh right. Sure." She slipped her phone back into her handbag and stood up. "I'll send you a cookie bouquet. With a little card that says, 'Thanks for sexually harassing me.'"

Emma slipped past me in the hallway and back to the bar without a backward glance. I followed her ass with my eyes appreciatively. Well, appealing to her sense of fairness failed. I hadn't really expected it to work anyway. Mostly, I just enjoyed teasing her. Plus, I wanted her properly worked up for phase two of my plan.

9

WARD

K<small>ATE APPEARED JUST</small> before last call to check on the main bar. "How are things?" she asked, looking around with a self-satisfied look on her face. "It looks good in here. Is everyone getting along yet?"

Emma, who happened to be within hearing range, shook her head grumpily and made a face. She stomped off irritably.

"What did you do?" my sister asked accusingly. I shrugged. Down the bar, Willie wiped down the bar and pretended not to notice anything, as usual. Kate's comments weren't for him anyway. I had yet to meet a person who Willie couldn't get along with. Hell, it probably wasn't even limited to humans. He could become best friends with a werewolf.

"Well, I suppose it can't be helped," my sister chirped. She was so happy to have help with the rush of customers that I felt guilty for not hiring another waitress sooner. She gave me a peck on the cheek and skipped off again, obviously proud of her hiring decision.

With Kate gone, it was time to put phase two of my plan into motion. The next time Emma came around, I had a question ready for her. "So, tell me, Emma, do you consider yourself to be more like the people in the bar right now or the people at the party earlier?"

Emma looked up at me in confusion. "What do you mean?" The look on her face was less polite than her words. It said: why are you babbling at me?

"I mean, are you more like those elitist jerks that work at the university or are you a regular person? A fun, normal person?"

"Are you trying to get me to admit if I'm an elitist jerk?" She rolled her eyes. "Not gonna happen."

"I was thinking about what you were saying before the party, about academia. About how they look down on people like me and my sister. And Willie. Do you look down on me, Emma?"

"What do you think?" She wasn't giving an inch. Her hand had found her hip, and she was looking at me sideways with one hand supporting a tray. She looked like a sassy, classic pinup in that pose. I had a spot on my bicep that would look great with her tattooed on it. I'd be sure she was wearing that Tinkerbell costume, too.

I smirked at her, imaging how furious she'd be if I actually did get that ink. "I think you're too short to look down on me without a ladder, but I'm asking you *metaphorically*." I was proud of my use of the word.

"I'm not an elitist," she said, setting down the tray of empty glasses and soiled plates she was carrying. "And I'm not a jerk. I know a few though." She looked at me with that one eyebrow cocked up again.

"Hmm. I'm not so sure you are normal. I think you might be a phony elitist."

"I really don't care what you think," she replied, grabbing the water pitcher and clearly planning to get out of my presence as quickly as she could. I wasn't about to let that happen. Particularly because I knew she had no customers left. I'd checked. I might be obnoxious, but I wasn't irresponsible. And I wouldn't jeopardize Emma's tips, either.

"Sure, sure," I continued, "but tell me, do you think you could try doing new things without getting all judgmental?"

"I do new things all the time." She waved a hand rudely at me, trying to get me to shut up and leave her alone. No such luck.

"Really? When did you last get out of your comfort zone?" I made sure to make my voice as condescending as possible, trying to get a rise out of her, and leering like it was the last time she let me get on top of her.

"I'm not in my comfort zone right now." She shifted from foot to foot uncomfortably, unintentionally proving her point. Thankfully, I'd anticipated this response and had the comeback all lined up and ready to go.

"That hardly counts. Nobody enjoys working. When did you last get out of your comfort zone when you weren't getting paid?" I pressed. I drummed my fingers on the bar as I waited for her response.

Her response only took a moment. "Easter. I had to visit my great-aunt Ethel. Her house smelled like rotten meat, cat pee, and old people. She also thinks I'm nine."

I smothered a smile. It seems like everyone has a great-aunt Ethel. Mine was a second cousin named Bill, and he had an animal hoarding problem rather than a memory problem, but the issue was the same. The last time Kate and I saw Bill, he'd tried to give us a pair of goats. Like we needed a goat for the bar, let alone two? I forced myself to get back on track.

"That doesn't count either. When did you last get out of your comfort zone when you weren't getting paid or doing it out of familial obligation?" I looked down at her with interest.

She stared up at me in confusion. "Why? Why are you asking me all these questions? Am I still interviewing for the job I've been doing for two days now?" She sounded irritated at me, but she wasn't storming off, either. This was my chance to spring the trap. A feeling of guilt bubbled up, and I ignored it. This was in everyone's best interests. Especially mine, but even Emma's. She'd see that eventually.

"Not exactly. I just want to know if you would be willing to take a chance on something, or if you're as locked up and blinded as those professors."

"Locked up? Blinded? What are you trying to say?"

Understandable. It sounded dumb, even to my ears. And I slept through most of college on a bus from one game to the next.

"Hmm. Okay. Hold on. Let me think of another way to say it." I thought about how to say what I was trying to say. I'd never been great at explaining my thoughts to people. Things were just clearer in my own head. I wasn't a poet like *some people*. Surprisingly, Emma waited politely while I organized my thoughts. "You know, they're like monks or something," I finally tried. "They're, what's the word for locked up monks? Cloistered. In their thinking."

For once, Emma looked like she was actually considering what I was saying. Her response, when it came, was unexpectedly thoughtful. "I suppose that I can understand what you mean. It's a good analogy, actually. Like a cloistered order or something, a lot of academics do go out of their way to avoid contact with the 'real world.' That way they can focus on their devotion. But no, I don't think I'm like that at all. I still very much live in the real world."

"Are you willing to prove it?" I challenged. I raised my eyebrows at her, in unison, since that was the only thing I could do.

"Huh?" Her little upturned nose crinkled with her confusion. It was adorable. Like a little rabbit. A very cute, and judge-y, rabbit.

"Prove it. Come out with me tomorrow. The bar is closed. Meet me outside of the bar, like two regular people going out to spend an ordinary day. Prove you aren't stuck up."

Emma's lips parted in surprise. "Ward, are you asking me out on a date?" She looked horrified. Or shocked. Or both.

I laughed rudely in her face and she scooted back from me. "No. Not at all. I'm performing an experiment."

She scowled at me. "Excuse me? An experiment? *I'm an experiment?*" The idea clearly didn't appeal to her at all. Which was, after all, part of the point.

"Yes. A very scientific experiment. You see, I want to see if you really are down-to-earth enough to work here. For science and for the sake of the bar."

"And if I refuse to go on your little experimental non-date?" Her tiny little fists were back, balled up at her sides in anger. She was positively quivering with it. I had a feeling that she'd just about hit peak irritation. If it didn't happen immediately, it would happen very, very soon. She'd be storming out the door, never to return. I backpedaled a bit.

"It's not a date," I repeated in a reasonable tone. "I'm just trying to determine if you're a good fit. I take my bar and its vibe very seriously. This bar is my livelihood. If you won't try new things... well, then you would've just proved to me that you are, in fact, an elitist snob, wouldn't you?"

Her fists loosened in surprise. She knew she was caught. "This is manipulative, and you know it."

"Yeah, it is. I know that. I also know you want to prove you aren't like *them.*"

She stared at me. Thinking. I could practically hear her brain working, trying to figure a way out. If there was one thing I'd realized about Emma, it was that she didn't back down from a challenge. I saw the exact moment when she came to her decision.

"I'm only going to meet you in a well-lit, public space. And you better not touch me again without my permission. Oh, and if I'm going to do something 'normal' with you, you have to do something 'elitist' with me. I think that's only fair, don't you?"

Huh. I hadn't been expecting that. Still... "I have no problem at all with that."

It was easy to agree to her terms when there was no way I'd have to go through with it.

"Good," she said, smiling at me like I'd just made a big mistake. "Then you're on."

"It's a date," I replied, "but you know, not really."

"Whatever, Ward," she said. Emma looked at me like I was an idiot and then walked away without another word. Somehow, even though I'd won, my victory felt hollow.

10

WARD

PART of me wondered whether Emma would really go through with it, but the address she texted me matched the one on her employee paperwork (yes, of course I checked). I looked up the apartment complex just off campus on Google Maps before heading off to meet her the next morning and found myself looking at the reviews the way I would if Kate told me she wanted to move there.

Landlords in this area are all sleaze-bags, one review said. *My apartment has more cockroaches than I thought could physically coexist with one another in four hundred square feet. It's a Malthusian nightmare in the making.*

I didn't know what a Malthusian nightmare was, but roaches sounded nightmarish all on their own. Austin has some of the biggest cockroaches I've ever seen. They can easily get four or five inches long.

The next review was no better: *My next-door neighbors are crackheads. They routinely steal my Amazon deliveries, then forget and try to sell me my own stuff. I did buy a nice bike from them that one time though. It's a really good bike.*

Delightful.

Either the local raccoons are having raves on the roof now or the undergrads that live next door figured out the fire escape was unlocked, complained the last review I read. *If you can afford to live anywhere else I'm sure you already would. But if you have to live here, avoid the third-floor units.*

Emma's place sounded like a dump, but the pictures actually looked okay. The location, just east of campus, was pretty prime, but it bordered on a relatively nasty part of town that gentrification had somehow missed. I chalked up the bad reviews to entitled, pampered kids living off mom and dad. It wasn't until I drove up that I truly understood how much ugliness a wide-angle lens, good lighting, and Photoshop could disguise.

The vacant property that separated the apartment complex from the interstate was overgrown, but it did nothing to stop the deafening sound of semi-trucks going past at seventy miles per hour. I saw a few mangy feral cats hanging around on the dry grass. The parking lot was cracked and ruined, making half of it unusable as weeds took the area back for nature one pothole at a time. As for the complex itself, it had seen better days. I'd estimate that those days were probably well before Emma was born, sometime in the early eighties. Next door, a particularly sketchy looking bodega advertised cabrito tacos and, weirdly, haircuts. There was no way in hell that I'd let my sister live at a place like this, even if it meant her moving in with me.

As I approached her apartment, Emma opened the door before I even knocked and immediately stepped out and locked it. She must have been waiting by the window, watching. I was almost touched until I saw her frowning face.

"You can't come inside," she said by way of a greeting. "My roommate is sleeping."

It was past noon and an obvious snub, but I was too focused on her outfit to do much of anything but shrug and stare.

Unlike her plain work outfits that were clearly designed to blend in—dark pants, solid color T-shirts—today Emma wasn't dressed conservatively. Instead, she had chosen to stand out. She was wearing a short, strappy sundress that showcased every inch of her figure.

Her delicate shoulders were covered with a light smattering of freckles, I noticed, and they extended down her collar bones and atop her exposed, impressive cleavage. Had she always had freckles? I didn't remember. The amount of skin I now had to admire and appreciate was overwhelming. Like a starving man offered an all-you-can eat buffet, I was overcome by the selection of long, slender limbs, full curves, and exposed neck, back, and shoulders.

My fingers itched to count her freckles and find out just how far down her body they decorated. To find out if her skin was as velvety soft as it looked, and if her hair was as silky. Alarm bells started going off in the back of my brain, warning me that I was about to get myself into trouble. But even as my brain tried to talk sense into me, another organ had taken over doing the majority of the thinking.

"Earth to Ward? See something you like?" Emma teased, echoing my comments from the day before. She spun around just to rub it in, revealing an extra inch of creamy white thighs. "You seem a bit distracted."

I wasn't going to take her bait. She knew she looked amazing. The color of the sundress, burnt orange, made me instantly suspicious. "You talked to Kate about this, didn't you?"

Emma batted her long eyelashes at me. Beneath, her green eyes were mischievous. "No. What makes you say that? Afraid I'll snitch on you?"

"I'm just shocked you know the school's color. Have you ever been to a football game before?" I asked, certain that the answer was no.

"Me? No." She looked unsurprised by my selection. "We're going to one today though, aren't we?"

"Yes, we sure are." I looked down at her with as much of a frown as I could muster when her tits were so prominently on display. "And we're staying for the entire thing. If you'd like to back out, this is your chance. Otherwise, I don't want to hear any whining out of you."

She rolled her eyes at me as we walked down the stairs. "Oh please. Taking me to a football game is the worst you could come up with? I was worried it was going to be hillbilly hand fishing or something."

I made a mental note to look up 'hillbilly hand fishing' as I had no idea what that was. I was born in a sprawling suburb of Dallas. Plano was not exactly the backwoods. "We're aiming for normal, not Texas Chainsaw Massacre."

She was obviously fighting back a smile. "Glad to hear it, but normal is relative," she said eventually.

"I'm no math genius or anything, but I remember from middle school that a bell curve has a big hump in the middle. Given the number of people who like football, I'm pretty sure that I fall closer to the center of that hump than you."

"I'm no math genius either, but I do know that a normal distribution of preferences would all depend on the sampling," she replied condescendingly. "I'm willing to bet you've got a bad case of post-hoc alteration of data inclusion based on arbitrary or subjective reasons."

Huh? Her face indicated that she'd just delivered a knockout punch in our argument. Clearly, there was only one reply. "I know you are but what am I?"

"You don't know what that means, huh?"

I bit back a laugh. "Obviously, it means you accidentally ate a thesaurus for breakfast." My curiosity quickly got the best of me. "Okay, what does it mean?"

"It means your friends probably suck too."

Damn. That was a legitimately sick burn. And I walked right into it, too.

"You're being awfully mean today."

"Turnabout is fair play," she told me.

Any guilt I felt for talking her into this faded as we walked. A woman this stubborn couldn't be forced into doing anything. Perhaps she was as genuinely curious about me as I was about her. Or maybe she really hated me and was just going along with my plan to make today miserable for both of us.

11

WARD

IF THERE IS one thing that I could get all soppy and poetic over, it would be the joy of going to a football game. Seeing it all through someone else's fresh eyes should have been even better. Unfortunately, Emma did not approach this experience with childlike glee and an open mind. Her mind went straight to the gutter.

"So, tell me the truth, Ward, what is it with the players slapping each other on the butt all the time?" Emma asked as we followed the herd of people into the stadium.

I looked down at her in disbelief, and a couple of heads turned our way, hiding smiles. "That's seriously your first question? Butt slapping?"

She returned my gaze with obvious amusement. "Yes, it is. Are you dodging it?"

Yeah Ward. Are you dodging the question like a pussy?

"No." I shook my head at her defensively. "It's just a really silly question."

Grow up Emma.

"Inquiring minds want to know. I've always been super curious about this. Come on. Tell me. Why slap one another on the butt? It's really weird!" She did look honestly interested.

Thinking up an answer that didn't sound stupid or weirdly sexual was a bit harder than I thought it would be, but it came to me after a moment. "It's a playful, harmless way to cheer somebody on. It has nothing to do with anything but the game." Emma looked totally fascinated, so I continued. "There are actually unspoken rules, too. Time and place are obviously limited to the actual game. No staring, no squeezing, no lingering. Never bring the slapping to the lockers or the showers. Unless the two dudes are both into that, I suppose."

"It's about camaraderie," a random guy in the crowd added.

"Yeah, it's just, like, a team building thing," his buddy agreed.

Emma looked at me, then at the men who'd chimed in, and then back at me. "But why the butt? Why not the shoulder? Or the arm."

"Why not the butt? If everyone is cool with it, why is that weird? You're the one making it weird," I said, shrugging. "It's just another body part if you think about it." The differences between a friendly butt slap and Carl grabbing Emma's ass in the bar were huge.

She blinked. "I guess you have a point. There doesn't *have* to be anything weird about it."

"I'm not saying it *can't be weird.* It for sure can get weird. Very quickly. Obviously, if some guy was just going around butt slapping all the time, or doing it inappropriately, that would become a big problem."

"So, it's just like cheering then? You don't cheer constantly right? It's only at, you know, the appointed intervals."

The ridiculous idea of a giant sign illuminating above the field after a touchdown that said 'the appropriate cheering interval has commenced' flashed through me.

Emma looked happy with herself for figuring it out, and I didn't want to ruin it. "Yeah, just like that," I replied.

"Wait, you have tickets, right?" she asked as we approached the ticket taker.

I dragged them out of my pocket and looked at her with disappointment. "I may not eat a thesaurus each day for breakfast, but I'm not a complete idiot."

Emma looked at me seriously. "Ward, I don't think you're an idiot." Oddly, I actually believed her, at least in the moment. Still, I handed the tickets over without comment and led her silently toward the elevators. Maybe Emma didn't think I was an idiot, but she definitely didn't think I was on her level. About anything.

"Where are we going?" she asked, gesturing behind us. "Aren't the seats out there?"

"We've got box seats," I explained. "There are a few benefits to being the former quarterback. One of them is access to the best seats in the house."

Before we could make it to the elevator, Emma drew us both to a stop in front of a huge mural that happened to have me in it. "This is getting weird," she said, pulling out her phone to snap a picture. Another picture to her left caught her interest. I was in that one too. "Really weird."

I looked at the mural uncomfortably. Whoever painted it made me look sort of puffy and unusually pink. My head was also attached to my body at a strange angle. "Yeah, it's definitely weird to walk past giant pictures of yourself," I admitted. I touched Emma's elbow to get her moving again toward our seats, and, for once, she didn't jump or scowl. She just followed behind me as we entered the more exclusive area of the stadium. She stared around herself with wide eyes, taking it all in.

"Okay, so are you going to explain the rules to me?" Emma asked eventually. "I really don't know a thing about football other than the thing about the butt slapping."

"Of course," I replied, shaking my head at her strange fixation. "But first, beer and food. The refreshments are an important part of the football experience."

Emma bit her lip and turned pink. "I don't like beer,

wine, or soda. Or fried food most of the time. Also, I'm a pescatarian."

Was that like a Pentecostal combined with a Lutheran or something? I hadn't figured Emma for the religious type, and I didn't know what kind of dietary rules that might bring. I knew she drank liquor. "And I'm a Methodist," I replied carefully. "Do you have a lot of food rules in your church?"

Emma eyes went wide, and she giggled at me. "No. I—" she giggled some more, and I frowned, feeling like I was missing something. "It means the only animals I eat are fish... no mammals or birds or anything. I'm an *almost-vegetarian*."

Why didn't she just say that? I raised my eyebrows. Somehow, I was not surprised that Emma would be a fussy eater. It could have been a lot worse though. She could have been a vegan. Or she could have been one of those girls that only ate tossed salads and raw juice. I went out with a girl like that once. *Once.*

"That's fine," I told Emma confidently. "We can still find stuff you can eat. They have practically everything here."

It took some hunting around the food options in the club area, but we eventually settled on beer and chicken wings for me and a mixed drink and cheese pizza for Emma. She nibbled on a slice of her pizza as we settled into our seats.

"This isn't too bad so far," she admitted, looking around at the plush seats. "What happens now?"

What was she expecting? Strippers and monster trucks?

"Now we watch football. Actually, we eat, drink, talk, and watch football. What exactly did you think would happen at a football game?"

"I don't know," she said with a shrug. "I guess I thought it would be dirtier or louder. I thought it would involve more testosterone-laden nonsense."

I'd be more than happy to show you something loud, dirty, testosterone-laden later tonight. I pushed the thought away. *Focus, Ward.*

"That's all coming. It is going to get quite a bit louder," I warned her. "There will be cheering. And singing. And maybe also screaming and swearing depending on how the game goes. But it's fun."

"You're going to sing?" She looked more excited than she should about the prospect of me singing.

"We're *both* going to sing," I corrected.

She shook her head. "No way. I don't sing. You don't want to hear me sing." She seemed sure about this.

"It's not American Idol," I told her. "I won't judge you, even if you're totally tone deaf. Trust me, I don't sing well either. It's really more like cheering anyway."

She still looked skeptical but took another deep drink of her vodka tonic as if she needed it to work up her courage for her upcoming solo. "When in Rome," she replied after swallowing it down. She made the little hand signal that University of Texas students used to represent the school mascot, a longhorn steer, and grinned. "Go team go!"

"That's the spirit. Now you're catching on."

* * *

"...AND that means the game is officially now half over. It's called 'half time'. Now they're going to take a short break to rest and figure out the strategy for the second half," I told Emma, sitting back in my chair as she watched curiously while the players departed the field and the marching band got ready to do their thing.

I was breathless from explaining every play to her in as much detail as I possibly could. The people seated within earshot probably hated us both, but I didn't care. Emma had questions about *everything*. It was a bit exhausting, but also quite cute that she was so eager to figure out what was going on and learn all the little details.

"Do you want to go grab another drink?" I asked. She nodded.

"I actually don't mind this," she said as we made our way back to the bar, shocking me speechless. "I certainly didn't think that I would, but this watching football thing is sort of fun."

Given the type of reaction I'd been preparing for, a

lukewarm response was far beyond my expectations for this afternoon. I found myself smiling.

"I'm glad you aren't having too terrible of a time," I said. My voice might have been dry, but I meant it. I didn't want to make Emma completely miserable, even if I'd told myself that was the initial plan. At my sarcastic tone, Emma looked at me and turned pink. She looked more than a bit embarrassed.

"I'm sorry, Ward. I didn't mean—" she started to say, only to be interrupted.

"Ward!" A familiar voice called—yelled actually—from behind us. We both twisted around to see the speaker rapidly approaching us.

"Cole?" I asked in surprise. "I'll be goddamned."

"Hey man," he said, hugging me hello and reminding me that in the world of football I was actually on the *smaller* side. "I thought I might find you here!"

Cole, my former teammate and old friend, had the life I might have had if my body and shitty luck hadn't ended my career prematurely. He was currently playing for the Packers.

"What are you doing in Austin?" I asked. "And why didn't you call?"

Cole shrugged. "I'm just in town today. I had an early meeting and then I figured I'd catch the game." He looked at Emma curiously. "Are you going to introduce me to your friend, or do I need to do it myself?"

Emma was watching our exchange with interest and seemed to be asking me the same question with her big green eyes. Suddenly, I found myself not wanting to share her with Cole, but not introducing them would be plain rude.

"Of course," I replied as smoothly as I could. "Emma, this is Cole Rylander. He and I played for the Longhorns at the same time. Cole, this is Emma Greene."

"Pleased to meet you, Emma," Cole said, shaking her hand. He looked at me for further explanation of our relationship, but I really had no idea how to define Emma and me at that moment. We weren't quite friends, we weren't just coworkers, and we weren't on a date. We also weren't enemies, at least not exactly. So, I just smiled possessively down at her and he nodded slightly in acknowledgment, a barely there widening of his eyes indicating my good taste.

"Likewise," Emma was replying, oblivious to our subtle bro code. She was smiling her customer service smile and I wondered if she'd ever heard of Cole before (he was fairly famous). I felt surprisingly proud that not only had I figured out when her smiles were real and when they weren't, but that Cole didn't earn a real one. But I did. In fact, I'd received a number of real smiles today.

"This is Emma's first football game ever," I told Cole. He gasped in mock horror and grabbed at his heart dramatically like he was having a heart attack.

"Tell me you're kidding," he pleaded.

Emma giggled as I shook my head solemnly.

"I know, I know," Emma said in an exaggerated tone. "It's heresy."

"Well, if you're going to get your football cherry popped," he remarked dryly, "I suppose you could do worse than Ward."

Emma's jaw dropped open at his crudeness. She turned bright pink. I couldn't stop my laugh. After a second, Emma shook her head and laughed too. Cole didn't mean to be gross, it was just his personality. She was really trying not to be uptight.

"Gee thanks," I said to Cole, raising my eyebrows at his poor word choice. "You're such a true friend to talk me up in front of a lady like that."

"Hey now, I'm an excellent wingman," Cole argued. He looked like he was about to bring up his past assistance, probably the story from freshman year about that exchange student from Sweden again, but thought better of it. "Although, if you piss me off, I could tell her stories from when we lived together that would probably make her run for the hills."

"You two were roommates?" Emma asked, now looking doubly interested. I nodded warily. I knew Cole wouldn't say anything too terrible, but he seemed to have a broken social filter. He might screw me over entirely by accident.

"Don't believe a thing he says," I told her, shooting a

warning glare at Cole. "I'll go grab our drinks and be right back."

By the time I returned, Cole was halfway through the story of how he met Kate. It was always a crowd pleaser.

"...And she was completely covered in glitter," he explained. "Head to toe. She looked like an angry disco ball."

"Well, you did mail a box full of three pounds of glitter to her," Emma argued. "I'd be pissed off too." I suspected she'd heard at least parts of this story from Kate's perspective.

Cole shook his head defensively. "No! I mailed it to Ward's home address. I didn't know he had a sister, or that she'd think it was hers, or that it would accidentally explode on her right before her senior prom."

"And she drove for two hours just to yell at you?"

"I wish. She shows up at three in the morning, this glittery, furious, teenage girl in a prom dress, and before I even know what's going on, before I'm even awake, she curses me out at the top of her lungs, throws something cold and wet all over me, drops a bottle, and storms off."

"Something cold and wet?" Emma asked, disgusted. Apparently, Kate hadn't told her the whole story. "Do I even want to know?"

"Probably not, but I'm going to tell you. Did you know that Cabela's sells genuine, bottled doe urine for hunters? I *didn't* know that. But now I know what it smells like to be covered in ice cold deer piss at three a.m. The fact that she refrigerated it was really a special touch."

Emma giggled. "I bet you didn't mess with Kate ever again."

"I lived in fear of her for years." He looked around as if she might pop out of the crowd and throw animal pee on him again. "But Ward and I bonded over the experience and became friends."

Emma shook her head in disbelief. "I can't believe Kate would do something like that. I mean it's obvious that she's got a temper on her, but that sounds... somewhat extreme."

"She was different back then," I chimed in, handing Emma her drink. I felt obliged to stick up for Kate, since she wasn't there to defend herself. "Younger, obviously, but also going through a tough time. Our mom was dating this guy she really hated and there was some serious drama at home, she was getting teased in school, and I wasn't around for the first time. It just wasn't a fun couple of years to be Kate."

"Oh," Emma said, looking more understanding and sympathetic. "Well, I'm still going to try and stay on her good side. I don't want to get the Cole treatment."

"You and me both," I told her, grinning. "Come on, half time's almost over."

"See ya' round, Ward," Cole said. "Say hey to Kate for me." A look flashed over him I wasn't familiar with, but it disappeared a second later. "It was nice to meet you," he added with a smile to Emma. We shook hands, promised to stay in touch, and I whisked Emma away. It felt good to have her back to myself in our seats. Because I wanted to focus on the game and our experiment, I told myself. Obviously.

12

EMMA

WE WERE LEAVING the stadium after the game when Ward was spotted by what was obviously a gaggle of sorority girls. The girls swarmed around him like piranhas and squealed excitedly while I stood by like an awkward, forgotten seventh wheel. Their voices were shrill, but universally reverent.

"Oh my God! You're Ward Williams!"

"You're a legend!"

"Can I take a selfie with you?"

"You're *so tall*."

"I can't believe you're just, *here*. Like it's no big deal. I feel like I'm in a dream."

Ward accepted their high-pitched, fawning attention with a bemused patience. I could barely contain my disgust for their antics, but they weren't sparing any energy on me whatsoever. I might as well have been invisible, because I was quickly pushed to the side. Literally. Before long, Ward had been invited to the sorority afterparty and more or less promised an easy night filled with nubile, worshipping coeds.

Wow. Just, wow.

This must be one of those advantages to fame that Ward was talking about earlier in the day. No wonder Ward had developed such an outsized ego. Given the fact that the girls were basically begging him to get drunk and fuck them (possibly to fuck *all of them* at once by the way they were hugging and hanging on one another, that part was a bit unclear to me), it was a surprise he wasn't *more conceited.* I couldn't imagine what life must have been like on campus for him. And that wasn't even during his professional career. The idea was mind boggling.

Ward shook his head and gently disentangled himself from their posse. He didn't seem the slightest bit put out not to follow the sorority girls to whatever bacchanal they invited him to, and I must admit that it made me feel damn good that he'd picked me over them. I walked a bit more confidently at his side as we left them behind. For his part, he looked somewhat embarrassed that he'd been swarmed by the sorority girls. I decided I wasn't ready to tease him about that yet. I wasn't sure I even could. He'd done nothing but exist and hadn't encouraged them.

In the absence of teasing, we found ourselves walking in silence.

"What?" I asked as we began the short journey back toward my apartment (it was easier to walk than drive, given the location). He'd been staring at me, clearly wanting to say something but holding back.

"I'm just surprised is all," he admitted, looking a bit sheepish. "I guess I thought this would all be a lot... harder. That there would be a lot more whining and moaning. That you'd be all stiff and unwilling to learn or give it a chance."

"That's what she said." I'm not sure what possessed me to channel an eight-year-old boy, but Ward laughed at my dumb joke anyway. I liked the sound of his laugh. It might have been the first real laugh I'd heard from him, and I found myself smiling from ear to ear.

"Maybe you're secretly normal after all," he said, shaking his head and staring at me in what might have been wonder. "You must have just been really sheltered growing up or something."

Sheltered? "Why would you think that? Is it just because I didn't know the sports trivia of the great Ward Williams?"

He rolled his eyes. "Hardly. The older I get the fewer people recognize me or, at least, the fewer people care. To be honest, I actually don't like the whole public figure thing anymore. It was fun at first, but now... it's just a huge pain in the ass more often than not."

"I can only imagine." The number of people that stared at Ward at the game like he was superhuman had been a bit bizarre, and I was only experiencing it secondhand. "It must have advantages though, right?"

"Oh, for sure. I'm not saying that I don't reap the benefits. My football career has opened up a ton of doors for me over the years, and it still does. It's just weird when I go out to buy ice cream in my pajamas at two in the morning and end up signing autographs with a stranger outside of the twenty-four-hour Walmart."

I winced in sympathy. Having done that exact thing (minus the autographs, obviously), I could not imagine the inconvenience of social interaction when a half-pint of rocky road was all I wanted.

"I still want to hear why you think I'm sheltered," I pushed. I hadn't forgotten. That accusation required an explanation.

Ward took a second before he answered me. He looked like he was choosing his words carefully, probably to avoid making me angry. "You're an innocent person. Clearly, you're smart and young, but it seems like you've spent a lot of your time on your studies and not a lot of time doing anything else."

"I work," I argued. I'd seen some weird shit in the restaurant industry, too. Unfortunately, some of it was *literal shit.*

"I know," Ward said. "You work hard, too. I've seen you in action. That's not what I mean."

"You wouldn't believe the number of masters and doctoral students who get supported by their parents the entire time. A lot of graduate students have never worked a non-academic job in their lives. Some never will. There are a lot of trust funded people in academia."

"I'm not trying to be rude," he said, clearly sensing my unease. "So, don't take it the wrong way. It's really sort of cute that you're so... you. But your parents, they're college professors or something, aren't they? Did you grow up in a small town?"

I frowned. "No. Well, okay, my dad *is* a professor, but my mom is actually a librarian. And the town's not that small. It's a liberal, university town."

"So, I think it's fair to say that you grew up in a bit of a bubble. Where are you from?"

I looked down at the sidewalk. "New Haven, Connecticut." When I glanced up at Ward, he was staring at me like he'd totally figured me out.

"Yale is in New Haven, isn't it? Did you go there for your freshman year?"

I nodded at him. "There's free tuition for the children of faculty members, and I saved a lot of money by living at home, too. But it's not like you're probably thinking. You don't get special treatment, or easy admissions, or anything like that. I earned my way into Yale, and I earned my GPA."

Ward shrugged. "I don't doubt that. But I wouldn't judge you if it were true that you got special treatment, either. You're talking to someone who never had a chance at graduating except for athletics. I never read a single book in college. We athletes do get special treatment and easy admissions by the way. Very special. I'm not even sure what I majored in. I think it was Kinesiology? Might have been underwater basket weaving for all I know."

"That sounds about right. It was even like that at Yale." Athletes are treated like gods at universities everywhere. They bring in so much money through ticket sales, I guess it makes sense, even if it isn't fair to everybody else. I'm sure my disapproval showed on my face, but at least Ward was honest about his academic achievement (or lack thereof).

"What made you come all the way down to Texas?" Ward asked. "I bet you could have gotten into another Ivy. UT is a good school, but it's not that good."

We'd arrived at a crosswalk. I kicked at the little rocks on the asphalt before I answered his question. "There were two reasons I chose to come here. I wanted to get as far away from Adam as possible, and the University of Texas offered me a free ride for the rest of my undergrad, which is basically unheard of in the humanities. My parents weren't particularly happy," I told him, not sure when I decided to stop being sassy and start being honest. "They would have preferred Harvard, naturally."

Ward merely nodded and grinned. "My parents would

have preferred Harvard, too. But neither me nor Kate had a snowball's chance in hell of being accepted there." He laughed a bit at the prospect.

A sudden rumble of thunder made us both look skywards. The fall afternoon had become cloudy during the game, and the first few drops of rain began to fall as the light turned. By the time we hit the opposite side sidewalk, it was coming down in sheets. That's just how the weather in Texas is sometimes. One minute it's pleasant, and the next, tornados, flooding, and hail. Luckily for Ward and me, we were just getting rained on, but we didn't make it two more blocks before we were both dripping wet. My feet were soaked up to the ankles from stepping in puddles.

"Shit," Ward cursed, grabbing my hand and pulling me underneath a nearby oak tree. Its leaves weren't enough to stop the rain, but they helped provide a bit of shelter. "Here, take this." He took off his jacket and settled it around my shoulders before I could react. "You're going to get soaked to the bone in just that little dress."

"Thank you," I said, wrapping the jacket around me as tightly as I could. It smelled like Ward: masculine and clean. The cool rain had me wishing I'd worn better shoes, pants, and most importantly, *a bra*. The thin fabric of the sundress went semi-transparent in the rain and I could see Ward looking and then pointedly *not* looking at my rock-hard nipples, which were now clearly visible for all the world to see. Public nudity wasn't really my thing, so having the jacket made me feel much better. "You're really quite a gentleman when you aren't being a big jerk."

Ward laughed at me, shaking his head in disbelief. "Does that smart mouth of yours get you in trouble a lot up in your ivory tower?"

"Sometimes," I admitted as we trotted along through the rain. Ward would probably consider this a quick walk, but I was almost jogging. His legs were much longer than mine and it was a struggle just to keep up. "But usually not. Many academics have very poorly developed social skills. It comes with the territory. The English department is better than most, but that's not really saying much."

We'd reached the end of our odd little non-date and were now just standing awkwardly outside under the shelter of my complex's roof.

"Do you want to come upstairs and dry off?" I asked. I must have been seized by some kind of temporary insanity when I made that offer, but once it was out of my mouth, I wasn't going to retract it. Instead, I felt myself turning bright pink when Ward searched my face for something he was looking for. He must not have found it there, because he shook his head. He smiled.

"I've got to meet Kate for dinner," he explained. "We always have Sunday dinner together." It was almost certainly a lie to let me down easy and I felt foolish. I smiled politely at him, and he smiled politely right back at me. The seconds ticked by, becoming awkward.

"See you tomorrow then," I told him, suddenly eager to get away from Ward. "Thanks for taking me to the game. It was fun. Really."

"See you tomorrow, Emma," he replied, looking like he didn't quite believe me that I enjoyed the game. I stripped off the jacket and handed it over, feeling extremely exposed. And not just physically. It was an uncomfortable sensation, like I'd let down my guard in some important way and Ward hadn't reciprocated. I flew up the stairs and away from him.

Once I locked the door behind myself, stripped, toweled off, pulled on pajamas and threw myself down on the couch in defeat, my self-doubt and insecurity came back in a rush.

Are you really that eager to roll over and spread your legs for him again, Emma? One afternoon where he doesn't talk down to you and you're ready to be another one-night stand for someone you shouldn't trust? When will you learn your lesson?

This was exactly the type of behavior that got me into trouble last time. I'd spent three years trying to keep myself from being an easy mark, to avoid the sort of impulsiveness that got me crushed last time, and I'd almost ruined it. I suppose I should consider myself lucky that Ward wasn't even interested. He probably had a sorority party to get to.

13

EMMA

I SPENT the rest of the afternoon and evening trying to anesthetize myself with trash TV and junk food. But no amount of *Bones* reruns and empty carbohydrates could banish Ward's face from my memory, or the thought that he might be three sorority girls into the party by now. I couldn't seem to get him out of my brain. Eventually, Rae came home and plopped down next to me on the couch. She grabbed a handful of pretzels from the little misery buffet I'd set up and looked at me expectantly.

"Tell me everything," She ordered. Between her New York accent and her severe, blunt bobbed red hair, Rae could be very intimidating sometimes. She could definitely channel the 'Law and Order' cops when she wanted to.

"Huh?" I asked innocently. "What are you talking about?"

"*Bullshit,* or as Ivan would say, *codswallop.* You know what I'm talking about. You've been acting oddly ever since you started your new job. And today, you took off with *a man.* You thought that I didn't notice, but I did. I saw him. And you. Together." She sounded like she'd just solved the crime of the century and was positively vibrating with excitement.

Slow down, detective.

"I can go out with men," I replied noncommittally. "You do it." Maybe if I made the situation look like no big deal, she'd drop it.

Rae just grinned at my accusation. "Yes, but I've become a boring relationship girl," she said, although her voice was somewhat wistful. She'd been dating her boyfriend, Ivan, for about six months now. They had been disgustingly cute and in love, although I think the 'honeymoon phase' was wearing off. Actually, considering that he practically lived here now, I really ought to be charging him rent. "Come on, Emma. Let me live vicariously through your exciting, new romance and tell me about your date. Please?"

"It wasn't a date," I protested. "He's just someone from my work. There's nothing romantic going on between us. Really." I didn't want to tell Rae, who was also in graduate school, about Ward's desire to determine if I was 'normal.' Or our one-night stand.

"Hmm. Are you sure it wasn't a date?" She looked at me

with an extremely skeptical look on her face. "You've been known not to notice when someone is interested in you."

Unfortunately, this was true. One of our classmates had confessed his love to me at the department Christmas party last year. Apparently, *everyone* knew about his crush but me. I'd thought he was just friendly! This time, however, was different.

"Yeah, I'm sure. It's totally platonic."

Rae still didn't look convinced. "Is he gay or something?"

"No. He's not gay."

"Is he a Catholic priest?"

"Um no. He's not a priest." That was just funny. I tried to imagine Ward in the whole priest outfit and couldn't.

"And he asked to spend time with you outside of work?" She clearly thought I just didn't understand the concept of a date. But Rae had a real tendency to oversimplify things.

"Yeah, he did, but—"

She interrupted me. "Then you're just plain wrong about what transpired this afternoon. I don't need any other details. He's hot, you're hot. You, my dear, just went on *a date*."

"It really wasn't a date," I repeated. Rae was jumping to conclusions. She rolled her eyes at me.

"Okay. Sure. I'll set that aside for now. What did you two do on your *entirely platonic outing*?"

I squirmed a bit. "We went to a football game."

Rae gaped at me. "I'm sorry. Did you just say that *you* went to a football game?" You would have thought I'd just attended a satanic ritual. To be fair, until recently, the two were equally probable.

"Yes," I said proudly. "I did." I'd successfully gotten out of my comfort zone. Ward could say what he liked about my narrow-mindedness, but I'd risen to the occasion. Now we'd both get to see if he would do the same.

"You must really be into this guy," she said, shaking her head. Rae and I had a similar dislike of football.

"You're seriously misreading this situation, Rae."

"One of us definitely is, but I'm pretty certain that it isn't me." She looked down her nose at me and then burst into giggles. "Okay, so what's his name?"

Finally, a question that I could actually answer. "His name is Ward Williams."

"Nice name. Strong. Alliterative. And you work with him at the bar?" She was fishing for details.

"Yes," I said, but then my conscience forced me to elaborate "Actually, Ward doesn't just work there. He owns the bar."

That earned me a raised eyebrow and a small frown. Her expression looked much more serious all of a sudden. "So, what you're telling me is that you're now dating your boss?"

"You may somehow be hearing that, but that is literally not at all what I'm telling you."

Rae was beginning to frustrate me. In particular, I was not a fan of the way she was looking at me. Like she knew better and was excited for me. Her superiority reminded me, ironically, of the way Ward sometimes looked at me.

"And you're certain that you don't find him the tiniest bit attractive?" She asked after a small pause. "I saw him, you know. So, don't lie. *He's absolutely gorgeous.*"

"I never said I didn't find him physically attractive." I was just annoyed enough to admit it. "But I'm not looking for anything serious, and I don't think he likes me that way at all."

Rae's mouth turned into a small 'o' shape. "So, it's just a hookup situation? Well, why didn't you just say that?"

I sighed, getting more worked up. My voice clearly indicated my irritation—it was shrill even to my ears. "No! It's not a hookup thing either. It's not any type of thing. Look, I think we should stop talking about this now."

Rae sat back and nodded. "Okay. I can see I'm making you unhappy. I didn't mean to. You know me. I just get excited."

"Don't worry about it."

Rae and I were well on our way to becoming great friends, and I depended on her for a lot of things, even if we clashed sometimes. Unlike Ward, she could admit when she was wrong, apologize, and we'd just move past it. That was one of the things I liked about Rae, even if she used my conditioner and drank stinky tea. She didn't feel the need to *constantly* push my buttons.

"Oh, so do you know the new professor or something? He keeps asking me about you," Rae asked after a moment. Unlike me, Rae had a great TA gig this semester with Dr. Lieu. Her curiosity was innocent, but I needed to tell her everything if she was going to be anywhere near Adam. I didn't want her to get put in the middle of any of his bull-shit. And I also didn't want her telling him a goddamn thing about me.

"Oh God," I said, cringing. "I'm going to need alcohol for this."

14

EMMA

AFTER EXPLAINING THE WHOLE SAD, humiliating saga of Emma and Adam to Rae over a bottle of prosecco, she was second-hand furious, and I was drunk. I slunk back to my bedroom in disgrace, feeling even worse about myself than I had before. I caught a look at myself in the mirror and found myself staring.

It's not like I was objectively ugly, mean, boring, or stupid. I wasn't perfect, but I certainly wasn't physically repellent, and I tried to be a good person. I just couldn't seem to find anyone that wanted a relationship with me. The guys I liked only ever wanted to hook up with me. I thought for a while that it had something to do with Adam, that he'd marked and ruined me somehow, but as much as I wanted to blame him for everything wrong in the world, I didn't think it was his fault.

It was me. Something about me clearly just screamed that I was easy prey for jerks. Since moving to Texas, I'd had three very nice-looking men in three years tell me they liked dating me but 'wanted to try out non-monogamy' after a month or two. *I just wasn't enough to hold their interest.* Was it some combination of personality and looks that I lacked? I really didn't know. The few dates I'd been on where the guys seemed interested in something long term had fizzled. I just wasn't into those guys, even when I felt like I should have been.

In my inebriated state, the disturbing truth was becoming clear to me at last. I preferred hot guys that were bad for me. The ones I wanted were always the ones that were trouble from the very start. Hot guys could easily play the field, and so they did. I just happened to be on the field because I had an exclusive attraction to *manwhores*. I was a manwhore-sexual. The nice guys, the ones who want to get married and build a house with a white picket fence, those guys just didn't do it for me. I wanted... well, I wanted Ward. And Ward clearly wasn't from the picket fence group at all.

For reasons that weren't remotely rational, I took a few pictures of myself in the mirror in a white tank top and shorts, examining them for obvious flaws. I was too scared and not drunk enough to text one to Ward, but still drunk enough to think it was a good idea to text him at midnight. My fingers were texting before my brain caught up to them.

Emma: Hey. So, did you go to the sorority party after you left?

The buzz of the response arrived swiftly. Almost as if Ward were waiting for me to text him.

Ward: Seriously? Do you know what time it is?
Emma: Is that a yes?
Ward: No. I didn't. I went home, changed, and went out with Kate, like I said. I'm much less exciting than you seem to think.

I could almost see him shaking his head at me through the text message. He'd be disapproving but smiling. And God, that sexy smirk of his. He made me feel things when he aimed that smirk at me. Good things. Bad things. Things that I wanted—needed—more of.

Emma: You didn't want to go to the party?
Ward: Why do you ask?
Emma: I have a curious disposition.
Ward: Curiosity killed the cat.
Emma: Aha! I see I've got you thinking about pussy.
Ward: Whoa. Christ. Emma... are you drunk?

I giggled like an idiot when I read his question and took another sip of the cheap prosecco. It slid down my throat and encouraged me.

Emma: A bit. Yeah.

Ward: You're too honest sometimes, you know that?

Emma: I thought it was good to be honest.

Ward: Someone less honorable than me might try to take advantage of you in this situation.

Emma: Maybe that's exactly what I'm aiming for.

His reply took a full thirty seconds of staring at the little 'typing' icon. I held my breath until the message dinged.

Ward: I feel like I should remind you that I'm your boss. Although I like where this is going.

Emma: Yes, I'm well aware.

Ward: Which part?

Emma: All of it. I know you don't date. I know you only like one-night stands.

Ward: You're probably going to regret this when you're sober. Don't say I didn't warn you.

Emma: Consider me officially warned.

Ward: Are you going to invite me over then? If this is a booty call, I want to know up front. I'd also need to stop for condoms unless you have some.

He didn't pull his punches. I liked that about him. He went right for what he wanted. And at the moment, he wanted me. I bit my lip, considering. Imagining. In vivid detail, I could picture what would happen if I said yes to

Ward tonight. I'd have to send Rae away though. I'm not quiet when I... Another sip of prosecco went down my throat before I replied. This is why they call it liquid courage.

Emma: I'm not that drunk.

At least, not yet. Another long sip of prosecco. It was sweet and tingly on my tongue. I fidgeted on my bed while I waited for him to reply.

Ward: Oh, I see. So, what, you're just teasing me to be cruel?
Emma: Not at all.
Ward: Are you alone?
Emma: Yes. Are you?
Ward: Yes. Extremely.

I was extremely alone too. My body was screaming for the sort of release my vibrator just wasn't capable of. It was screaming for a man, but not just any man. I wanted Ward. Part of me wanted him to invite himself over so I wouldn't have to. I felt like I was spiraling out of control and I willed the feeling to stick around long enough for me to get off. I needed it, even if I wasn't brave enough to ask for it.

Emma: Then how's this for cruel?

I sent him the picture I'd taken earlier in the mirror. In it, I was staring up at the camera, lips parted, and eyes bright. My nipples were hard and dark pink through the fabric of my white top, and I was pushing my tits together and up with one arm underneath, clasping my midsection. My blue sleep shorts were short and tight enough to reveal the folds of my sex.

Ward: Fuck. Emma, you... this is a bad idea.
Emma: You don't like my picture? That hurts.
Ward: No. I fucking hate it. It's the worst. Send me another one without that awful top.

I debated but couldn't quite do it. I even tugged off my top and posed with the camera open. But I couldn't pull the trigger. I'd never sent someone a nude, or even partially nude picture of myself. My body clenched at the thought, though, deep inside. It left a slow, throbbing ache between my thighs. I was imagining him imagining me. Was he touching himself? Stroking? I wanted to touch him. I rubbed my legs together restlessly, but it did nothing to help the ache between them.

Emma: You first.
Ward: Absolutely. With pleasure.

The picture he sent made my fingers slip on my phone, dropping it on my own face like an idiot. When I recovered enough to peek at it again, my mouth fell open in true disbelief. In it, Ward was shirtless, and wearing only a pair of black boxers. The muscles of his abs and chest were just as perfectly sculpted in the picture as in my memory, and he had that sexy cut where his hips met his torso. His face wasn't visible, but his erection clearly was, straining thick and long against the thin fabric. I ran my tongue across my lips, imagining. He was *massive*. No matter what happened with Ward, I'd be saving this picture. Suddenly my remaining clothes were feeling extremely heavy, hot, and uncomfortable. I wriggled out of my shorts until I was in just my tiny, black thong.

Emma: Wow. I'm... I'm speechless. Those sorority girls don't know what they're missing.
Ward: Quit talking about them. I don't want them. I want you. I'm waiting for my picture. I've been thinking about your tits since I first laid eyes on you again.
Emma: Really?
Ward: Really.
Emma: I've been thinking about you too. More than I want to admit.
Ward: I know.
Emma: This isn't a good idea, is it?

Ward: No. It isn't a good idea at all. But I need that picture. I sent you one. Are you too scared?

It was a challenge, and God help me, I've always loved a challenge. But... I still had a shred of dignity. Or was it self-preservation? Something made me hesitate.

Emma: Swear to me that you won't show it to anyone? Ever?
Ward: I would never.

My sex clenched. I believed him. I took the picture of myself in a daze and sent it with my breath held. I'd covered my nipples and supported my heavy breasts with my arm, but with just the thong, there was very little left to the imagination.

Ward: Fuck. You're going to be the death of me.
Emma: Is that a good thing?
Ward: Depends on whether you think my survival is a good thing.

My phone's ringtone startled the hell out of me, and I nearly jumped out of my skin. The number belonged to Ivan, Rae's boyfriend.

"Hello?" I answered, confused as to why he'd be calling me at midnight. Or at all.

"Hey, Emma?" Ivan's voice was muffled over the sound of sirens. "Sorry to call you so late. Rae's phone is off, or maybe she's sleeping, but I got into a minor wreck on I-35. I'm fine and no one's hurt but my car is fucked. Can you go wake her up? I need a ride."

My brain readjusted from lust to crisis management in a few painful seconds. By the time Ivan finished speaking, I was already pulling my clothes back on.

"Oh my God, Ivan, that's awful. Yeah, I'll go get Rae right now. Can I call you back in two seconds?"

"Sure. Thanks Emma. Talk to you soon."

Emma: Hey, I've got a minor emergency I have to deal with. My roommate's boyfriend was just in a car accident. Gotta go.
Ward: Shit! Do you need anything?
Emma: No, it's ok. No one's hurt. I just gotta go now.
Ward: Please don't drive. You're too drunk.
Emma: I won't drive. Rae's sober.
Ward: Promise?
Emma: I promise.
Ward: Ok. Be safe.
Emma: Good night.
Ward: Good night Emma.

Reluctantly, I closed the chat window and grabbed my shoes. Frustration spread through my body from toes to fingertips like a poison. Ivan might have just saved me from making a huge mistake, but at this moment I was uncharitably hoping he had whiplash and a black eye. I pushed my lingering achy horniness to the back of my mind. I knew it would still be there later, waiting for me. That and my picture of Ward.

15

EMMA

THE NEXT TIME I saw Ward was two days later. Because I didn't know what to say, and because I'm a lot less brave when I'm sober, I didn't say anything. Not even 'hi.' I just nodded a greeting, tied on my apron, fixed my smile in place, and got to work. For the next few hours, my words to him were limited to the absolute minimum necessary to do my job. With every terse interaction, I could see Ward getting more and more suspicious. His eyes followed me around the bar, something unknown but intense burning brightly behind them. I should have known the silent approach was doomed to fail.

"You're avoiding me again," Ward announced when he found me on my break. He leaned against the wall and stared at me expectantly.

I couldn't very well deny it. I nodded and looked down

at the laces of my boots. They were interesting, my shoelaces. Very, very fascinating with their loops and their knots... "Yeah. Sorry."

We stood there in silence for a moment before Ward sighed.

"Do you want to talk about it?" he asked. When I peeked up at him, his expression was frustrated. I hardly needed to ask what he was talking about.

"I'm not that kind of girl," I finally managed to say.

"What kind of girl?" Ward asked. He now looked confused as well as frustrated. My heart pounded in my chest like I'd been running a marathon. I swallowed hard before continuing.

"The kind you think I am."

"What kind of girl is that?" Ward looked genuinely perplexed, and it made me feel even worse.

"The carefree, casual kind." I replied, shaking my head. "The kind that texts dirty pictures like that, or who sleeps around and then goes back to work like nothing happened. I'm just not that freewheeling. I don't like one-night stands. That one time... it was a mistake. So was texting you."

Ward was quiet for a moment. His face was puzzled like he was trying to solve a particularly difficult math problem. Eventually he shook his head and sighed.

"So, are you telling me that you wish it never happened? Fine. We'll just forget about it." His voice was entirely mild. Understanding even. But he looked uncomfortable for the very first time I'd ever seen. It was an expression that didn't suit him.

I took a deep breath. To steady myself. To buy me a moment to figure out what I wanted to say and how to say it. It didn't help. I rushed forward before I lost my nerve.

"I don't do the just casual sex thing with guys. I can't. So, yeah, I guess we should just forget it."

"Okay. Consider it forgotten." Ward shook his head, but I didn't know if it was disappointment, irritation, or relief, in his eyes. "If you change your mind, let me know." There was just enough heat left in his gaze to remind me of what I was missing.

I felt like I was being ripped into thirds. A piece of me that was simmering just under the surface was screaming for him to tell me he didn't want just casual sex either. Another piece was grateful he was letting me off the hook before he kissed me, and I gave in. A final piece didn't mind being a casual hookup as long as I got to be his for an hour or two. None of the pieces was fully satisfied by this conversation.

"Okay," I said. My voice was small. I folded my arms around my midsection and wished I could be anywhere else.

"Okay. Does this mean you're going to stop looking at me like I ran over your puppy dog?" Ward stared at me intensely.

"Is that how I've been looking at you?" I hadn't realized.

My lips curled upward into an involuntary smile. I suppose I had been acting strangely.

"Yes! Jesus. You've got these big sad eyes on you tonight. It's making me feel like a murderer or something." He smiled back at me, and my spirits lifted just the tiniest bit that he wasn't going to hold any of this over my head.

"Sorry. I can go back to being mean to you. Did you like that better?"

His laugh was a bitter, humorless little bark.

"I won't say that I *liked* that, but it was a lot better than feeling like a monster."

"You're not a monster." I was staring back at my shoelaces again. "I just... I don't want to do the hookup thing. I always end up getting hurt." I couldn't be someone's dirty little secret again. It would break my heart to bits to be Ward's.

"That's not a crime either. You're allowed to change your mind." He was frowning but did not look angry with me. That was a relief. And a mystery. I wanted to ask what he was thinking but doubted I'd get an honest answer. I'd just rejected him. From his perspective this was probably very frustrating, and baffling. He probably just thought I was a tease.

"I really am sorry if I gave you the wrong idea about me."

"You don't owe me any explanations. I've already

forgotten about it." He smiled then and I knew instantly that it wasn't real. It didn't reach his eyes.

So, I'm that forgettable? Of course, I would be. Why should I think otherwise? "Okay. Well, I need to get back to work."

Ward didn't stop me, and I scurried off, feeling like an idiot.

The night seemed to drag on and on after our conversation. Things between Ward and me felt forced and unnatural, although I was smiling and so was he. At least I knew where I stood with Ward now, and I supposed that was a lot better than just sleeping with him and then hoping he might want to date me afterwards. Somehow that wasn't making me feel better though.

Kate appeared about halfway through my shift to ask me to cover for her tomorrow.

"Why, have you got a date?" I asked interestedly. She blushed and nodded. Of course, she had a date. She was absolutely, stunningly beautiful. Like Ward, Kate was tall, with fair skin, blue eyes, and dark hair. Her features were more delicate than his, but just as gorgeous. I don't even think Kate wore any makeup. She didn't need to. The genes in that family were something else.

"Do I need to threaten him first?" Ward asked from across the bar. "Put the fear of God in him so he behaves?" He cracked his knuckles for good measure and made a 'mean face.'

Kate rolled her eyes. "No, Ward, you don't." She looked at me and grinned. "You hit the jackpot being an only child."

I grinned. "Yep. I got all the attention."

"If only I could have been an only child," Kate said wistfully. Then, in a lower voice that Ward couldn't hear, "Our dad wasn't ever around. Ward has always looked out for me, and apparently still hasn't grown out of it. It's wonderful except when it's infuriating."

"He loves you," I said, just as quietly. "You're lucky to have such a close relationship with a sibling."

Kate nodded in agreement, then rolled her eyes dramatically. "He can be really, really annoying though."

I giggled. "I'll bet." Having seen how seriously Ward took any threat to me—just a cocktail waitress—I could only imagine how protective he would be of his sister. Anyone should think twice before messing with Kate, not that she *needed* any protection. The woman was a force of nature all on her own. Ward may own the bar, but Kate ran it in most substantive ways. They were like a CEO and a COO. Kate made the schedules, inventory decisions, vendor choices, hiring decisions, promotional materials, and took care of all the tiny details of running the day to day.

"What are you two whispering about over there?" Ward asked. He looked between us with suspicion.

"We're talking about you," Kate said, sticking out her tongue. "I'm telling Emma all your secrets."

Ward smirked and shrugged. "Oh, is that all? That's fine. I'm a very simple guy. I don't have any secrets. What you see is what you get with me."

"That's actually true," Kate said, faking sadness. "You are simple. I know mom always said you rode the short bus to school because you were special, but even you were bound to figure it out eventually."

Ward grinned. "At least I'm pretty."

"Pretty ugly," Kate retorted.

"I thought so too, until I saw you."

"At least I'm not stupid."

"I know I'm talking like an idiot, I have to, or you wouldn't understand me."

"There you go, talking about yourself again."

If this was how they bantered as adults, I could only imagine them as kids. Their poor mom must still be exhausted.

As I made my rounds and served my endless stream of customers, I found myself envying Kate and Ward's sibling relationship. They each had someone that was well and truly in their corner. The next time I swung around the bar, I heard Willie and Ward discussing Kate's upcoming date.

"She's going out with that finance douche again," Ward was telling Willie. "She told me that the last time they went out she didn't feel like they connected, but she's still going to see him again. I just don't get it."

"Maybe he's somehow redeemed himself since then," Willie offered.

"I think he's a waste of her time. He sounds boring." Ward looked bored just talking about him, whoever he was.

"Boring's not a problem if they aren't spending their time together talking."

Ward frowned but didn't argue with that. Despite what Kate said, it seemed like Ward did recognize that his sister was an adult (even if they both behaved like kids). "I just think she deserves better."

"Of course, you do; she's your sister. No one will ever be good enough."

"Yeah, that's probably true. But if she was really happy, I'd put up with him."

Ward saw me listening and raised his eyebrows. I just smiled politely and continued on my way.

Eventually, Ward and I settled into an uneasy détente. The hours dragged by and turned to days. Ward didn't tease me, and I didn't bait him. Perhaps this was how our interactions would have been if we hadn't slept together three and a half years ago, but it still felt forced and uncomfortable to me.

It wasn't until right before our next mutual day off that I worked up the courage to corner him in the office one evening.

"I've decided where we should go," I told him, pretending that things hadn't been weird for an entire week.

"Huh?" He looked up from his paperwork in confusion.

"Did you forget already? I went to a football game. Now it's your turn to do something *out of your comfort zone.*"

The look on his face told me he had either forgotten or thought I had.

"You aren't scared, are you?" I challenged. I melted into the chair across from him, crossing my legs and watching him carefully.

"Me? Never. Bring it on." He laughed. His bravado was really something, but after spending so much time carefully observing him, I could see just the smallest amount of hidden worry. And perhaps, although maybe I was imagining it, excitement.

"Good. Does tomorrow work for you?"

He nodded. "Sure. Do I need to wear a pocket protector?"

I rolled my eyes. "No, I mean, you can though. If you want to." I couldn't imagine it.

"Other hints? Dress code? Anything?" He was fishing. That wasn't fair.

"You didn't give me any hints." I pouted.

"I'm a walking hint for football. Come on, give me something. Anything."

I shook my head. "No way. It's a surprise."

"Alright, I guess that's only fair," he acknowledged. "When and where?"

"You can pick me up at twelve again," I told him, grinning. I stood up to leave. "I'm glad you didn't chicken out."

"That's funny," Ward said, his drawl more pronounced when he talked slowly like he was doing now. "I was going to tell you the exact same thing."

16

WARD

EMMA WAS DRIVING ME CRAZY. She'd been standoffish and wary all week. I could accept that she had changed her mind after our ill-advised near phone sex session (that I had every intention of turning into a late-night visit to her bed). I could appreciate that she'd been willing to be honest about it and tell me she regretted it and wanted to move on. And I could admit that I was sorely disappointed. What was driving me crazy was that the more time I spent around Emma, the more I wanted her.

When I arrived at her apartment complex the next day at noon, Emma didn't shoot out of the front door like a rocket, and I actually got to knock. The woman that opened the door, a tall, fierce-looking redhead, was not Emma.

"You must be Ward," she said with a thick east coast accent, looking me up and down with skeptical eyes.

"Come on inside. She'll be right with you. I'm Rae, her roommate."

"Pleased to meet you," I replied, going for charming as I looked around at the Ikea-decorated living room. The space was small, but clean and neat. Exactly what I expected from Emma. "How long have you lived with Emma?"

"Only a few months but long enough to know how great she is." Rae smiled at me in obvious warning. *Hurt her and I'll hurt you,* her expression said. She perched on the edge of a chair and watched me with narrowed eyes. Like Emma, Rae had green eyes, but hers had none of Emma's sea green soft dreaminess. She was all business. An uncomfortable silence filled the little apartment.

After about thirty seconds, I couldn't continue our staring contest. This woman was making me nervous. "How's your boyfriend doing? I heard he was in a car accident."

"See for yourself," Rae said, pointing at the man who'd just limped out around the corner following a toilet flush. "Ward, this is Ivan. Ivan, Ward. You know, Emma's *friend*." The emphasis clearly indicated that she wanted me to unpack the relationship between us, but I couldn't even explain to myself, so I focused on Ivan.

Ivan was tall, skinny and wearing a leg brace from ankle to thigh. He inched forward to shake my hand. "Hi, good to meet you," he said. His grip was weak, and he immediately looked down at his phone when we drew apart. He didn't have any of Rae's menacing attitude, but he didn't seem interested to meet me, either. Given the choice, I'd take disinterest over dislike any day. He had an accent as well, but I wasn't sure where it was from. English? Scottish? I'd never been particularly good at accents. He could be Australian for all I knew.

"Same," I said, gesturing to his knee, although he was now staring at his phone. "Did you hurt your leg? I thought Emma said no one was hurt in the crash."

Ivan grimaced and leaned against his crutch. "I didn't realize how bad it was at first. But, yes, I seem to have tweaked a knee ligament." He shook his head, still without looking up at me. "I suppose I shouldn't have done that last line at the party."

Rae gasped and Ivan looked up to roll his eyes at her dismissively. He finally glanced at me as if to say, "Women, am I right?"

What he actually said to Rae was worse. "God, could you be any more of a killjoy?" he snapped. "Besides, it's not my fault everyone here drives on the wrong side of the road."

I felt myself really disliking Ivan. Not only was he a jerk to his girlfriend, but he could have killed someone with that attitude. I had a bad feeling he might have been serious about being coked-up behind the wheel, too. He was exhibiting all the tell-tale signs of being a spoiled, rich asshole. An uncomfortable silence descended.

"I destroyed all four of my knee ligaments on the left side," I told him to make some attempt at polite conversation. "I know how much that hurts. I hope you heal quickly." Knees are delicate, fickle, cruel creatures.

"All four? At once?!" Ivan's voice was horrified and he actually looked up at me, which was the reaction that only someone who'd ever seriously injured their knee could truly understand. I nodded, not wanting to get into my career-ending injury with an unpleasant stranger. I had ligaments from three different organ donors and one pig in my leg. Thankfully, Ivan didn't dwell on the circumstances. "That sounds horrible. I've got an appointment with a surgeon next week to take a look. I'll probably wait to go home to have surgery though, if I do need it. I'm not sure I want to have surgery in a foreign country that doesn't have good healthcare." He made a face that suggested he thought the US was a third world country.

"Oh? Where's your home?"

"London." Ivan looked wistful at just the mention of his homeland.

My first guess had been right. That accent was British. Emma might think I was a total dunce, but I knew some things about the world. Too bad she wasn't here to witness my small victory.

"So, you work with Emma at the bar, isn't that right?"

Rae asked, clearly looking for details on me. I got the feeling that her snobby boyfriend's appearance had just distracted her from her interrogation of me. I also got the feeling she was embarrassed of him (I would be).

"I do, yes. How did you meet her? Through school?"

"Yes, all three of us are doing our graduate work at UT."

Emma arrived then, coming in through the front door and looking rushed and sheepish. "Sorry I'm late!" She said, peering curiously around at her roommates and me. "I went to run a quick errand and it ended up taking *forever*. I got caught behind one of those old ladies that want to pay with a giant stack of expired coupons. It was excruciating."

I smiled at her. "No problem. I got a chance to meet Rae and Ivan."

She smiled back, but with a nervous, almost hysterical edge. "*Wonderful*. Ready to go?"

I nodded, and Rae looked at us appraisingly. Her frown at me indicated that she wished she'd had more time to inspect me. "Be safe kids. Call me if you need anything, Emma."

"I hope they weren't mean to you," Emma said as we walked down the stairs to my truck. "Rae in particular can come off a bit abrasive. Especially around new people."

"They were perfectly nice. I'm not sure Rae likes me much, but I think she's just protective of you." In reality, I'd disliked Ivan much more than Rae. At least Rae wanted to make sure I was worthy of her friend. Ivan just seemed like a dick, and I felt kind of bad for Rae because of it.

Emma shook her head, sending her blonde hair waving. She was wearing it down today, and I wanted to touch it. "She's just a New Yorker. They're less immediately friendly than Texans, but if you had stuck around long enough, she'd have thawed out. She's really quite sweet under her hard shell. Like an M&M."

Emma probably even believed that. I let it drop. "So, where are we going?" I asked as I opened the passenger door to my truck for Emma. She looked at my vehicle in surprise.

"This thing is a tank," she said. "How am I supposed to get up into it?"

"One foot here," I pointed, "grab here," another point, "other foot here," I gestured. She followed my instructions and hoisted herself up to swing into the seat. It was one of the most adorable things I'd ever seen. She settled in with as much dignity as she could muster.

"But really, why do you need a truck this big?"

"My mom lives on a ranch now. Sometimes I lug supplies out to her."

"So, it's not to compensate for insecurities in other areas?"

I laughed. "Not a problem I suffer from. *Besides, you've got personal and photographic proof.*"

She flushed crimson. I'd really missed her blushes over the last week.

"So, where are we going?" I repeated.

Emma grinned, and challenge slipped back into her expression. Her confidence was back in the blink of an eye. "We're going to an art exhibition."

Ugh. Kill me now. "Great."

17

WARD

DESPITE THE FACT that I owned and operated a bar just off campus, I'd never visited the Blanton Museum of Art that sat just on its southern edge. Emma led us toward the towering multistory building with a big smile on her face, and her enthusiasm began to transfer even though I'd never given a single shit for art before. She was all smiles this afternoon, and I liked it. I wanted to grab her hand but resisted. I wouldn't make the first move.

"What are we going to see?" I asked, curious if there was something specific she wanted to see. In a building this large, we could easily lose an afternoon without some sort of plan.

"There's a visiting exhibit I've been wanting to go to. It's called 'Medieval Monsters: Terrors, Aliens, and Wonders.'"

"Monsters?" I wondered aloud, and she nodded.

"Yeah, you know, griffons, sea serpents, mermaids, dragons, devils, demons, all that stuff that terrified the peasants and gave their children nightmares."

Maybe this wouldn't be so bad.

"I like monsters," I said carefully. This earned me a chuckle.

"I thought you might." Her voice was bland.

Inside, we navigated up through the permanent collection to what Emma wanted to see. The first painting was a massive picture of what looked like an enormous, awkward weasel with scales and way too many feet. Half a peasant was hanging out of its gaping, toothy mouth. Everyone in the painting had extremely awkward facial expressions, like the artist wasn't sure how to convey anything but confusion. Even the monster looked somewhat surprised to find it had eaten someone. Its chubby body told a different story.

"What is that even supposed to be?"

Emma shrugged and looked at the little card. "It looks like a furry snake to me. It's called 'Taming the Tarasque' and was painted in 1500."

I looked it up on my phone for more details. "Oh, that's actually kind of sad," I told her after a moment of reading. "Wikipedia says there was a legend of a beast that was terrorizing villagers. Many knights died yada yada yada. Eventually it was tamed by Saint Martha who played it hymns and prayed over it. Afterward she led it back to the village where the villagers attacked and killed it out of fear, even though it was being nice."

"Sounds about right."

"Well, on the upside, after that Saint Martha converted the pagan villagers to Christianity and everybody lived happily ever after."

Emma smirked at me. "Everybody but the Tarasque."

"Well, yeah. He kind of got the shitty end of the deal."

Moving on from the Tarasque, we walked on through the exhibit. There was a wide variety of weird, silly monsters represented. Some of them were just bizarre.

"Imaginative," I remarked as we passed by a topless mermaid who had wings, legs like a chicken, a harp, and a ton of drowned men around her.

Emma looked at her face. "She looks very sad."

"I'd be sad too if I had chicken legs, a big scaly tail, and no shirt."

"It says she's a siren," Emma said. "The poem that goes with it apparently warns men to avoid the temptations of beautiful women who use their looks to hide their sin and lure men to their doom."

"Sounds like good advice," I offered.

Emma shook her head. "All these monsters are just ways that peasants were scared into obedience. Especially this one."

"How do you figure?"

"By vilifying beauty, men can argue their superiority to

women. They can pretend that women are sinful sources of lust, and so the men bear no responsibility. All these artworks are just about controlling people through fear and faith." She pointed to the next drawing, three funny-looking guys wearing pointed hats and conferring with what looked like a devil. "See, that one's just literally Jewish men talking to Satan. Blatant antisemitism."

Yeah, I could see her point.

"What about this one?" I asked, pointing to a particularly grisly picture of a man being flayed alive while grinning like the process was tickling him. I found this one to be the creepiest of the bunch.

Excited to prove her point, Emma swept past me to read the card, and I caught a whiff of her coconut-scented hair. In an instant, I was removed from any academic discussion and reminded of who I was with, and why. Suddenly, the fact that we were alone in the gallery seemed incredibly important.

Emma seemed oblivious to the shift in my attention from art to her. "This one's the Martyrdom of St. Bartholomew," she told me. "I guess what I would say about that is it's an example of the supernatural being used as a way to represent the awesome power of faith. St. Bartholomew is so infused with, er, holy power that he doesn't care that he's getting his skin peeled off like a peach. He's super ready to meet God, and so his power is inspiring to others."

I struggled to keep up with her interpretation. I had no practice with art appreciation, although it was easier than I'd feared. Perhaps Emma was just going easy on me. "But there's no monster in this one."

Emma smirked. "The people torturing him are the monsters."

I looked at the faces of the torturers in the picture. "They look weirded out that he's smiling."

"Wouldn't you be?" she asked, shrugging. "I think I'd be really creeped out if someone I was torturing kept smiling like that at me. He looks way too into it."

I laughed. "I like to think I wouldn't ever *flay somebody*. I imagine the entire process would weird me out."

She smiled. "Fair enough."

We'd made it through the entire exhibit and wandered into another section of the museum. This area was filled with painting after painting of naked women in various poses.

"This is even better than the monsters," I joked. Emma rolled her eyes.

"What do you like about these?" she asked, clearly challenging me to come up with something better and smarter than 'I just love looking at naked women.'

"I just love looking at naked women." *Oops.*

"Is that all?" Emma pushed.

I frowned. "Is this a test? Did I fail? I know what I like."

"It's not a test," Emma said. She shrugged. "I don't really

enjoy looking at naked women, which is probably why I find these all pretty boring. It's just boobs, boobs, boobs. I don't subscribe to the idea that there has to be some great reason behind why someone likes art. If you like it, you like it. If you don't, you don't."

"Does that mean I did okay at your high-brow activity?"

"You did a great job," she said. "Really. I couldn't ask for anything more." I felt irrationally proud of myself.

We meandered downstairs and got lunch in the little café. Emma insisted on paying for my food, seeing as I paid for our food at the game. Since this wasn't a date, I reluctantly allowed it.

Emma pushed her salad around without much enthusiasm. Once out of the exhibit, she'd turned quiet. Her eyes, usually so clear and transparent about her emotions, were guarded. My curiosity quickly got the best of me.

"What's bothering you?" I asked her.

She looked at me in surprise. "I really thought I was doing a good job of hiding it."

"Maybe I know you better than you think." We had been spending more than forty hours a week with each other lately. You do get pretty used to someone's moods.

She smiled at me as if to say, *I doubt that.* "Promise you won't judge me?"

I nodded. "Friends don't judge."

"Are we friends?" she asked, surprised.

"Aren't we?" It felt like the wrong word, and I immediately regretted it, but I couldn't think of a better one. Plus, I really wanted to know what Emma was keeping from me.

"Okay," she said, smiling a tiny little smile. "Well, remember my ex from the party a couple of weeks ago? Adam? Well, he's been trying to get me to come work for him again in the English department. The professor that I'm working under for my dissertation is on maternity leave, which has put me behind in my research. If I were to go work for Adam, I'd be able to get a teaching stipend, continue my research, and potentially graduate faster. I wouldn't have to work at the bar. He keeps sending me these long emails trying to convince me to call him."

I had a lot of thoughts about that, but all I said was, "That all sounds good, though, right? Graduating quickly is what you want, right?"

She nodded and made a face. "I guess so."

"So, what's the catch, then?"

She looked embarrassed. "He obviously wants to sleep with me. To restart our twisted relationship. It's not an explicit part of the offer or anything, but I just know that's what he wants. It's all he's ever really wanted from me." She sounded bitter, but mostly just tired. I hated the look she had on her face, too. It made me frustrated on her behalf.

"And you don't want that." I'd seen them together and I could tell she didn't want him.

"No. I don't. He didn't treat me so great the first time around. He used me and cheated on me. I know he's just pursuing this extra because you kissed me, and he saw it. Now he's *jealous*. It's not even really about me."

I wanted to ask about that, figure out exactly what he'd done to hurt Emma and then fix it somehow, but I resisted asking more questions. It wouldn't be right to pry. And it wasn't my place. She'd share what she wanted to share with me and no more. That's what *friends* did.

"So, what are you going to do?" I asked her. "Are you going to go work for him? If I need to find another waitress, I need to let Kate know ASAP."

Kate was going to have a cow if we lost Emma after only a few weeks. We'd both been reaping the benefits of having Emma around. Despite my initial misgivings about Emma, she really was a fantastic waitress. The customers loved her, Kate loved her, Willie loved her... and me? I couldn't stand the thought that I might never see her again.

Emma shook her head and relief shook me. "No. I'm not going to do it. It's just stressing me out."

"Have you written him back?"

"No. I'm giving him the silent treatment."

"That's probably the most mature thing you could do. Let him make a fool of himself. If he continues to harass you, report him to the university."

"You sound just like Rae."

"Great minds think alike. Just stay away from him and he'll give up eventually."

Emma nodded. "That's what I'm trying to do."

"I'll go slash his tires if you want. Call him in the middle of the night and threaten him? Egg his door? Toilet paper his front yard? Mail him some glitter? You know, generally scare him off."

She raised a blond eyebrow. "I know you're just trying to be a good friend, but I don't think that's necessary at this point. Also, some of those are felonies."

"You just let me know."

She smiled weakly at me. Anything that kept Emma away from that Adam creep. If it required a felony, well, that was just fine.

18

WARD

FRIENDS. I wished I could take it back. But the word was out there now, hanging between us like an obstacle. A wall.

Emma didn't seem to notice. If anything, she seemed much more at ease than she had been before. We walked back toward my truck in the late afternoon sun, taking our time and enjoying the weather. We passed a small art gallery that was advertising a free show.

"Want to check it out?" I offered. I didn't really want to look at any more art, but I found myself desperate not to let this day end.

"Sure," Emma replied. "These things usually have free booze."

She was right. I snagged a couple of glasses of the free champagne sitting atop the makeshift bar and joined her in front of the first piece on display. The plaque below stated that the piece was entitled 'Gossamer.'

"What am I looking at?" I whispered in her ear. "Is that what I think it is?"

"If you think it's a ball of human hair, then yeah," she whispered back. Her soft voice sent shivers down my spine.

A gigantic ball of hair nailed to a large canvas was exactly what it looked like. It resembled something that would come out of a badly clogged drain, but bigger. Much bigger. Nearby, a young woman with a buzz cut was being congratulated by her friends. I had a bad feeling that I was looking at her hair. *All of her hair.* Emma and I exchanged a wordless, disgusted look. *Why?*

We moved on to the next piece. This one was much less upsetting. Just a picture of a cat lying on a garbage pile. Everything was made of little pieces of colored paper. Kind of boring, but okay. It was recognizably a cat. A long, written explanation for how the cat was a metaphor for women's representation in modern media accompanied the piece. The bits of paper were apparently collected from women's fashion magazines. Emma rolled her eyes.

"You're not a fan of this one?" I asked her in a whisper.

"It's a bit on the nose," she replied. She looked unimpressed.

"Snobby much?" I teased gently.

"Guilty as charged," she admitted with a smile. She

took a swig of her cheap champagne and wrinkled her nose at the harsh taste. "Very, very guilty as charged."

The third piece in the gallery involved the projection of a water texture onto black and white photographs of dogs jumping into water and swimming. They'd been photographed in such a way that their faces were distorted and funny looking. I recognized the backgrounds of the photos as being Barton Springs, a local swimming hole famous for its freezing cold water and native salamander population.

"Okay, I really like this one," Emma admitted, smiling at the silly pictures. "These are pretty adorable."

I nodded. "Yeah, this one's my favorite too. Anything with dogs will always get high marks from me."

"Emma, is that you?" A voice behind us asked. Emma turned, her body tensing at my side.

Two women and a man looked us both up and down. The first woman was wearing a loud, flower print Kimono and aggressive makeup. Next to her, a petite brunette wearing all black peered at us through aggressively ugly coke-bottle glasses. At their side, a gaunt fellow with an artistic, asymmetric haircut looked at me with far more interest than Emma.

Great, more of Emma's friends?

"Hi, Ivy," Emma said in her customer service voice. This wasn't the voice she used for friends. I reevaluated the three. Not friends. "It's great to see you. Hello, Jannie. Hi,

Simon." She turned to me. "Ward, these are some of my classmates. Ivy, Jannie, and Simon are also in the English department. They're master's students."

Emma's tone was guarded, so mine was too.

"Nice to meet you," I said pleasantly enough, shaking hands with each of the three. They had universally weak handshakes. Simon, after apparently determining that I was here with Emma, drifted off wordlessly with a sad shake of his head at me. He needed to brush up on his social skills if he wanted to score. Ivy and Jannie, on the other hand, seemed very keen to socialize. They seemed intensely interested in the both of us.

"I haven't seen you around much lately, Emma," Ivy said in what was clearly a falsely-sweet tone of voice. "We've missed you. Where have you been?"

"I'm taking a semester long sabbatical while Melissa is on leave," Emma said simply. "I hope to be back full-time in the spring."

"Oh, how frustrating for you," Ivy crooned. "Well, at least it looks like you've been putting your time to good use. I heard from Adam Barnstead that you're working in *a bar*. And what do you do, Ward?" Ivy's voice was mean-girl cruel.

"I have a few business ventures around town," I answered. I didn't really want to reveal any personal information to this woman staring down her nose at Emma.

"Ah, business. How very ordinary." You'd have thought I

had just admitted to slaughtering puppies for a living or something. I may have thought Emma was snobby when I first met her, but I don't think I realized until this moment how much I'd misjudged her. Compared to her eccentric peers, Emma was positively ordinary. And unlike Ivy, I don't think of that as a bad thing.

"We thought you might have quit," Jannie said. She was practically sneering at Emma. "After all, you and Barnstead have quite *a history*."

"Excuse me?" Emma said, wide-eyed. Her voice had risen an octave. Jannie, sensing danger, shut the hell up and looked uncomfortable. Ivy was less careful.

"Well, yes," Ivy said, smiling like a crocodile. "Rumor is that you were his muse and prize student until he just couldn't resist your advances anymore. You seduced him and the torrid affair that followed led to him leaving Yale and his fiancée. Apparently, even though you've mastered the sweet and innocent impression, you're *really quite the homewrecker*." She whispered the last part like it was something to brag about.

"*Is that what he's telling people?*" Her voice was livid. And loud. Around the gallery, people glanced over at us. Emma was flushed a brilliant and unhealthy red-purple. It was time to go. Preferably before Emma exploded.

"Oh, well, it's all just rumor, of course. I wouldn't take it too personally." Ivy shrugged and smiled. "See you around."

Ivy and Jannie waved cheerily and wandered off. Perhaps they had someone else to torture. Emma looked heartbroken.

"Let's get out of here," I suggested, and she didn't protest. I pulled her out of the gallery by the hand and we made it all the way back to the car before she spoke.

"He's making me out to be some kind of slut."

"I'm sorry." I didn't know what else to say. It sucked that he was starting rumors about her. No matter what the truth was, he shouldn't be talking about her behind her back. That was just shitty.

"I liked him, and he made me feel older and more mature," she told me, blushing furiously. "I was a virgin. He told me he loved me. I didn't know he was engaged to someone else, but I knew it was wrong to sleep with my professor..."

"You don't have to explain yourself to me," I told her. Although I wouldn't deny that I was curious.

"I want one person to know the truth," she said, shaking her head sadly. "He used me like a toy. Told me not to tell anybody. I thought it was fun to have a secret, but he wasn't who I thought he was." Her anger had faded while she spoke. Her green eyes just looked sad now.

"He just didn't want his fiancée to find out."

"Right. And the university. It's against the code of conduct for professors to sleep with students."

"For obvious reasons."

"It wasn't obvious to me at the time, but yes. It's a very unhealthy dynamic for a nineteen-year-old and a forty-year-old to sleep together. Especially when he controlled my GPA."

Gross. I kept my opinion to myself. It wasn't her fault.

"You have nothing to feel guilty about," I told her. "He took advantage of you, not the other way around." She smiled thinly at me.

"Rationally I know that. But why do I feel so crappy then?"

"You're the siren," I told her. "Remember? You said that society punishes women by turning their beauty into something dangerous to men. It's not really your fault, but you're made to feel like it is."

Emma was quiet for a long time. When she looked up at me, her green eyes were soft again and her smile was less forced. "You're very smart, Ward. You pretend that you aren't, but you are."

"Do you mean that?"

She nodded. "Yes, I do."

"Well, then thank you. Did I help any?"

Emma laughed. "A little bit, yeah."

I'd take a little bit. If it was all I could get, I'd be happy with a little bit. I had to be. After all, we were *friends* now. So why did I feel so bad?

19

WARD

"DON'T TAKE ME HOME," Emma said as I started up the engine after a few minutes of awkward silence. "I don't want to go home right now. Drop me off at the library or something. Just don't take me home."

"The library?" *Did she really want to read right now?*

"Anywhere," she said. Her voice was soft and pain-filled. "Just not back to my apartment."

We were still sitting in the parking lot. I looked over at her, unsure. Emma seemed upset and I didn't know what to do to fix it. Before I could say anything to her, she pulled my shirtsleeve to make me face her, and then she kissed me.

Her lips were soft, warm, and eager. I didn't stand a chance to resist her. Without thinking, I scooped her up from her seat and pulled her over the console and into my lap. She was so small it was hardly difficult. She leaned against me, teasing me senseless with her mouth and sighing contentedly when I held her tighter and tighter.

It had been years since I made out with someone in a car. I felt like a teenager, and my heart pounded in my chest like it was the first time when she let me cup her tits and knead her round ass in my palms. She fit perfectly in my hands. She was whimpering, nuzzling, and urging me on as I touched her, rounding second base and heading for third. My brain was already planning how I could maneuver her in order to fuck her within the narrow confines of the cab. I could put her in the back or bend her over the dash. But first, I needed her out of her skinny jeans. I started on the buttons and worked down the zipper. I felt her lips curl into a smile against mine.

Stop.

Somehow, I managed to obey the little voice of conscience. I pulled back.

"Emma, wait a second." My voice sounded pained even to my own ears.

"What's the matter?" she asked, playing with the hair behind my ears. Her voice was low and throaty. She kissed my throat and my cock ached, throbbing and desperate for her touch. She bit down gently on my neck, just a little nip, and I moaned.

"This isn't a good idea. You're upset. More than I think you realize."

She pulled away and tugged the buttons on her shirt open, baring her lacy, red bra for me. "Do I seem upset?" It took me a long, long time to rip my eyes away from her perfect, round tits. With great effort, I kept my hands on her waist.

"No. I mean, yes. I--you're too emotional at this second and I don't want you to regret this later."

"You think I don't want you?" She grabbed my hand and led it between her legs and down the front of her unzipped pants. Her matching red, lacy panties were soaking wet. Ready. She pushed her sweet pussy against my palm, grinding and looking for friction. My breath caught in my throat. "I want you," she purred.

"I want you too. I just think this is a bad idea." It took all of my strength to choke out the words.

"Are you seriously turning me down right now?" Her hands went for my belt, and I grabbed them.

"You'll thank me for turning you down when you're back in your right mind. You said you don't like casual hookups. That's all I can offer you."

A flash of annoyance entered her eyes. "I know what I want."

"So do I. I don't want to see you make an impulsive mistake your gonna' regret just because someone said something mean to you."

Hurt and rejection were obvious in her eyes. She seemed to melt into herself and scrambled awkwardly back to her seat. I felt a thousand times worse. She righted her clothes and stared directly ahead like looking at me was too awful.

"Emma?" I ventured.

"Yeah?" She was still staring straight ahead.

"Should I take you home now?"

"Sure." Her voice was expressionless. She'd closed down completely.

The five-mile drive back to her apartment took the longest ten minutes of my entire life. I was so tense I was surprised I was able to drive. Emma was utterly silent throughout the drive. I knew that she was unhappy and hurt. I knew that she would be feeling rejected and deprived. I just didn't know what to say or do about it.

When we pulled up to her apartment, Emma shot me a look that hurt my heart and made my head ache.

"Emma, I'm sorry—" I started to say, but she shook her head.

"Don't say anything," she said. "You can't make it any better. You're only going to make it worse now if you pity me. If you're really my friend, please just let me go."

I nodded.

She didn't say goodbye, she just ran. She was out of my truck and climbing the stairs faster than I thought she could move. I didn't even have a chance to open the door for her, although I got the feeling it would be an unwelcome gesture.

She probably hated me now. I couldn't blame her. I watched her go and sat in the parking lot for a long, long time. I'd seriously fucked up, but I didn't know what else I was supposed to do. Take advantage of her when she was upset? That would have been definitely, one hundred percent wrong. She'd been taken advantage of before, by Adam. I didn't want to be like him. But I wanted Emma.

I needed advice, and the only person who could give it to me was going to be seriously pissed off. Kate would not react well to me pursuing Emma. Reluctantly, I drove home. Alone.

20

EMMA

I woke up the next morning and had to talk myself into getting out of bed. I felt like I'd been hit with an emotional sledgehammer. Between Adam and Ward, I was just about to swear off men forever. I'd finally decided to hook up with Ward and he'd turned me down? What an asshole. My pride hurt from the rejection, even though I knew I'd be regretting sleeping with Ward right now if he hadn't turned me down. The last thing I needed was to cry over Ward again.

The only good thing about this day was that I didn't have to see Ward. I took a long shower to try and clear my head and resolved to be productive. I would buy groceries. I hadn't done that in a while and I could only mooch off Rae for so long.

A polite knock on my door interrupted my disconsolate hunt for shopping bags. I opened the door, squealed, and immediately tried to slam it. Ward edged a gigantic foot in before I could. Before I could stop him, he was standing in my living room like he owned the place. He was so big that he made my apartment look tiny.

What the fuck?

"Good morning to you, too." His voice was amused, and I seriously wanted to murder him.

"God dammit, Ward. Why are you here?"

"I'm here for two reasons." He held up two fingers and I wanted to jab them into his eyes.

He shouldn't be here at all. "Shouldn't you be working today?"

"I called in sick." According to Willie, Ward hadn't missed a day of work or taken a vacation in almost three years. I didn't know what to say.

"Why are you here?" I finally managed to choke out.

"I told you. Two reasons. Reasons worth calling in sick."

"Okay, I'm waiting." I had both my hands on my hips and was tapping my foot impatiently. "What are your two reasons?"

"The first is to offer myself to you. *Sexually*." He smiled at me with the sort of smile that could make a nun rethink her vows. It wasn't doing anything for me at the moment.

"I'm sorry. You're what?"

"I'm here to fuck you. However you want me to, for as long as you want me to. If you still want me to, that is." He seemed perfectly serious. I couldn't help but laugh.

"Oh, you're definitely fucking with me."

"No. I'm not. I'm really, really not. I realize that yesterday I was wrong and stupid to say no. You're phenomenally hot, and if you're still willing, I'm ready. So, let's go. Where's the bedroom?" He looked around curiously.

"This isn't funny, Ward." I didn't appreciate being made fun of. Yes, I'd been impulsive yesterday, and yes, it was a bad choice, but this was just plain mean.

He pulled his shirt over his head. "I'm not joking."

I swallowed hard and my heart beat faster. "You're making fun of me."

"Trust me, I'm totally serious." He stepped closer to me and I retreated to the other side of the room. "I want you. Now."

"Stop it. You've made your point."

"I'm not here to make a point. I'm here to fuck you." He pulled an entire box of condoms out of his pocket. "I came prepared, too. We can go all day."

"Gross. No. Too late. I'm not interested. You had your shot with me."

"So, you're turning me down now?" He looked comically rejected.

"Not just that. I'm throwing you out. Leave. Leave now."

"Are you sure?" He looked me up and down. "I promise I can make you scream."

"Maybe in disgust and horror."

"Hardly. I'm at your mercy here. I want you. Let me prove it to you." He got down on his knees. "Please?"

A little hysterical part of my brain was screaming that shirtless Ward was on his knees, begging to fuck me. I told it to shut the hell up.

"No. Get out." I was yelling. My hands were balled into fists at my sides.

"That's what I figured," he said. His smile was knowing, and it made me even more upset. He got up and put his shirt back on and I bit back a pang of disappointment. "I knew you'd change your mind."

"I changed my mind because of what you did yesterday."

"Sure."

"You know what, I ought to thank you for turning me down. Because you're disgusting. You're probably diseased. You don't deserve me."

"Yes, I'm sure that's all true except for the diseased thing." He looked smug. "I get tested regularly."

One part of me said 'gross,' while another filed the information under 'good to know.'

"Why are you still standing there? Leave."

"Oh, because I haven't told you about reason two."

"Spit it out!" I was all out of patience.

"I'm going to take you fishing."

My jaw went slack and I stared at him. "What?"

"You, me. Going fishing." He mimed a cast of an invisible fishing pole.

"No." I shook my head. "We are not."

"Yep. We definitely are."

Ward was pushing me to my absolute limit. I feared I was literally going insane. "Get out of my house."

"Okay. Just put on your shoes and we'll go."

"I'm not going anywhere with you."

"Yes, you are. We're going fishing!"

"Why the hell would I want to do that?"

"Because you're my friend and I want to help. I know for a fact that going fishing is the cure for a bad mood. And you, my friend, are in a terrible mood. Aren't you?"

No point in denying it. "You called in sick to take me fishing?"

"I called in sick to fuck you. That was definitely my primary intention. But since you aren't interested, yes, we'll go fishing instead."

"I have plans," I lied.

"What?"

"Grocery shopping."

"Grocery shopping?" He looked around at the bags I'd strewn about the living room. "Well, guess what? We can get you some fish *while we're fishing.*"

"I don't want any fish."

He shrugged. "We'll throw them back then."

"It will hurt the fish."

"It doesn't hurt them to be caught. They're just fish. You know, you eat fish."

"I've got very important grocery shopping to do."

"Do you really want to go grocery shopping by yourself? Wouldn't you rather go fishing with me?" He smiled at me sweetly, and my resistance wavered.

I wanted to throw Ward out, but the part of me that wasn't an immature, horny jerk realized what he was doing. He was honestly trying to cheer me up. He'd taken time off to cheer me up. That was nice. Bizarre, but nice. Infuriating, but nice.

"I've never been fishing before in my life," I stuttered.

"I'll teach you." He grinned. "It's gonna be really fun. I promise. It will put you in a better mood."

"You really took time off to go fishing with me?" Part of me really couldn't believe it. Ward was nothing if not a workaholic. Kate had to force him to keep a regular schedule or he'd work seven days a week. It was only by her insistence that he took *weekends*.

"I told you, the fishing thing was my fallback plan. Plan one was—"

"Yes, yes. Fucking me. But you knew I wouldn't agree to that." I rolled my eyes at him.

"A man can still dream. You haven't changed your mind again, have you? The offer stands."

"No. I don't want to fuck you." *I want to strangle you. Sort of.*

"So, are we going fishing?" He looked at me expectantly.

I could barely believe it. I shook my head and stared at him in disbelief. "Yeah. I guess we're going fishing."

21

EMMA

"THIS IS A VERY NICE BOAT," I said loud enough to be heard over the noise of the engine. I was still looking around my new surroundings with interest. "It looks brand new."

I don't know much about boats, but this one seemed fancy. It had a shiny blue and white paint job, white pleather seats, a nice shaded area to get out of the sun, and an engine that pushed us along the smooth surface of the lake fast enough to push my hair back like a dog sticking its head out the window.

"I bought it a couple of years ago, but I feel like I never get a chance to use it," Ward admitted. "It's basically still new."

"So, what are you looking for?" I asked Ward as he slowed the engine to a putter.

"It's more of a feeling thing," Ward said. "I'll know when we get to the spot where the fish are."

I arched an eyebrow at him but said nothing. It sounded a bit farfetched, but maybe Ward did have a sixth sense for where the fish were. We'd find out soon enough. Eventually, he cut the engine and nodded like he was listening to something I couldn't hear.

"Yeah. Right here. I've got a good feeling about this spot."

"You're the boss," I told him with a shrug. "Now what do we do?"

"Now we fish." He looked at me like that should have been obvious to me.

Ward showed me how to bait the hook, cast the line, and reel it back in. It was a bit gross with the live worm wriggling from the hook all sad and impaled, but it wasn't hard. Once we both had lines in the water and beers in our hands, I looked over at him.

"What happens now?" I asked.

He shrugged. "We wait for the fish to bite, drink these beers, and talk."

"That's all?"

He laughed lightly. "What were you expecting? Sharks?"

I smiled at him and shook my head. "Not in Lake Austin. I still can't believe you called in sick to take me fishing."

"Maybe we both needed a break." Something about his answer seemed evasive, but I didn't push. He looked happy.

"Did you grow up fishing?" I asked Ward after a few minutes of companionable silence. This was the most relaxed I think I'd ever seen him. He took a long sip of his beer before answering.

"Yeah. With my grandfather. He would take me out sometimes for 'man training.' Those were some of my favorite memories with him."

I tried to imagine little Ward fishing. I bet he was really excited about it.

"What exactly does one learn during 'man training'?" I questioned.

Ward grinned. "All kinds of things. We went camping, fishing, and hunting, sure, but he also taught me some basic mechanic skills, gardening, how to tie a tie, how to dance, all that good stuff."

"That does sound like fun. My parents weren't very outdoorsy. I was in Girl Scouts for about five minutes, but I hated every second of selling cookies." Even the memory was cringe-worthy.

"You were a shy kid, huh?" Ward guessed.

I nodded. "Very." Approaching strangers to push cookies on them had been mortifying for me. I sold exactly two boxes. One to my neighbor and one to my teacher. My mom quickly got frustrated and told me if I wouldn't ring the doorbells, I couldn't stay a Girl Scout. By that point I was happy to hang up my uniform.

"I was shy too," Ward said, surprising me. "It wasn't until I got to middle school and started getting any good at football that I came out of my shell."

"I have a hard time imaging you as shy," I told him. Ward was the polar opposite of shy. He was the most extroverted person I think I'd ever met.

"Well, once I was out of the shell, I never went back. I wouldn't have fit. I shot up about eight inches in two years."

Yikes. "That actually sounds painful."

"It was. It made my shins ache at night. But then I was taller than everybody and that was cool."

"I imagine you were pretty much king of your school, being a star football player and all that."

"It wasn't bad, no." Ward's attempts at modesty were pretty weak. He looked pleased with himself.

"Did you date the head cheerleader?" I asked teasingly.

He grinned. "Maybe. Maybe her sister, too."

"Were you the Homecoming King? Prom King?"

"Maybe."

"Class president?"

He shook his head. "Nah. Too much work."

"Yeah, it sounds like you had it really rough," I told him.

He smiled. Suddenly I sat forward, thinking I felt something on my line, but it was nothing. I giggled as I sat back. "False alarm," I told him. "No fish." He grinned at me.

"What about you?" Ward asked. "What were you like in high school?"

"Besides shy? I was, um, incredibly studious and needlessly serious," I said. "We probably wouldn't have gotten along."

"And we get along now?"

"Good point." Although we were getting along fine right now.

"I think I would have liked you in high school," Ward said after a moment. "I've always had a thing for the super-sexy, no-nonsense type."

I rolled my eyes at him. "I'm pretty sure I would have hated you. Popular guys have always irked me."

"Maybe I would have grown on you."

"Or maybe you wouldn't have spent a second on me, since you had twenty cheerleaders to choose from." Did my voice sound bitter? I felt that way.

"Cheerleaders can get boring after a while," Ward said lazily. "Always with the cheering, the giggling, and the pom-pom shaking."

"Isn't that what most men like? Simple, pretty girls to worship them?"

"I mean, yeah, absolutely. It was great while it lasted. I can't speak for most men, but at least for me, it was all a lie. The second my football career fizzled, the girls disappeared. Including my fiancée."

"Oh," I said softly. "Yeah, Kate told me about that. I'm really sorry that happened to you."

"Don't be. I'm better off," Ward said with a shake of his head. "Jessie wanted to date a football star, not Ward Williams. We're both really lucky she figured that out before she became Mrs. Ward Williams."

"I guess so," I murmured. "Still sucks though."

"Yeah, it did," Ward agreed. "There's nothing quite like lying in a hospital bed knowing your entire world is ending when your girl up and dumps you. I loved her. She only loved the idea of me. The reality was apparently very disappointing to her."

"And I thought I had a good reason to have trust issues," I remarked. That earned me a smirk.

"On the upside, I don't have to see her anymore. I haven't seen her in years and probably never will again. Your ex followed you across the country."

I groaned. "Don't remind me."

"You'll figure it out," Ward promised me. "I know you will."

"How?"

"You're smart. Way smarter than me."

"You say that, but it isn't true. You're plenty smart."

Ward looked at me and smiled. "It's okay. I don't mind that you're smarter than me. I'm way taller and stronger than you are."

"That's certainly true." The way he'd manhandled me

in the cab of his truck flickered through my mind. He'd picked me up like I weighed nothing at all. With his strength and my flexibility... I shook my head to clear it.

"Fish!" Ward cried, sitting forward and reeling in his line. He pulled up an empty hook. "Well, shit."

We slowly worked our way through the beers in the cooler and worms in the can. We didn't catch a thing for about three hours.

"I'm not sure your feeling about this spot was accurate," I told Ward as I baited another hook.

"Hush. Don't jinx it," Ward said. "This is gonna be the time."

I settled back into my seat. "Okay. Okay."

Moments later, I felt a tiny nibble on the end of my line. Maybe Ward was right. I wiggled it back and forth, feeling the tension. Yeah, there was definitely something on the end of the line.

"Ward," I whispered excitedly. "I think I've got a fish."

"Okay, start reeling it in," he said, "just a little bit at a time."

Carefully, I reeled up the line. Ward got a net ready. From the depths of Lake Austin, a shape began to emerge. It was heavy. The fish was big, oblong, and white. It was... not a fish. It was a shoe. More specifically, an old, nasty tennis shoe.

"What the fuck?" I laughed. "No fair."

Once he got it in the net, Ward snapped a picture of it with his phone. "Catch of the day."

He took a picture of us, too. It was a cute picture, two smiling happy people having a nice day at the lake. We looked like friends, not touching and only close enough to fit in the frame together. I guess that should have made me feel good to have made friends with Ward, but it didn't. The picture just made me feel lonely.

22

WARD

"What do you like about being in school?" I asked Emma. We were down to the last few bait worms. The survivors wriggled around in the cup helplessly. They didn't know it yet, but their fate was already decided.

She shrugged, squinting into the sunlight to look over at me. "Why do you ask?" Her green eyes glowed in the light like they were lit from inside.

Because I want to know every detail about you.

The little voice in my head came from nowhere. I told it to shut the hell up before it got me into trouble, but just like the bait worms, I suspected my fate was sealed.

"I'm just curious," I said casually, "I spent my whole life waiting to get out of school, but you've spent your whole life trying to stay in it."

"I like to learn," she said simply.

"There's got to be more to it than that. Getting a PhD sounds like torture to me. You couldn't pay me to do it, let alone *make me pay to do it.*"

Emma sat quietly for a bit before answering. "Did you read *The Chronicles of Narnia* when you were a kid?"

"The ones with Aslan the lion and the British kids that went through the wardrobe?" I grinned at her. "Of course. My mom read them to me. I liked that the kids got to be kings and queens." I had fuzzy, happy memories of sitting with my head in her lap as she read them to me right before bed. This was when Kate was just a baby and I had to beg, borrow, and steal every moment I could with my mom. I eventually stopped disliking my little sister for monopolizing our mom's attention, but there had definitely been a few years when we were both small that I wished I was an only child. The reading time I spent with my mom before bed was still special in my memory. I could almost feel her hand on my forehead and hear her voice in my memory, even now.

"Do you remember the first book in the series? *The Magician's Nephew*?" Emma's voice was wistful.

"Um... not really." It had been probably twenty years since I thought about these books. The actual plots had become extremely mixed up in my head. "Was that the one with the evil talking ape or the one with the prince and boat?"

"Neither. Those were different ones. This was the first

book, set before the other ones. In *The Magician's Nephew*, the two English kids find these rings that bring them to this place that they called 'the wood between the worlds.' It was where they first found Narnia, and also the world that the evil White Witch was from." I nodded vaguely, remembering not liking that book as much as the others. Fewer battles. Emma continued, "Anyway, that image has stuck with me all this time. That there were all these worlds out there, all these different stories. Not just Narnia. Other worlds too. And you needed the rings to access them, but if you could get it, you could escape Earth and have adventures."

"And you thought that school would get you there?" I guessed.

"Well, yeah. That's how the magician figures out how to make the rings. He studied and experimented. It turns out I interpreted the whole allegory wrong, and C.S. Lewis wasn't trying to say any of that, but it worked for me." She shrugged. "I know that it's silly, but I've always had it in my head that I can get to 'the wood between the worlds' if I keep at it."

"What do you mean it wasn't what C.S. Lewis was trying to say?"

"Well, he was writing a Christian-themed fantasy. He says in his writings that the 'wood between the worlds' is located in Aslan's country. That's essentially heaven, right? The wood between the worlds is where God—Aslan—can enter and exit the different worlds, and presumably where dead souls pass through on the way to Aslan's country. It isn't meant to be used by magic-using humans to have fun adventures. In fact, the magic-using humans who access it get into trouble. Magic is evil and unnatural, after all."

"Wait. What? It was a Christian-themed fantasy the whole time?" I blinked. That was news to me. "Magic is evil?" Everything in those books had magic. *The animals talked.*

"You didn't notice the Christian themes?" She smirked at my ignorance.

"No." I doubted my mom even knew they were Christian-themed fantasies, though I'm sure she would have approved if she had known.

Emma giggled at me. "You didn't think it was odd that all the animals in Narnia celebrated Christmas? What about all the apple-themed imagery? Or the fact that the evil character is a witch? Aslan even tells the kids at one point that 'in their world, Earth, he is called by another name.'"

"I was just a dumb little kid!" I said defensively. "I wasn't exactly looking for hidden Christian messages. Even if I had been, I wouldn't have known what they meant. I just liked that the kids got to wear armor, fight battles, talk to animals, and have fun adventures. I suppose your parents explained all the metaphors and stuff to you?"

Emma nodded and then giggled again. "They did, yeah.

When I said I wanted to go to 'the wood between the worlds,' they were *really* worried about me. They thought that I wanted to commit suicide or something, since the only time you were supposed to go there is when you're dead. They were relieved when I told them I really just wanted to go to school and read and write."

I smirked at her. That was a very Emma-type story. "Your parents must be very proud of you for going for your PhD."

She shrugged uncomfortably. "They like that I'm following in their footsteps. But..." she trailed off and looked suddenly nervous.

"But what?" I probed.

Her little sigh was frustrated, and her hands gripped her fishing pole a little tighter. "Sometimes I wonder if I'm doing the right thing by getting my PhD." Her admission was soft.

"What do you mean?" I was surprised to hear that Emma had any doubts. She always seemed so focused when she talked about her studies.

She pushed her hair back from her eyes while she looked for the words. I waited as patiently as I could. "I feel like the more time I spend around academics, the more I realize they're all mostly just huge phonies."

I didn't know what to say, so I didn't say anything. I had always thought my teachers were secretly full of shit—*especially my English teachers.*

Eventually, Emma added, "It's like they think they have everything figured out. They pretend that they're so much better than anyone who just reads for fun, because they're *analyzing and interpreting* everything. I mean, it's good to try and understand what you're reading, but you can't act like you *know* what someone was trying to convey in their writing on a subconscious level. It just feels like it sucks the joy out of reading sometimes, but they act like they're superior humans because they don't enjoy anything but negativity and criticism. And God forbid you ever disagree with them."

"I always felt like my English teachers were trying to suck the joy out of everything," I admitted. "I liked reading as a kid, but then later on it was just a chore. The more I hated reading something, the more my teachers acted like I was dumb." I remembered making many a diorama in school that felt like huge wastes of time. And my essays were always terrible, too, mostly because I hated writing them. Kate and I were both solid C students in high school. We did the absolute minimum to get by and only went to college on athletic scholarships.

"Exactly! It's so fake. So many people pretend they're intellectuals when really, they're just snobs that want you to agree with them. There's legitimate literary criticism and then there's bullshit, pointless, self-indulgent criticism that just tears another person's art or opinion down. I've met some very distinguished professors that think they're doing the former when they've really spent their whole careers cultivating the latter." She looked around herself uncomfortably, as if one of her professors might be scuba diving beneath us and listening in.

"As long as you know the difference, it seems like you'd be in the clear though, right?" I feared I was quickly getting out of my depth. There were literal libraries full of things I didn't know about literary criticism. Emma didn't seem to notice my worry. She was clearly too focused on her own insecurity to worry about mine.

"That's what I'm concerned about. If I spend too much time around academia, I might end not being able to tell the difference between *thinking critically and critical thinking.*"

"I wouldn't worry about that," I told her. "You're a genuine, honest, good person. I'm sure you'll always know the difference." I may not know about much, but I believed Emma was a good person. She might be *a little bit* on the snobby side at times, but there were much worse qualities that a person could have. Plus, she was currently out fishing with me. So, she clearly wasn't too set in her ways.

"You're a genuine, honest, good person, too," Emma said to me, worry coloring her voice, "and you still ended up engaged to Jessie."

Ouch. I felt myself wincing, and then saw Emma's eyes turn huge in apparent guilt. Her cheeks turned that familiar pink.

"Oh God. Sorry, Ward," she said, placing a tiny palm on my arm. "I really didn't mean to..."

I shook my head at her, making myself smile to reassure her. She looked horrified. "No, no. You're right. I did end up mixed up with someone toxic and fake." I stared down at her hand, enjoying her touch and then feeling deprived when she pulled away a second later. "I really fucked my life up good for a while."

She was still frowning and unsure. "No, you didn't do anything wrong. You just thought she was someone better than she was. That's not a weakness. You gave her the benefit of the doubt because you were in love."

The truth was, I just thought she was pretty and I was stupid enough to believe her when she said she loved me. Jessie's true loves were money and attention. She only loved me when I could provide those things. "Being gullible is definitely a weakness, I'm able to admit it. We were happy for a while, though." I cast my line out into the water a bit more forcefully than was really necessary. The bobber hit the water with a distant little splash.

We both watched it, lapsing into an uncomfortable silence. I thought the conversation was over, until Emma asked, "What was it like when you were in love with her versus someone else who loved you back?" Her voice was soft and wistful. "Can you tell the difference when it's real?"

"What?" My heart was pounding all of a sudden.

"What was it like? I thought I was in love with Adam,

but he didn't care about me. I've never been in love with anybody that loved me back. So, I wonder if it's a different feeling." She looked genuinely curious to know the answer.

"I'm sorry to disappoint you, but I can't help you there. Other than Jessie, I've never been in love. I've never been in love with anybody that loved me back, either."

"We're quite the pair, aren't we?" Emma's voice was a bit bitter.

"I guess we are."

Somehow, the thought didn't make me feel alone or bitter. If anything, it was nice to know someone else understood, even if it meant we were both damaged goods.

23

EMMA

"Did Kate tell you she broke up with that guy she was seeing?" I asked Ward, wanting to change the subject away from Jessie as soon as possible. I don't know what I'd been thinking to bring her up in the first place. Ward was clearly still not over her. He was as wounded by her as I was by Adam.

Ward's face told me that he hadn't heard the news about Kate yet. "Good riddance," he said after a moment, grinning from ear to ear and looking relieved. "I really didn't like that guy. Speaking of phonies, he *definitely qualified*."

"Really? I never met him." All I knew was that Kate said he was bad in bed and boring to talk to. I wasn't going to tell Ward about the underwhelming sex. Some things were not meant for her brother's ears.

"The guy, who I literally only met once for fifteen minutes, told me he owned two Rolexes." Ward looked disgusted by the prospect of this man's conspicuous consumption. I didn't know anything about Rolexes other than that they were expensive.

"What, was he wearing one on each wrist?" It didn't sound like a good look.

Ward laughed. "No, but he probably would if he could. He just talked about them."

"Maybe he was just trying to impress you so that you'd like him and think he was worthy of Kate?" I offered half-heartedly. It did seem tacky, at the very least.

Ward rolled his eyes. "I don't think he was trying to impress me." He certainly didn't sound impressed. "I do think he was trying to *intimidate me.*" He didn't sound intimidated either. I imagined that it would take quite the man to intimidate Ward. Ward generally *did* the intimidation.

"I haven't had a real watch in years," I mused. "I just use my phone. If I don't have my phone, I'm just late." I shrugged my shoulders and watched my bobber floating on the water. Had it moved? No, it was just my imagination.

"I don't think he was trying to make sure I knew how on time he always was." Ward's voice was dry.

"Yeah, probably not," I agreed. "Well, it sounds like Kate won't be seeing him again. She said he was really boring. All he ever talked about was finance stuff."

"He was probably bragging about his salary." Ward looked completely grossed out. "Kate's not the type to be impressed by money. We were never well off growing up and she got teased in high school about it because most of our school was from a much richer area. She hates it when people act all superior just because they have money."

I nodded. I'd known Kate for long enough to be certain that her heart was in the right place about a lot of things, including money. She wasn't one to be swayed by money, or even be very impressed by it. It was just a thing that was nice to have for Kate. The fact that her brother was able to pay off all her student loans in her sophomore year had been a huge deal for her, but she never bragged about Ward's money or seemed to take it for granted. She worked her ass off, lived modestly, stayed in college and finished her degree. To this day she was working at the bar and saving up her pennies. One day she'd have enough to finance her dream of owning and operating a boutique, but she'd sworn back in college that she'd never ask Ward for money, and as far as I knew, she never had. I wasn't even sure if Ward knew that's what Kate wanted.

"It must have been weird for your family to have you suddenly get really rich when you were playing in the NFL, huh?" It would have been like winning the lottery.

Ward's face was bemused. "You can say that again." He drummed his fingers on the railing of the boat in a display of apparent discomfort. "I had a lot of second cousins and friendly acquaintances come out of the woodwork looking for handouts."

"That must have been really bizarre." I couldn't even imagine how I'd deal with it. Probably poorly.

"It was awful. I hated those conversations. There's no nice way to tell your cousin you haven't seen since junior high that you aren't going to buy him a monster truck." From the look on Ward's face, this was a real conversation he'd had.

"Did you buy any monster trucks at all?" I felt like I had to ask. Ward seemed like he might drive a monster truck if it were an option. Hell, his regular truck was a monster, and it was still technically just a normal vehicle.

"No, but I did buy my mom a Ferrari for Mother's Day." He looked proud of it, and I couldn't blame him. I would buy my mom an expensive, fancy car if I could, too. Although she'd probably insist on something dull and practical instead. Like a used Volvo station wagon or a Prius or something. Trying to imagine my mom behind the wheel of a Ferrari wasn't possible. She'd hate something so ostentatious.

"That's actually really sweet," I said, shaking my head. I liked that Ward had such a good relationship with his mom. "Did you buy her the ranch she lives on, too?"

Ward nodded proudly. "Yeah. That was right before I blew out my knee. I'm really glad I was able to give that to her. She loves it. She always wanted a lot of land and animals. She loves it, and it's a good business, too."

"Does she ride and rope cattle and stuff?" I knew virtually nothing about ranching other than that it usually involved a lot of cows. It was a very Texas type thing to do, which meant that I had very little interest in it. I saw a cow once. It was unattractive.

"It's an alpaca ranch, so no." He grinned. "They wouldn't let you ride them. And they're too small."

"An alpaca ranch?" I tried to imagine it.

"Yeah, you know, from South America. They're like little lamas." He gestured the size of an alpaca as being about four feet tall.

I frowned. "I know what alpacas are. But why would you want an alpaca ranch? Do you eat them?" They didn't look particularly meaty. But what did I know? Maybe they were delicious?

Ward laughed so hard he almost lost his fishing pole to Lake Austin. "No. God no. They have wool. Kind of like sheep's wool. But much softer and warmer."

That was somewhat less disturbing to my vegetarian sensibilities.

"So, your mom raises alpacas now?" For whatever reason, this fact had never come up with Kate over the entire life of our friendship. All I remembered was that Kate had mentioned her mom was an emergency room nurse. That must have been pre-alpaca ranching. How I managed to go so long not knowing my friend's mom was a professional alpaca farmer was baffling. Perhaps Kate was embarrassed? That was the only explanation I could come up with.

Ward clearly didn't have any shame about the situation. "Yes, she does." He looked extremely pleased with himself that he'd made that happen.

"Well, to each their own. I'm glad she likes her alpacas and her ranch." I shrugged and took a sip of my beer, grateful that Ward had thoughtfully packed some fruity beer for me. Ranching sounded like a miserable existence.

"The alpacas spit when they get angry, scared, or horny. And they smell very, very bad," Ward added, smiling at me as if trying to imagine me raising alpacas. "You'd hate them." His voice was amused but certain.

"I'm sure that I would." I couldn't really see myself enjoying spending time around livestock of any variety. I hadn't even liked ponies as a kid; they frightened me. I'd cried at every petting zoo I'd ever visited in my youth. The spitting and the smelliness of the alpacas didn't help their case much, either.

"The babies are really cute, though."

"I'll take your word for it." I shook my head at him. "So other than the alpaca ranch and the Ferrari, you didn't buy anything else crazy?"

Ward looked suddenly uncomfortable. He dragged a huge hand through his dark hair, messing it up even worse than the wind already had. "I bought a ton of crazy stuff actually. And I dated several girls that were the female equivalent of Kate's finance bro."

"They had two Rolexes?" I guessed.

"They did once they started dating me." He looked embarrassed.

"Ah, I see." Ward had liked to spoil his girlfriends. There was technically nothing wrong with that. I smiled at him. "You know, it's not a crime to spend money on the people you care about."

"That's true," Ward admitted. "I just wish I'd realized that the girls who hung around football players sometimes cared much more about the money than me."

We were talking about Jessie again. No matter what we talked about, she seemed to find her way into our conversations. She was like a heat seeking missile killing our buzz. I wished I could erase her from Ward's memory so that she couldn't hurt him anymore. She'd done enough damage to the man's views on women, life, and love. She didn't deserve to come fishing with us, too. She wasn't invited.

"At least once you stopped playing you would have learned who your real friends were." It was probably cold comfort, but at least he knew the truth now.

Ward laughed bitterly. "I definitely did." He impaled a bait worm on his fishing hook with a bit more force than was probably necessary. "I found out who was really my friend basically overnight. It was a much smaller number than I thought." There was definite pain in his voice.

"I don't have a lot of friends," I admitted after watching Ward cast his line out over the water. "But I'm pretty sure that I know they're all real." I found myself looking over at Ward fondly.

He returned my smile long enough that I got embarrassed and had to drop my gaze. I stared out at the calm green water of the lake instead, feeling my cheeks tingling with a blush. Whenever I was with Ward, I seemed to spend a good three quarters of the time blushing like an idiot.

"Me too," he said after a minute. His voice was mild, but it filled me with something that felt like hope, but somehow also felt like nervousness. "And that's worth a lot more to me than anything money could buy."

24

EMMA

WE DIDN'T CATCH any fish, but by the time we left the lake behind, I was feeling a lot better. Ward seemed happy, too. I found myself thinking about his initial offer on the drive back. I pushed that to the back of my mind with some effort and focused on something else that had been rattling around in my head.

"Hey Ward?"

"Hmm?" He'd been humming to himself although I don't think he realized it.

"Do you like running a bar?"

He looked over at me in surprise. "Yeah. I like it." For a minute I thought that was all I was going to get from him, but then he added, "I didn't ever think this was how my life would turn out, but I really can't complain."

"You thought you'd play football forever?" Having now

done some Googling on football, I understood that at twenty-five, there was a good chance that Ward would be retired no matter what his career in the NFL had been like. Average careers in professional football only lasted between three and six years. Many don't last that long.

He laughed. "Yeah. I mean, rationally I knew that I'd eventually get too hurt or too old, but I definitely didn't have any sort of a plan for once I quit. Looking back, that was really stupid." He looked only slightly chagrined.

"You loved it?" It was obvious that he did.

"God yes. I wish I could explain it to you, but there's really no way."

"Try. I'm really curious. Was it just the competitive thing you enjoyed? Teamwork? The thrill of winning?" It was *just football*. I didn't say that, of course. It clearly meant a lot to him.

Ward's face was wistful. "All of it. I was the happiest I'd ever been when I was playing for the Longhorns. I was in the best shape of my life, working like a dog, and loving every second of it."

"I'm sorry you had to quit." Although secretly I was also very glad. Some of the injuries that he could have sustained were horrific. I'd gone down some dark internet rabbit holes, and those brain injuries were no joke. Also, I probably never would have seen Ward again if he was still playing. And, a cruel little voice crowed in my head, he'd be married to Jessie.

He shrugged. "I've made peace with it. I was lucky to walk again after my injury, so I try to keep things in perspective." Part of my cyberstalking involved watching Ward's career-ending injury on YouTube. It was completely horrific. I've never seen a leg point that many directions at once. Legs aren't meant to do the things his was doing in the video clips.

"But running the bar doesn't make you as happy as football did."

"Nothing will ever make me as happy as football did." He seemed one hundred percent sure of that fact.

Not even love? That made me sad for him. I didn't know what to say. We lapsed into silence for a bit.

"What about you, Emma? What makes you happy?" Ward asked. He seemed relieved to turn the tables on me. Little did he know, I'm extremely simple in my tastes.

I smiled. "I like writing. Compared to you, I'm very easy to please."

"There has to be more to it than just that."

"Not really. It's simple. I just want to write and learn how to do it better."

"You don't need a PhD to write."

"No. I don't. That's true. But I feel like I'm learning a lot that's valuable to me as a writer and a thinker." It sounded sort of lame when I said it out loud, but it was true.

"Do you want to teach?"

"Maybe someday. Right now, I primarily want to learn. I

guess I'm still trying to figure out what I really want." I shrugged.

"That's okay, too. You're young. You've got time to figure out what makes you happy." He was smiling at me in that way that made my heart pound again.

"So do you."

He nodded, but I knew he thought his chance for happiness had come and gone. It made me ache for him. I lay my head against the window of the truck and zoned out. The day wasn't hot, but the sun out on the boat had been bright. It felt good to be in the shade. I closed my eyes for just a second...

"Emma?"

I jolted awake. We were parked in front of my apartment. The sun was now shining from a different direction. Time had clearly passed.

"Oh. Sorry." I sat up and pushed my windblown hair over my shoulder sheepishly. "I didn't mean to fall off like that. How long was I asleep?"

"Half an hour maybe. I didn't have the heart to wake you." Ward was looking at me affectionately and it made my heartbeat race. "We've been sitting here for about ten minutes."

Yikes. That's a bit embarrassing.

"I didn't snore, did I?" Sometimes I've been known to snore, but usually only when I have allergies. Or when I'm drunk.

"No, but you did drool a bit."

I gasped in horror, touching my mouth and chin just to be sure. "I did not!"

He chuckled at me. "No, you didn't. I was just messing with you. You slept like a baby. It was cute."

Great. I love being cute.

I stretched, and my neck made a loud popping noise, causing Ward to chuckle. "I feel better."

"Yeah, naps are wonderful sometimes, aren't they?"

"That's not what I meant. I feel better generally. Thanks for taking me fishing." I grinned. Fishing wasn't bad. I might even go fishing again sometime. But only if Ward was there with me.

"You're welcome." Ward fidgeted in his seat. "I had fun too."

"I can't believe all I caught was that dumb shoe." Not a single fish was caught on our so-called fishing trip. All we did was drink beer in a boat and talk for three hours. Not that I was complaining. This was the nicest afternoon I'd had in a long, long time.

"You did good for a beginner."

I smirked at him. "Yeah, I did. At least I caught something. You didn't even catch a shoe."

"I got you to come fishing with me. That's my achievement of the day. Even if it was the fallback."

"Right, because you were so sure I'd pick option one." I

rolled my eyes, but I was definitely considering it. I'd been low-key considering it all day.

"I told you. A man can dream." He looked me over with enough heat behind his eyes to make me flush again. That's all I seemed to do with Ward, blush, blush, blush. He knew just how to make me do it.

It was time for me to get out of the car now. Time to go inside, maybe do some chores. Alone. I bit my lip. I thought about the consequences of being responsible and smart, and the possible benefits of being impulsive. The cost benefit analysis warred in my brain for about two seconds until my hormones beat my fear into submission.

"Ward, what would happen if I told you I still wanted option one?"

He froze. Looked over at me. The bright blue of his irises receded as his pupils dilated, drinking me in with all the available light. My heart pounded, filling my ears with the noise of my own pulse. The seconds ticked by at half their ordinary speed while I waited for him to say something. One torturous second. Two seconds. Three. I was going to die. Finally, he spoke.

"Your place or mine?" Ward's voice was uncharacteristically soft, and almost amused. It was almost like he knew that I'd end up right here, asking for what I knew would only get my heart broken. Maybe he really did know me better than I thought. Well enough to guess what I'd barely admitted to myself.

His gaze was free of judgement or manipulation. It only held attraction and the promise of more. A dull, throbbing need started up in me, blurring out any second thoughts. All I wanted was him. And right now, even if it was only for right now, he wanted me too. I could let that be enough, couldn't I? If I went into this without my hopes up, could I escape the pain? I felt like I ought to be able to. At that second, with him looking at me the way he was, I felt like I could do anything I wanted. I felt like I could fly.

I knew I was making a stupid decision. A decision I was going to regret. But with Ward looking at me like that, knowing that he was at least an okay guy, *at least my friend...* I was at least making my bad choice with both eyes wide open. I couldn't resist him. There was never a chance in the world that I might.

"Well, we're already at mine."

25

WARD

EMMA LED me up to her apartment. It looked the same way it did when we left it several hours earlier, but somehow being in Emma's space now felt so much more intimate than it had before. Maybe it was just the way she kept looking at me over her shoulder, like she was expecting me to disappear. Little did she know that there was nothing—nothing—that could drag me away.

She didn't waste time on the pleasantries. No offers of coffee. No chit-chat. We were past that, anyway. After checking to make sure her roommate was gone, she glanced behind to make sure I would follow, and opened the first door on the right down her tiny hallway. Her bedroom was exactly like I'd imagined, and yes, I'd spent plenty of time imagining it. More time than I probably should have. Possibly hours at this point.

Ever since she texted me that picture of herself, topless and wearing the world's tiniest little thong, I'd been imagining her on those neat, lacy bedsheets. I'd imagined doing all kinds of dirty things to her on them, usually with my phone in my left hand and my cock in the other...

And now I was here. It was real. Surreal. More surreal than Emma cheering at a football game and going fishing. More surreal than the Tarasque monster from the museum exhibit. Even more surreal than that girl's weird hairball art.

"What are you staring at?" Emma asked, touching her face like she might have a piece of food or stray pen mark.

I shook my head at her. The truth slipped out before I could come up with some charming line. "I'm just hoping you aren't about to laugh in my face and tell me to get out."

She stepped in closer. "I'm not that much of a tease."

"Good." I closed the distance between us in a single step, grasping Emma's slender waist and pulling her the final inch forward against my chest. She looked up at me dreamily, threading her little arms around my neck.

"This isn't a bad idea, is it?" she whispered. "You'll still be my friend after this, won't you? Nothing has to be weird, right?"

There was that word again. Why the hell did I ever say that? But at the moment I was beyond any complex emotions. Even worrying. She was already in my arms.

"Everything will be fine," I promised her, even though I

knew it was a lie. I wasn't her friend in the first place, not really. I'd never wanted to be her friend, not since the moment I laid eyes on her. "Don't worry. We can go back to being mean to each other tomorrow."

She nodded. "Okay."

Then I was kissing her soft, warm mouth and everything else faded away. Emma's kisses were less urgent than the night before, but just as teasing and somehow sexier now that we could take our time. And I took my time with her, carefully claiming every corner of her. At least for this moment, she was mine. I wanted her to feel that way and so I stole her breath to prove it.

By the time the back of her calves collided with her mattress, I'd peeled her flimsy T-shirt off her and helped her do the same to me. She was wearing another lacy bra today. This one was sea green, like her eyes. It was very pretty, but it needed to be gone. Immediately.

I've never been a huge lingerie lover. By the time I see it, I always just want to tear it off. It didn't matter how pretty, sexy, or elaborate Emma's lingerie was, this fabric was keeping me from seeing Emma, and I *knew* she'd be prettier. Better. This piece of lingerie, however, seemed to lack the usual closure. My fingers fumbled around helplessly on her back as I tried to find it.

"It's in the front," Emma murmured against my mouth. Her lips had turned upward into a smile. She probably liked me like this. Desperately wanting her. Even though we were barely started, my cock was rock hard and straining against the material of my jeans. But as badly as I wanted to be pounding into her, growling her name and making her moan mine, I wouldn't dare skip the details.

Now that the mystery of Emma's bra was solved, I slid the closure apart and got my first look. Emma's perfect, soft, teardrop shaped tits spilled forward. They fit perfectly in my hands. For a woman so damn short, she had all her curves exactly where they ought to be. She arched into my palms with a shy smile on her face, and I worked each pink nipple into a stiffer point with my thumb and forefingers.

"These are going to get me into trouble," I told her seriously, pinching her a bit harder until she gasped. "You've got quite a lot here for me to play with."

"We've got all night," she answered, easing herself backward onto the bed and pulling me with her.

All night isn't going to cut it. It won't be nearly enough.

I didn't say it, of course. Instead, I lowered my head down and licked her, before sucking her soft, warm nipple into my mouth. I was greedy for her, and she was eager for it. Her little fingers held the back of my head steady, buried in my hair, urging mc on. She spread her legs beneath me and I settled in between them, carefully attending to her chest until each nipple was a wet, hard, dark pink point.

Satisfied with the way she lolled back against the mattress, breathing hard, I tugged off her shorts to reveal more matching lingcrie. Did she coloi coordinate all her underwear? I'd never met a woman who did that before, but I was willing to bet she did. It was such an Emma thing to do. The sea-green panties joined their matching bra on the ground.

She was totally smooth and hairless between her creamy white thighs, courtesy of some waxing studio somewhere. I've never really understood why women feel the need to do that, it sounds painful, but I would never complain. It made her feel even slicker when I rubbed her soaked pussy, parting her legs even wider to touch her swollen little clit.

Emma's eyes slipped shut while I petted her there, and soft, airy little noises escaped her that I didn't think she realized she was making. She arched her back and lifted her hips against my fingers. Her mouth parted when I slipped a finger inside her, in and out, and then a second. I was only giving her shallow, gentle thrusts, though. Not enough to get her off, especially without spending more time working on her clit. Just enough to make her whimper and sigh and stare up at the ceiling like I was driving her out of her mind. Just enough to tease her.

"Do you need some more?" I whispered against her neck. "Tell me what you need me to do with this perfect body of yours."

I wanted to hear her ask for it. Needed it.

"I need you please," she said in her bedroom voice, turning to look at me with half-hooded eyes. She'd never looked sexier with her hair mussed up around her flushed face. I kissed her soft lips, two fingers still inside her.

"What do you need me to do to you?"

Another shallow thrust. Another little moan.

"I need you to fuck me. Please. Now."

26

WARD

SHE DIDN'T HAVE to ask twice. I stood up just long enough to slip off my jeans and roll on a condom. Her bright eyes widened as she stared at my hard cock.

"Go slow, okay?" She told me when I got on top of her, keeping my weight on my elbows to avoid crushing her. "It's, um, been a while for me, and you're..." she trailed off blushing, seemingly too embarrassed to say 'big.'

"Okay." I nodded. I knew it could be uncomfortable for some women to be with me, particularly at first. I'd do my best not to hurt her and I knew we'd fit. We had before, and we would again. I notched the tip of my cock against her hot wetness, heard her soft inhale, and drove home slowly, inch by inch.

Her most intimate muscles squeezed around my cock

like a vise, and I struggled with my promise to go slow. My whole body was urging me to move, to thrust hard into her and find the right rhythm to release us both, but I didn't. I was good to my word. Although it almost hurt to stay still, I waited, watching her face for any sign of discomfort or pain. After a second she nodded, took a deep breath and opened her legs wider.

That was all the invitation I needed and could wait for. My first thrust into her was slow, but not very gentle. She made a little noise that told me that she was *not* in pain. She lifted her legs up and wrapped them around my hips after a moment, digging her fingertips into my forearms and moving up against me. Within moments we'd both given up on slow.

Slow was highly overrated anyway. Soon Emma was urging me on, pushing against me with just as much force as I was giving her. She wasn't quiet when she got close. She found her rhythm quickly, slipping one hand between us to give her the friction she needed against her clit. There was something phenomenally sexy about watching her get herself off while I was pounding into her, and her high, breathy noise and pulsing muscles nearly pulled me over the edge right along with her when she came. I hadn't had nearly enough of her yet.

Once her aftershocks slowed to a halt, I pulled out of her and flipped her on her stomach. It wasn't hard to do, she was loose-limbed and pliant now. Her round ass was silky soft under my fingers. When I spread her legs and reentered her from a prone position, her pussy clenched around me again, taking me in like she missed me. I know I missed her. I'd been missing her my entire life.

"Fuck, Ward," she moaned again and again. I loved the sound of it.

And I loved her like this, facedown and totally submissive. She rocked back into me, lifting that fantastic ass with each little upstroke and whimpering out my name again when I pushed deep back in. I pushed her hair aside and bit the back of her neck, and was rewarded by an even louder, sexy moan. She was bucking underneath me like a wild animal.

When I slipped my own hand between her legs to give her clit attention, she ground against me shamelessly. She moaned a second orgasm out from my fingers, and her sweet little pussy clamped down around my cock with pulsing spasms. This time I couldn't withstand the force of it. I came into her so hard I saw stars, emptying out all thought and feeling in an instant of blinding pleasure, and she was still whimpering and convulsing underneath me when my vision came back.

"Christ woman," I said after I rolled off her onto my back and caught my breath—probably a full minute later. "If that's your idea of slow and gentle, I don't think I'd survive fast and rough. I thought you were going to fuck me to death, and you weren't even on top."

Emma giggled, snuggling up under my arm and onto my chest. Her little hands were folded up under her head, and she looked up at me with soft, happy eyes. I pushed her fluffy hair out of her face and was rewarded with a kiss on my nose.

"Yeah, but what a way to go," she replied with a grin and a bemused shake of her head.

I planted a kiss on her forehead, feeling sleepy and relaxed. The happy, comfy sex hormones were still cascading through my body, keeping any fear or doubt at bay for the moment. I tried to savor the feeling. I knew it wouldn't last forever.

I'm not sure how long we drifted there together in semi-sleep, but eventually I became aware that Emma had pulled on her panties and my T-shirt and covered us with a blanket. Something about the way she looked in my T-shirt was infinitely sexier than her lingerie had been. She looked so comfortable. And she looked so mine. That was what it was. In lingerie, she could be anybody's. This was better. In my T-shirt she could only be mine. It was far more intimate and more real.

It had been a long, long time since I had considered staying the night with a woman. Not since Jessie ripped my heart out and convinced me that relationships were just lies. Relationships were manipulation pretending to be commitment. If love was real, it wasn't for me.

As a result, my time with the women I took to bed was generally measured in hours. Any more than that and I ended up regretting things when they inevitably got weird. The woman would get attached, start getting expectations... I did my best not to give them the wrong idea, and some were playing the same game and just out for a good time, but I'd still learned my lesson once or twice over the past few years. If I waited until the fun stopped, I was in for nothing but drama and pain.

I was very much a leave-before-the-party-ended type of guy. Leave while you're still having fun. That's what my mom always said about birthday parties when I was a kid. I'd found that her sage advice applied just as well to hookups.

"Are you going to stay for a while?" Emma asked lightly, reading my mind. Her voice was hopeful and inviting, but not pushy. She looked over at me carefully. "I can order us some pizza if you want. Rae is staying over with Ivan tonight."

I needed to tell her no, to get out of there before I got myself in real trouble, but I seemed to be paralyzed. Besides, I was still having fun. There was no harm in staying a bit longer. Right?

"Sure, pizza sounds great," I heard myself telling her. She smiled at me and grabbed her phone to order.

"Any toppings you don't like?" She asked me.

"To be honest, I don't remember," I said, shaking my head at her. "I think you might have literally fucked my brains out." And I wasn't particularly clever to begin with. I was probably functionally impaired now.

"Oh good, then you won't mind if I get pineapple and olives." She looked excited.

"Wait, *what*? No. Don't you dare." Surely, she was joking.

"It's really good. See the pineapple adds sweetness and acidity, while the olives—"

"Nope. No. No way. That's horrible." There was no way she could talk that up. I might be dumb, but I wasn't *that dumb*.

"Okay, half what I want and half..." she trailed off looking at me expectantly.

"Pepperoni," I answered. Obviously. "With ranch dressing." The way God intended.

Her nose wrinkled at my condiment preference and I shook my head at her in dismay. She had literally no leg to stand on. She was legless.

Pineapple and black olives? That wasn't a pizza. That wasn't even a food. It was a fucking travesty.

Emma ordered her franken-pizza (having to repeat her revolting order three times to what I imagined was a horrified pizza shop employee) and stared up at the ceiling dreamily. Despite her bad taste in pizza, she looked completely relaxed and happy. Happier than I'd ever seen her in the few weeks we'd been working with each other. Given how tense and tightly wound she'd looked this morning, I liked to think I'd helped with her new-found good mood (although I may have played a role in the foul one too).

Don't kid yourself, Ward. My insecurity chimed in. *You didn't just do some kind of selfless, good deed. You're treading on thin ice. Get out. Get out now.*

I ignored the negative little voice. Emma snuggled back in under my arm and reported that the pizza would be arriving in approximately forty-five minutes.

"Okay, I'm gonna nap until then," I told her. This earned me a sexy pout from Emma. "What?" I asked. "Are you so cock hungry you can't wait for a man to recover?"

She giggled, and her eyes glinted mischievously. "No. But I was going to go take a shower." My ears—and other parts—perked up in a hurry. "How am I gonna wash my back if you're just in here sleeping?"

"Oh! Well why didn't you say so," I told her, sitting up and pulling her over my shoulder in a fireman's carry. I was repeatedly surprised by how light she was. Carrying her around was a lot easier than my cousin Jaimie, who was about her height, but brawny and stocky. Granted, she also didn't try any weird WrestleMania moves like Jaimie usually did. Emma just laughed against my back and seemed surprised to be suddenly upside down. "Soaping you up is my specialty. Which way is your bathroom?"

"I'm pointing at it, but I guess you can't see me," she answered, her voice muffled against my back. "It's right down the hall. First door on the left."

27

EMMA

IF THERE'S anything in the world better than having a super-hot, naked guy wash your back after sexing you up, I haven't found it. Shower time with Ward was pretty much total bliss. Also, my boobs had definitely never been cleaner. I wished that I could bottle this moment for later use, or better yet, reproduction and sale. I would be so stupid rich if I could.

An hour later and we were lazing around on the couch, partially clothed, and eating pizza. There's something so soothing about the afterglow. It's *almost* better than the sex itself.

"So, tell me, if you didn't think you'd end up a barkeep, how did you end up owning the Lone Star Lounge?" I asked Ward in between bites of pizza.

He looked at my pizza disparagingly before answering. "I bought it during my first season in the NFL. Temporarily, I had more money than I knew what to do with. A terrible problem, I know. But during that brief period of being incredibly rich, I made a few investments. The Lone Star Lounge was one of them."

"You mean you own other bars, too?" That was a surprise. I couldn't imagine how he had the time. He seemed to give the Lone Star Lounge virtually every waking moment of his life.

Ward shook his head. "No. The Lounge is the only business. I also have a couple of commercial and residential rental properties is all. Enough to provide me a nice passive income without requiring any real work."

"You're a landlord? Yikes. Maybe you could teach mine a thing or two." He could certainly use the instruction.

"I'm not, no. I hire a property manager to do the landlord stuff. You have a sketchy landlord here, huh?" He looked unsurprised. I suppose my apartment complex could speak for itself. I couldn't wait until my lease was up and I could move somewhere, *anywhere*, else.

"Yeah, he's not exactly the greatest." My voice was dry. Mentally, I ran through the list of still-unaddressed complaints I'd emailed about: bugs, leaky air conditioner, bugs, broken ceiling fan, more bugs, broken garbage disposal, broken dishwasher. Oh, and bugs. So, so many bugs. "On the upside, I've learned a surprising amount about home improvement while living here."

"Really?" Ward looked dubious, which I did not particularly appreciate. I was perfectly capable.

"Actually yes," I told him. "I've learned how to take apart a garbage disposal, repair a leaking toilet, replace a showerhead, and fix a messed-up cabinet hinge. I also know a lot about roach bait."

Ward smiled at me. "That's a lot better than Kate can do. She called me once to help her replace her air conditioner filter."

"Was it up high or something?"

"No, I think she just didn't want to do it herself. Usually she lures me over with some easy task and then when I show up—bam—Ward, can you retile my bathroom? Ward, would you mind replumbing the kitchen sink into the new island that I also need you to build?" He shook his head. His smile, although long-suffering, was also indulgent. Also, his 'Kate' voice was hilarious.

"I wish I had an older brother to con into impromptu home renovation," I told him. "Kate's lucky to have you."

"Be sure you tell her that the next time you see her," Ward said seriously, but his smile broke through a second later. "She sometimes forgets."

"I don't think so," I said, thinking about all the nice things that Kate said about Ward when he wasn't around over the years. "She's pretty proud of you. I don't think you're likely to hear her say it, but she is."

He rolled his eyes. "Kate's not one of those people who's hard on the outside and warm and gooey on the inside. She's hard edges and throwing elbows all the way down. She bought me one of those 'world's best brother' mugs once when we were kids. Then when I pissed her off, she threw it against the wall. She was eight."

I giggled at the thought. It was totally believable to me, especially now that I knew about the Cole glitter incident. It was not a good idea to get between Kate and whatever it was Kate wanted. During our time working together in restaurants in college, I saw Kate put the fear of God in a woman who was talking on the phone while ordering a drink. She didn't even need to say a word. She just glared the woman into hanging up and profusely apologizing. "Kate's one tough cookie. There's no doubt about that. I'm hoping some of her toughness rubs off on me eventually."

"You're plenty tough," Ward told me. "You stood up to me. You've always stood up to me."

"I'm not tough," I admitted. "I'm just extremely snarky and irritable. There's a difference. How did you put it? Warm and gooey on the inside? That's me. I'm gooey inside. Like a marshmallow."

Ward smirked at me and reached out to brush a stray strand of my hair back over my shoulder. "I think you're great."

My heart thumped in my chest. *He likes me!* "I think you're great, too."

"Except for your pizza preferences," Ward amended. "That's just fucking disgusting."

I looked down at my food and curled my hands around my plate protectively. "I like it. This is actually an inherited pizza preference. My parents like it this way so I grew up with it. My cousins like it this way, too. The whole Greene family is out there ordering it. It's gonna catch on eventually. Just you wait. It's the next big thing."

Ward looked positively mystified. "There are more of you out there eating this *abomination*?"

"Slow down professor! Don't use those big words around little old me," I joked. Ward was still hung up on the pizza.

"That's my line," he griped.

"Oh, please. You're plenty smart," I scolded. "I've got you figured out. The whole sweet good ole boy thing is just a ruse to make the ladies smile."

Ward looked at me affectionately. "If you want to believe that, I fully support it. It's not true at all, but I like it."

I rolled my eyes at him. "If you really were dumb, your business would have failed a long time ago. Clearly you've got something figured out."

"You didn't see where I started from," Ward argued. "Trust me, I came very close to bankrupting myself after my injury because I didn't know how to adjust from unlimited income to zip. Actually, it's sort-of a miracle I didn't end up bankrupt. Almost eighty percent of NFL players declare bankruptcy within two years of the end of their careers."

"Wow, that's horrible. Why?"

"The same reason I did. You work your whole life, finally start seeing that fame and fortune start to happen, and it goes to your head. You spend money like it's going out of style. And trust me, it isn't hard to do. The lifestyle adjustment is beyond belief. You see what your teammates are doing and think that it's normal to buy three Rolexes and a Hummer. Then there's the women. There are a lot of women, and they aren't just interested in finding love." Ward's voice was bitter. Whatever this Jessie woman had done to him, the damage still hadn't healed.

"I can't even imagine," I told him. "As someone who intentionally went into academia, knowing perfectly well that the pay is abysmal, I just pretty much expect to be poor forever. The thought of being able to buy whatever I want... it must be intoxicating."

"Intoxicating is right, but really it's less like being drunk and more like being a full-fledged alcoholic. You even go through withdrawals." He was smiling, but it wasn't a very happy smile at all.

"But you didn't go bankrupt." I felt like Ward wasn't proud enough of that fact.

"That's true. I didn't. Thanks to the fact that I made a

few purchases that actually *generated* income for me, I managed to escape what happened to most guys."

"They ought to provide you guys financial counselling or something."

"Oh, they do. We got all kinds of warnings about saving money and making smart investments. But it's hard to listen to it when you're twenty-three and making millions of dollars a year."

"You sound like you feel really strongly about this issue," I told him.

"I just hate the idea that all these guys playing right now are just one compound knee injury away from losing both their dream job and their financial security. It's not fair to them. There's always somebody younger and stronger to take your place, so the league doesn't need to worry much about protecting players."

"Have you ever thought about doing something about it?"

He blinked at me. "What do you mean?"

I shrugged. "I don't know. Talking to other players, helping them to manage their finances responsibly."

"I told you, they have lots of guys buzzing around trying to help. Some of them are sharks, but some genuinely want to help."

"But you said that it's hard to listen when you're young and intoxicated by all the money. You could bridge that gap though. It would mean more if it came from someone like you instead of some old dude in a suit that talked down to them. You can relate to those guys. Maybe you could make them listen."

He looked like he was chewing it over. "Emma," he eventually said, "you really are very smart."

"Thanks," I said with a shrug. I took another bite of my pizza and closed my eyes in bliss. "Are you sure you don't want to try some of this? It really is good."

"Nope. No, I don't want to."

"And you say I won't get out of my comfort zone."

"After the football and the fishing, I am pleased to admit that I was wrong," he said. I grinned, but it faded quickly.

"But you still won't even try the pizza?"

"Not a chance." He looked at it like it might be poisonous.

"It will grow on you. You just need to give it a shot." I offered him a bite and he shook his head.

"It looks like it would grow on something." His superiority was beginning to grate on me. *If he would just try it, he might like it.*

"You're a pizza racist," I accused. "You're prejudging the pizza on the basis of appearance."

"That's... not even possible. Pizza has no race. It's pizza."

I stuck my tongue out at him, and he laughed. This felt

so normal. So good. As we bantered and chatted our way through dinner, my heart started to get attached. I didn't tell it to, I didn't want it to, but it was happening. Just like Ward wouldn't try my pizza, he'd made it clear from the start that he didn't do relationships. And he was stubborn as hell. When this ended, it was going to hurt. I just knew it.

28

EMMA

THE FACT that Rae was spending the night with Ivan was beyond lucky. Aside from the obvious, it allowed me the opportunity to break into her good liquor. After dinner, Ward made me a vodka tonic and himself a martini while I watched from the little breakfast bar. My kitchen had never looked better than with him in it. It had also never looked smaller.

"How tall are you?" I asked. He looked a bit surprised.

"You didn't look up my Wikipedia page?" He teased, sliding my drink across the countertop like he did at the bar. "I'm pretty sure it's on there."

"My driver's license says I'm five foot four," I told him. "I only trust primary sources anyway. Wikipedia can lie." I wasn't going to admit how much time I'd spent on Ward's Wikipedia page. It was a lot. Too much.

"You wouldn't be five foot four with your hair teased up three inches like a beauty queen," Ward said, smirking.

I rolled my eyes. "No, but a pair of long pants and some high heels fooled the Connecticut DMV when I was sixteen."

"I'm six-three," he said. "A full inch shorter than my Wikipedia page currently says."

"You should change it."

"Nah, I'll take it. I don't see you getting your license fixed."

"What's it like always being able to reach the tall cabinets?" My voice may have been wistful. My kitchen would double in usable storage if I were only two or three inches taller. As it was, step ladders got as much use in the kitchen as knives and forks.

He shrugged. "Good? I don't really think about it that much."

"Do you think the whole world is just really tiny? Is it like living in a doll house?"

"I'm not *that tall*. By football standards, I'm actually rather short." He flashed his white smile at me.

I snorted into my drink and Ward laughed at me. "Yes, so very short," I teased when I recovered my composure. "I'm surprised they let you play at all."

"What's it like being so tiny?" Ward asked, turning my question back at me. "Is it like living in a world of giants?"

"Yeah," I admitted, shaking my head in chagrin. The

world was not set up for tiny people like me. "It is. You know I'm too short to work a forklift? I also can't be a Rockette, a ballerina, a professional cheerleader, an astronaut, a police officer, or a fighter pilot."

"You'd be a really cute little astronaut," Ward said, shaking his head. "I have a bit of a thing for petite girls," he admitted, looking me up and down appreciatively.

I rolled my eyes at him. "Compared to you, pretty much all girls except WNBA players and fashion models are petite."

Ward seemed to realize this for the first time. "Yeah, you know that's true. I've only met a handful that are even close to my height. You actually might be onto something there. Maybe I just like short girls. Or maybe Jessie just ruined me."

"Oh, is she super tall?" I couldn't help asking. Ward made a face.

"Yeah. I mean, not weirdly tall or anything. But tall. Six feet give or take."

"Wow, that is incredibly tall for a woman. I would trade IQ points for inches to be that tall." I tried to imagine a life being six feet tall but couldn't. "Was she a model or something?"

"Yes. A model and professional volleyball player."

"How glamorous," I heard myself saying somewhat enviously. Ward winced. "We can talk about something else," I added. "I didn't mean to pry into your business." I shook my head to try and dispel the mental image I was developing of a towering Amazon wearing super-fashionable clothes while she broke Ward's heart as he lay in a hospital bed. *What a bitch.* The worst part was that I knew I'd be looking her up on the internet later, trying to find pictures of her and Ward together. My curiosity could be a real pain in the ass sometimes. At least when I'd been pretending that I didn't know Ward Williams, I'd been able to avoid all the Googling. Now I seemed to spend all my free time on Wikipedia.

For his part, Ward just shrugged. "It's all water under the bridge. We're both lucky that things worked out the way they did. If we'd gotten married before I got injured—or God forbid had a few kids—it would have been a thousand times worse."

"Yeah, you're definitely right about that," I told Ward. "My parents got a divorce when I was in middle school. It really did a number on my self-esteem for a while. No matter what they tell you in family therapy, the kid still feels like it's their fault."

"I'm sorry, Emma," Ward said. "That really sucks."

I shrugged and took a sip of my drink before I replied. It had sucked. "It was a long time ago. They get along better as friends than they ever did when they were married. I'm glad they did what was best for them as people, rather than trying to stay together for me. I'd much rather have two functional parents than two angry ones."

"I get that," Ward told me. Then he added, "which is just one of the many reasons I'll never get married or have kids. I'd be too afraid to screw them up."

"You really think you'll never do those things?" I asked. "I promise I'm not judging, I'm just not sure what I'll be doing next Tuesday, let alone five years from now, or ten. For all I know in ten years I'll have joined one of those weird cults where men have multiple wives, and everyone dresses like pilgrims. Maybe I'll end up having eight kids and three sister wives." Granted, that was *highly unlikely*, but there was still technically a non-zero chance.

"Something tells me you'd be a terrible cult member," Ward joked. Then his expression turned more serious. "But it's not like I'll just wake up one day and be a married father of three. There would be warning bells."

"Warning bells?" My now-alcohol influenced brain imagined tornado sirens going off as Ward approached a jewelry store.

"Yeah. I mean I'd have to, you know, get myself into a long-term relationship and stuff. As long as I avoid relationships, I figure I'm safe."

"That does seem like a sound enough plan," I murmured, shaking my head.

"It's worked so far," he said, shrugging. "Besides, it lets me spend time with lovely, fascinating women with whom I am totally and completely incompatible. Like you."

I blinked and smiled. I tried not to let that sting and

failed spectacularly. Ward must have seen it on my face. His lips parted, and his brow furrowed.

"I didn't mean anything—" he started, but I shook my head.

"Don't worry about it," I told him, getting up and rounding the breakfast bar to set my glass in the sink. "Long-term commitment isn't what I'm after either." I winked at him.

He laughed, and I saw the moment when he decided not to push it. It was probably for the best.

"And what are you after?" He asked, moving close enough to drop his own empty glass next to mine and tip my head up to face him.

"I'll give you three guesses. No matter what you say, I know you're clever. I bet you can guess."

29

EMMA

"Are you looking for... expert fishing instruction?" Ward teased, taking another half step toward me. Even under the nasty fluorescent lighting of my kitchen, his blue eyes were hypnotic.

"If I was, I wouldn't ask you," I told him haughtily. "All you taught me to do was catch somebody's old nasty shoe."

"Fair enough. Well then, are you looking for... someone to help you appreciate the *exceedingly interesting and culturally relevant* sport of football?" His voice had dropped a half octave and gotten softer, more seductive. I felt a smile spreading over my face and warmth starting in my center.

"Um, no. But look at you use those big words again. I must be rubbing off on you." I was close enough now to touch him, but I didn't. Not yet.

"Oh no, I'm down to my very last guess," Ward said

dramatically. "Well, let's see. You don't want me for my fishing experience. You don't want me for my football knowledge. That means you must want me for my... skill at art appreciation."

I giggled. "Yep," I managed, "that's it. Your skill at art appreciation." I nodded seriously.

"I know art when I see it," Ward told me with matching seriousness. "I am *highly skilled* at appreciating beauty." He ran a finger down my cheek to my jaw, tipping my face from side to side. "And I know just what to do with it when I find it."

My lips found his a second later, cutting off whatever his next smooth line was. His lips curved into a smile against mine, and I found myself pinned against the refrigerator a second after with his hands on my waist. He was sweet and insistent, teasing my tongue with his and erasing any insecurity or second-guessing. Thoughts in general receded to the edges of my mind, where I could deal with them later.

"Give me back my shirt," he whispered against my lips.

In that moment, any other thoughts were just a waste of effort. My focus was entirely on Ward, and on sensation. His hands left my waist to lift the hem of his T-shirt that fit me like a mini-dress. I raised my arms and let him pull it off me, exposing my naked skin to the cool air in the kitchen. I was down to just the thong. My nipples hardened instantly, and the cool of the fridge against my ass and back was broken only by his warm hands.

"This shirt looks better on you," he admitted, holding the T-shirt in his left hand before dropping it on the tired linoleum floor of my kitchen. "But you look better naked."

I tugged on his boxer-clad hips, pulling him closer and feeling the length of his erection press against me. His hard, thick cock didn't intimidate me anymore. Now that I'd been reacquainted with what a good fit we were, despite the differences in our heights, I just ached for him. My curious fingers dipped below his elastic waistband, seeking and finding exactly what I wanted.

I pulled him free and stroked him with both hands, looking up into his wide, eager eyes. His breathing sped up while I played with him, and I leaned up on my tippy-toes to kiss his neck with little nips and heard it coming even faster. His abdominal muscles tensed and rolled under his soft skin and he rolled his hips forward, thrusting into my grip. It made me feel powerful to see him reacting to my touch like this. Maybe it wasn't forever, but at least for now, Ward was mine. It felt especially exciting and transgressive to be doing this in the kitchen. Although Rae wasn't around, this was still a very private act in a public space.

Before I could get too carried away, he stilled my hands and knelt. His long fingers rolled my thong down my hips and off my legs. I kicked it away to join the T-shirt in the middle of the floor. I was already more than turned on enough to take him, but he had other ideas. He lifted my right leg wide over his left shoulder, exposing me. The cool air of the kitchen rushed between my legs, but only for a moment, since his hot tongue found me a moment later.

I leaned back against the fridge, overwhelmed by the feeling of his mouth on me. I'd had guys go down on me before, but it was never like this. Ward took things slow at first, reading my reactions. Learning me. He used his fingers to spread me even wider, finding my clit with his tongue and gently teasing around it, not putting any pressure where he knew it might overwhelm me until I was pressing my hips forward. Then he finally kissed me there, pushing against me with his tongue while he worked two fingers inside my dripping, desperate pussy.

I'd never thought it would be possible for me to climax this way, but my body was telling me that I definitely could. I felt my pleasure building inside, lick by gentle lick. It was almost too much, but I wanted it. I needed it. I leaned up and back, arching, seeking release from the growing pressure. Noises were coming from my throat that weren't even close to being words. When my climax hit, I was up on my tiptoes, fucking Ward's mouth and shaking like a leaf. He kept touching me, stroking in and out with those two fingers while I came down—clearly, we weren't done yet.

Now that I'd come, I felt cold and exposed. I shivered, and Ward was wrapping his arms around me again in an instant, kissing me with a tongue that tasted like me. There was a time that I might have found the taste unpleasant, but in the heat of the moment it was unbelievably sexy. His mouth had just worshipped me, just fucked me until I came for him. It was the sweetest taste in the world.

My wetness returned in a rush when his cock brushed against me. He'd been so patient, making sure I came first. It was only fair that he got some reward for his efforts.

"My turn," I whispered, shifting us so it was his back against the fridge. He looked down at me eagerly, and I folded his T-shirt underneath my knees as I settled down in front of him. I had no idea what I was going to do with so much cock, but there was no time like the present to find out.

I licked the tip eagerly, staring up at him while I did so. I delivered gentle, slow thrusts at first, shallowly sucking him and lavishing attention on the head. His hands buried themselves in my hair, and it looked like he was holding himself back from pulling me forward. So, I did it for him, drawing him between my lips and back down my tongue to the back of my throat. I swallowed hard when I felt my gag reflex start to react and was rewarded with an impressed moan from Ward. He liked that? Cosmo was right. I did it again. He *definitely* liked that.

I sucked on him with a greedy, eager rhythm, but he didn't let me control things for very long. He couldn't seem to keep his hands off me. Soon he was guiding me forward with a fistful of my hair, fucking my face more and more forcefully. Like he owned it. I was shocked that I was able to take the whole thing, but it was mind over matter. I wanted to do it, so I did. I wanted so badly to please him, and so I made it possible. He clearly appreciated it, warning me each time that he was going to pull me deeply onto his cock with a little squeeze on my hair.

I could feel his climax coming, see it in the way his body tensed. When the thick rope of come hit the back of my throat, he swore foully and clenched his eyes closed. I swallowed down every drop, content and exhausted. My jaw was probably going to ache tomorrow, but I felt like I'd just won the dick sucking Olympics.

My legs were unsteady when I got back to my feet, but I didn't have to walk. Perhaps sensing that I was about to collapse back down to the floor, or perhaps just because he could, Ward scooped me up and carried me back to the bedroom. He settled me into the bed and slid in next to me, like two nesting spoons.

"Now you can't tell me that wasn't art," Ward whispered to me eventually. I was almost asleep.

"Huh?"

"Never mind," he said, kissing my neck and drawing my back closer to his chest.

"Ward?" A thought had just occurred to me, and I forced back the wave of sleep.

"Hmm?"

"Will you stay the night?" I didn't want him to slip away without me knowing.

"Do you want me to?"

"Yeah," I said. "I want you to stay." I was just too tired, and too satisfied to come up with any cutesy answer that wouldn't make me sound desperate or clingy, or God forbid, like someone that wanted a relationship. I only had the energy to be honest.

"Then I'll stay," Ward replied. I wondered if he was too tired for dishonesty, too.

He said that he wasn't in the market for anything serious, and I'd learned the hard way to listen to guys that told me stuff like that. Adam had once told me that he was no good for me, and I hadn't listened. He'd told me from the very start that our relationship was a bad idea, and that he just couldn't resist me when he knew he should. If I had listened, I wouldn't have gotten my heart broken, ripped apart, and then set on fire. If I had listened, I would have walked out the door on day one instead of bending over a desk and letting him turn me into his toy. I turned away from every warning I was given, and I paid the price in tears.

At the same time, I knew that Ward wasn't like Adam. He wasn't using his power over me to manipulate me or control me in a way that was unhealthy or wrong. We were consenting adults doing adult things. Ward was just being honest about what he had to offer: sex and nothing more.

Ward wasn't prepared to be anything but a hookup to me. He'd been burned before and it was crazy of me to think that I could change his mind. But part of me couldn't help but imagine a world where Ward was as into me as I was into him. It would take a much stronger woman than me not imagine it.

In my fantasy world, Ward would realize that I wasn't like that mean bitch Jessie who kicked him when he was down. He would realize that I wasn't interested in his money, or his name, or even just his body. I was just interested in him, as a person. I thought he was great, and spending time with him made me absurdly happy. And then he would realize that he felt the same way about me. But that's all it was, a fantasy. Because Ward didn't seem to believe that anyone would want him just for him. Just like me, he'd been misused. And now he didn't want to put his heart on the line. I had to be grownup enough to accept that.

So, as I was drifting off to sleep, I made myself a promise. No matter what happened with Ward I wasn't going to repeat my past mistakes. I wouldn't try and make this something that it wasn't. I wouldn't be the crazy girl, the one that drove Ward even further into himself. If I wasn't strong enough to resist sleeping with Ward, I would at least be strong enough to resist falling in love with him. That would be the worst thing I could do, because I knew he couldn't love me back.

30

WARD

I woke up early, disoriented, and very, very cold. It had been so long since I shared a bed for actually sleeping that my body was just as confused as my brain to find myself in an unfamiliar place. After an initial adrenaline spike before I remembered where I was, I felt silly. I was perfectly safe.

Next to me, Emma was fast asleep. In sleep she had curled around herself like a kitten, making a tiny ball of naked limbs, and drawing the covers around her like a cocoon. I untangled just enough blanket to cover myself and she whined without waking up. I reminded myself to tease her later on for being such a covers hog.

The sun wasn't up yet, but once I wake up, usually there's no going back to sleep. Years of early morning work-outs had conditioned me to get up early whether I wanted to or not. I had become a morning person by necessity. I couldn't very well lift weights in Emma's apartment though, and I wasn't about to go for a run in her neighborhood. So, with a mighty yawn, I dragged myself out of bed and into the bathroom. One quick shower later and I found myself face to face with a woman who was not Emma in the hall-way. Rae.

"Fuck!" she hissed, clearly not expecting me. She looked like she'd just gotten home and was still carrying her purse and dry cleaning. Both slipped to the ground when she clutched at her heart. "Fuck! Fuck! Fuck!" She kept saying it like it was a magic spell that could make me disappear.

Nice to see you too.

"Sorry," I mumbled, clutching the towel around my waist a little bit tighter. I'd met my share of unenthusiastic roommates at women's homes over the years, so I deployed my patented diversion tactic. "Good morning, Rae. I'm going to make some coffee before I leave. Do you want some?"

She blinked at me suspiciously. "I've already had some, but I appreciate the offer." Her voice wasn't particularly grateful. If anything, her accent and attitude seemed to be telling me to fuck off and die, even if her words were polite. "I assume Emma's still asleep?"

I nodded. Rae was knocking me off my regular game. She was so *hostile*. I could practically feel the waves of dislike radiating off her tall, menacing figure.

"Okay. Let's just get this out of the way now," Rae said. I wasn't sure if she was talking to herself or me until she drew herself up to her full height and held out an arm to block my retreat back to the safety of Emma's room. "You had better not hurt Emma."

I felt myself frowning. It was too early to argue with anyone. "I don't want to hurt her. Did I do something to make you think that I did?"

She shook her head. "No. You haven't done anything... yet. But I've watched her last few attempts at dating make her sad. I'm tired of seeing my friend be sad because some idiot led her on."

"I'm not leading her on. And I'm not dating her."

"So, what, you're just hooking up with her?"

None of your business.

I shrugged. This was beyond uncomfortable. Did I really have to explain myself to Rae? She certainly seemed to think so.

Her next question was just as sharp. "Does she know you're just using her for sex?"

None of your business!

"I'm not using her for anything, and I'm not a liar either. I don't like where this is going."

"Me either. She's not the hookup type."

"Are you sure?"

"I don't want her to get hurt." Rae's skin was flushed almost as red as her hair.

"I told you I'm not going to hurt her."

"Emma doesn't do casual, friends with benefits stuff. It's not like her."

I rolled my eyes at her. I wanted clothes, coffee, and for this conversation to end. Not necessarily in that order.

"Okay, Rae. I think you need to back off now. Emma's a grown woman. She doesn't need your help. And I certainly don't need your approval." My voice was no longer friendly and reasonable. I wasn't going to be rude to Rae, but I was done playing along. She had no right to interrogate me. Emma and I could do whatever we wanted to do, and there was nothing she could do about it.

She blinked at me in surprise. Paused for a moment. "Okay. Fine. You're right." I waited for the next snippy comment, but it didn't arrive. I was surprised—no, stunned—that pointing out the obvious had worked.

"Really?" I wasn't sure I believed the sudden change in her mood.

This has got to be some kind of trick to throw me off balance.

"Sure. I was meddling. I know that's not cool. She wouldn't do that to me." She shrugged.

Was it possible that there was a reasonable woman beneath Rae's grumpy, pushy attitude?

"Can you let me through now?" I asked her, nodding toward her arm. She flattened herself against the hallway. Although her face still hinted that she might not trust me, she didn't look like she wanted to murder me anymore, so that was an improvement.

"Ward?" She said before I made it to Emma's door.

I turned. I knew it was too good to be true.

Now what? Just write me an email or something.

"Please be careful, okay?" Without her anger, it was obvious that Rae's motives really were on Emma's side. "She's sensitive." Rae's voice was soft, either because I was so close to the door, or because she was really worried about Emma.

"Sure," I replied, opening the door and escaping her as quickly as I could. I had no intention of doing Emma any harm. The fact that Rae thought I might be out to lead her on and break her heart made me frustrated. Emma said she understood what she was getting into with me. So why all of a sudden did I feel like I was lying to her?

* * *

I didn't ever make that coffee. Despite my best efforts to be quiet, Emma woke up while I was getting dressed.

"Hi," she said dreamily, startling me as I pulled on my shoes.

"Good morning, Emma."

She had amazingly poofy morning hair that stuck out at all angles. She looked well-loved. "You stayed. I thought for sure you'd be gone by the time I woke up."

I shrugged. That was my usual M.O., but she'd asked me to stay.

"Is it okay that I'm still here?" I asked, wondering if I'd misread her.

"Of course." She grinned at me suggestively. "I wouldn't just throw you out after shamelessly using you. I at least owe you breakfast!"

I rolled my eyes. After my encounter with Rae, I had the distinct impression that perhaps Emma had been the one thrown out with no breakfast before. "You gotta' stop stealing all my lines," I told her, not wanting to dwell on the thought.

A thump from the other room made Emma sit up in bed. "Is Rae already back?" She looked suddenly flushed and wide awake.

"Yeah. We ran into one another in the hallway already."

"Oh..." Emma looked mortified. "I'm so sorry. I should have warned you. I hope it wasn't awkward for you."

Given that I'd thought for a second that she was ashamed of me, I laughed. She'd been worried I'd be embarrassed? It would take a lot more than Rae to shame me for spending the night with a beautiful woman. "Don't worry. It was fine. I don't think she likes me much, but I'm a big boy."

"She can be abrasive. And she's not a morning person." The two women were very protective of one another. It was almost endearing except when I was stuck in the middle.

"It was fine," I repeated. "Really."

Emma smiled weakly. "Do you want to grab some breakfast with me at the taco place around the corner? I'd cook you something, but I don't know that I want to chance it with Rae here."

"Sounds good to me." I would never turn down a breakfast taco. "Do they have coffee?"

She nodded. "I think they even roast their own beans."

"Fancy."

"Even this neighborhood is finally getting on board with how expensive everything is in Austin." She grimaced. "Pretty soon I'm going to end up with two roommates."

The rapidly increasing cost of living and housing shortage had done nothing but benefit me, although people like Emma got the short end of the stick. "At least you get to have good coffee?" I offered. She rolled her eyes at me.

Emma rolled out of bed with a dramatic sigh, stretched, and then hunted around in her closet for something to wear to work. "Is it going to be weird at the bar now?" she asked. "I'm not sure what to expect, if I'm being honest. I told you I'm not usually the casual hookup type and it's true. I don't know the rules."

"The rules?" I frowned. "There aren't rules, that's the whole point."

She'd been holding two nearly identical blue T-shirts and deciding between the two, when she turned to stare at me. "But what about Kate and Willie? What about..." she trailed off, looking lost.

"That one," I said, pointing at the lighter blue shirt in her left hand. "And don't worry," I added. "Everything will work out." My voice sounded confident. I was proud that I sounded so sure.

She pulled the T-shirt I picked over her head and smiled at me, clearly not believing a word of what I was saying.

"I hope you're right," she finally mumbled.

So did I.

31

WARD

MY SISTER DIDN'T FIGURE it out immediately, but, within about twenty minutes or so, she knew. Kate always knows when something significant happens in my life. It's like some kind of weird sixth sense with her. Like she's reading my aura or some shit. Our mom is the same way. I never could get away with anything between the two of them.

"There's something up with you," she told me, trapping me in the office when I went to grab my lucky bottle opener. She closed the door behind her and stared at me like she was looking for evidence—or guilt.

"Oh yeah?" I tried for casual.

"*Oh yeah.*" She wasn't fooled. Her eyes narrowed. "Are you going to tell me, or do I have to figure it out? You've been really weird today."

This I had to hear. I'd only been there for fifteen

minutes. Emma wouldn't be arriving for another hour and a half. There was no way I'd already somehow done something to tip Kate off.

She raised her right index finger to prove me wrong. "First, you aren't early today. You're always early."

"I am not. I was late last week. Twice actually."

"Okay. But if you aren't late, you're early. You arrived suspiciously on time."

"And?" She had to have more than that.

"And you called in sick yesterday."

Oh, right. That was outside my norm.

"I was feeling under the weather."

"You haven't been sick since eighth grade."

I'd gotten mono in the eighth grade from Ashley Monroe, who got it from Cody Leander, who got it from Riley Ransom, and on and on. Our whole school was like a cautionary tale against making out under the bleachers. I'd been one of the lucky kids to get the bad version, laying me out flat for a full four weeks. It was the sickest I'd ever been in my life.

"Maybe my mono is acting up again," I told Kate, shrugging. "I feel just fine now."

She squinted at me. "You were shacked up with some girl, weren't you?"

Busted.

My face must have betrayed me because she rolled her eyes. "Very responsible managerial behavior boss-man."

Oh, she had no idea.

She poked up a third finger. "And third, you forgot your stupid lucky bottle opener."

I looked down at the brass, painted bottle opener in my hand that was shaped like a topless mermaid. It had been a gift from Willie when I bought the bar from him. He probably just got it at Target or something, but he said it was from his days in the Navy. It had served me well so far. I had developed sort of a strange attachment to the thing.

"It's not like I lost it," I told her. "I just left it here in the office. That's not weird at all."

She shook her head. "Sure, it is. You've carried that thing around in your back pocket at least fifty hours a week for the past *few years*. It's practically an extension of your body."

I shrugged.

"You know," Kate said, "that thing actually looks sort of like Emma."

The mermaid did bear a somewhat loose resemblance to Emma. I cocked my head. Emma's tits were better.

Something must have showed on my face because Kate sucked in her breath in horror.

"No!" she exclaimed. "*You are not sleeping with Emma!*" Was I really that transparent to her? She might as well just be reading my mind.

Having been caught, there was not a lot of point in lying to her. If I did, Kate would ask Emma. And I sincerely doubted that Emma would lie to her, because they were friends. I nodded, looking resolutely at the floor of my office. I was not going to be made to feel ashamed of hooking up with Emma. Not again. I'd already dealt with Rae, so at least I had practice.

"I don't need to explain myself to you," I told Kate. "I already got the fucking Spanish Inquisition from Emma's scary roommate this morning."

Kate was still staring at me with her mouth hanging open, too shocked to speak, so I took a deep breath and rushed on.

"Look, we're both adults and it's not—"

She cut me off. Her face had turned an unpleasant shade of bright red. "Is this part of some brilliant plan of yours to get rid of her? Are you messing around with her so she'll get pissed off and quit her job? That's really low, even for you. Just because I hired her and you weren't involved? Is she really that hard to work with? *She's my friend.*" Kate wasn't yelling anywhere near as loudly as she could, but she was definitely yelling. The daytime crowd in the bar would be able to hear her if they walked past the door. I needed to deescalate the situation before it caused a scene.

"Christ. No. I wouldn't do that. This has nothing to do with Emma working at the bar, or you hiring her to work here, or anything to do with you. It's completely unrelated to that." My heart thumped in my chest. "I just like her. Is that so wrong?"

Kate looked at me for signs that I was lying. "You're telling me the truth," she said after a second, as if she was surprised. "Huh."

"Gee, thanks," I told her. Picking up my junior prom date hadn't been as nerve-wracking as this. Granted, I'd been lying then that I'd have her home by ten, and that she'd still be "pure" when she got there... but whatever. Her family was more than a little bit nuts. And I wasn't the one who ended up deflowering her, and not that night. I forced my brain back to the present.

"Am I excused now?" I asked my sister, trying to figure out a way to get out of the situation before she found some other reason to yell at me.

Kate sighed. "I really wish you hadn't slept with her." She shook her head in apparent disappointment. "Emma's been hurt enough. And she's my friend."

"What, you can't be friends with someone I hooked up with? It's casual! It didn't mean anything. We're not going to make a scene or anything."

Kate looked at me like I was the world's stupidest man. "She's going to quit now. Within a week. I guarantee it."

"Why would you say that?" To be honest, I was a bit hurt that Kate thought I was so awful.

"Because it's obvious that she's into you."

"I'm into her too... which is why we—"

She cut me off with an angry wave of her hand. "No!" The shouting was back. When I put a finger to my lips and pointed at the door, she lowered her voice. "Look, I'm sure you think she's fun and sexy and whatever. But she... ugh, I hate that I have to explain such a simple concept to you! She has *feelings* for you. You know, like normal people do."

I paused. "You think so?" The idea that Emma had feelings for me, which should have terrified me, actually made my heart do a little pathetic flip-flop in my chest. That was new. I'd honestly thought that part of me was dead, murdered forever by Jessie.

"I can tell by your shocked and vacant expression that you didn't realize," Kate told me. "But yeah, she clearly does. And now that you've decided to turn her into your latest conquest, she's going to get her hopes up, and then get crushed, and then probably neither one of us is ever going to see her again. *That's why I wish you could have just left her alone.*"

I'd been ready to head back to the bar, but now I was feeling a bit lightheaded. I sat down in my office chair.

"I'll figure it out," I told Kate. "Don't worry."

She rolled her eyes at me and made a rude noise. "Yeah, okay. Whatever. At least I still have the stack of other resumes from the job posting. I might as well start scheduling the interviews now. Thanks in advance for making my friend hate me."

Kate stomped out, leaving me alone with my thoughts. Kate was smart, and she was disturbingly good at reading me, but there was no proof that she had any skill at all when it came to Emma. Kate had been studying me our whole lives, but she'd only known Emma for a fraction of that time. Maybe she was just misreading Emma.

Or maybe she was picking up on something, but it wasn't what she thought. I'd spent the past half-decade insulating myself against any chance of falling in love with someone, or having anyone fall in love with me, it would be just my luck that it happened anyway. Like some kind of perverse, cosmic joke, it would be Kate who would figure it out. Only *backward*. Kate, who couldn't ever seem to tell if someone was into her, even if the guy hired a skywriter and showed up with a dozen roses.

Emma didn't have feelings for me. It was the other way around.

Even though the thought ought to send me running for the hills, I found myself entertaining the thought of dating Emma. Of moving in with her. Getting a dog together and going on walks with it. Getting engaged. Maybe even, one day, getting married. I bet Emma would be beautiful in white...

Oh, shit. Why couldn't Kate ever be wrong?

32

WARD

OVER THE NEXT THREE WEEKS, Emma and I defied Kate's gloomy expectations. The bar had never been better. The general atmosphere there was better than usual, and customers seemed to be spending more time, and money, there as a result. The whole world seemed to be riding our gentle high. Although I was fairly sure that disaster approached, I wasn't going to question the present. I was happy. Emma was happy. Wasn't that really all that mattered?

Outside of work, we spent almost every waking moment together. I would have thought we'd both get sick of being together, but it only seemed to feed our hunger for each other. Rae got used to seeing me in the mornings. Emma learned where things were in my condo. Kate didn't learn not to make a weird, disapproving face every time she saw us together, but I think she was working on it. Emma and I did a lot of talking, in addition to spending hours between the sheets (and in the shower, and on the couch, and on the floor...). Life was good and neither one of us felt the need to say anything about dating, or relationships, or feelings. It was easy.

Until one morning, it wasn't. I woke up to Emma already up and tapping at her laptop to my right in the bed, sniffling.

"Emma, what's the matter?" I asked her, surprised to see her awake at six a.m. and even more surprised to see her puffy-eyed and upset.

She looked over at me and slammed the top of her laptop down. Blushing furiously, she set it on the bedside table like she'd been caught doing something bad. "Sorry, Ward. I didn't mean to wake you up."

"You didn't," I told her, pulling her close to me and feeling slightly encouraged when she nuzzled against me after a second. "Do you want to tell me why you're upset?" I couldn't imagine what she might have been looking at that would have her so worked up. It must have been very bad news.

"It's not a very interesting story." Her voice was muffled against my chest.

"Tell me anyway," I coaxed. She raised her head up to look at me, maybe to determine whether she could trust mc, and nodded.

Her story started with a sigh. "I submitted a few of my short stories and poems to a well-regarded literary magazine," she told me. "They liked one of my shorts and they published it in their fall publication."

"Emma, that's really great!" I knew that being published meant a lot to Emma. It helped her establish credibility for herself in academia, and it also helped provide validation to her that she was actually a good writer. We'd talked about it a lot over the last few weeks, mostly at my prompting. I wanted to understand Emma, and I had been feeling like I was making progress at doing that. But now I wasn't so sure. "Isn't that great?" I asked again, confused.

She laughed miserably. "Yeah, that part is great. I'm sorry. I'm explaining this all wrong. I'm happy that I got published. But I didn't even know that I made the autumn quarterly until I got this email. From Adam. He's telling me how much he liked my piece and that if I would just come and study under him at the university, he could see me doing even better work in the future. Then he goes into all the ways I could have improved the piece, and all the things that were wrong with it..."

What a dick.

"Wait, he wrote you a note congratulating you and then decided to tear you down? That's really rude."

Emma shook her head, which I felt rather than saw because she was now hiding under the covers. Her voice emerged from under the comforter. "You don't understand.

It's his job to help people like me become better writers. He's had dozens and dozens of pieces published in this magazine. He's brilliant. And his criticisms are all... good. Insightful, you know?"

"Emma, that's crazy," I told her, lifting the blanket and brushing her hair back from her forehead so I could see her better. She looked up at me miserably.

"I wish it was crazy," Emma said. "I do. If he were just one hundred percent wrong, I'd be fine with it. I could just write him off as an asshole and move on with my life. But he makes some really good points about where I could have improved the piece, and it just makes me doubt everything. Maybe I should go talk to him. I could use his help. Maybe he's right that we would work well together..."

I swallowed my snide comments about the fact that Adam clearly just wanted to get her into bed. He was gaslighting her and making her doubt her own talent. But even though I was sure I was right, if I said the wrong thing in this moment, it might be a disaster. I had no right to tell Emma what to do in her professional or her personal relationships. I was just a hookup to her, but I was also her friend.

"Do you think he would have written you this note if you two had never been together?" I asked carefully.

She blinked. "Not this email. But probably something. It's perfectly standard for department members to email grad students if they see them published. And it's also standard for them to offer feedback."

"What do you mean 'not this email'?" I had a feeling I already knew, but I needed her to figure it out for herself. I resisted the urge to be pushy, even though it was my natural response. Emma didn't react well to pushy. Our first interaction had taught me that much.

"Well, the email wasn't totally about the piece that I published. Some of it was about other things. He says that he misses me a lot. He talks about how it's hard to adjust to being here in Texas after living in New Haven. He just moved here. I think he's very lonely."

I swallowed my disgust. I couldn't care less that he was lonely. In fact, I liked it. I hoped that it continued. He deserved to be lonely. "Do you think it's possible that he's trying to mess with you emotionally?"

After a moment, she nodded. "Probably. And it worked." She looked upset, but also annoyed. "Offering me feedback is fine, but it's not normal that he would combine it with his weird little love letter, is it?"

"No. That's not normal at all."

"Should I write him back?"

I blinked. She was asking me? "I don't know," I told her. "If it were up to me, you'd forward that message that clearly shows what an ass-hat he is directly to his boss. Get him fired. He shouldn't be trying to trick you into anything, and that's exactly what he's doing. He's trying to appeal to your hope of being published and being a better writer in order to get you back into his bed."

I think my little monologue had shocked her. She sat up in bed and looked at me for a long moment. Her sea-green eyes were unreadable. "You really think I should do that? He'd probably be fired. He'd certainly be embarrassed and humiliated. This was a private message, sent outside of the university email system."

"Don't you think he should be punished? He's sexually harassing you."

She bit her lip, turning it a sexy, deeper pink. "I don't know. I mean, our relationship was always consensual."

Part of me wanted to convince her that if a guy was willing to do something like that after the end of a consensual sexual relationship, he was probably willing to pursue someone who wasn't willing. Another part wanted to convince her that sexual harassers generally didn't harass *only one* person. There were probably other victims of this guy running around feeling ashamed. But I didn't need to tell her any of that. She already knew. She just didn't want to admit it yet.

"I'm not telling you to do anything," I told her. "Scout's honor. But you asked me what I think you should do, and that's what I would do. I'd get his creepy old ass fired and then laugh while he was escorted out of the building."

Emma looked like she was really considering it, but

then she shook her head. "I can't. I don't want to destroy his career."

"Can I offer another option?" I asked. As much as I wanted to see the guy ruined, Emma still clearly had a bit of a soft spot for him. Not that he deserved it. I stifled my jealousy.

She nodded. "Sure."

"Why don't you write him back? Thank him for his comments on your piece and then tell him that you think the rest of the message is not okay. Make it clear, in writing, that he needs to back the hell off. Permanently. That way if you ever do need to go to the University about him sexually harassing you, you'll have the email."

Her mouth dropped open. "Okay."

I could barely believe my ears. "Really? You'll do it?"

She smirked, and the light came back into her eyes and cheeks. "Yeah. It's a good idea. You always make such a big deal about how dumb you are, but you aren't. I think maybe Adam doesn't actually hear anything that I say. But maybe if he reads it, he'll understand that I don't want to be with him—personally or professionally."

I grinned at her, delighted that she was going to write the guy and tell him to fuck off. Only nicer, of course, since she was Emma.

"So, am I allowed to read your piece?" I asked. "I mean, I know I won't have any criticisms, so you don't need to worry about that. I probably won't understand half of it."

"You want to read it?" She looked shocked and happy. "Really?"

"Of course, I want to read it," I said. "Is that okay?" I was proud of her for getting published. It was the equivalent of winning a bowl game to a writer. There was no bigger win for Emma than having people read her words.

"Yeah, I'll email you a copy." She looked excited and hopeful.

"Can I read the print version? It seems more important if it's in print, don't you think?"

"Yeah, it definitely does."

Emma smiled her biggest, brightest smile, and it made my heart throb. She was so beautiful it was ridiculous. I'd told her about the fact that she looked like my bottle opener and she'd curled her hair the night before to play up the resemblance. Now that she'd slept on it, she looked even more like the mermaid. I wished I could carry her around in my pocket the way I did the bottle opener.

Knowing that she was operating under the information that I had no feelings for her was beginning to eat at me, but I had no idea what to do about it. If she didn't feel the same way, and I told her I was in love with her, she'd bolt. And I wasn't sure I could stand losing her, even if I couldn't have her heart.

33

WARD

"I GUESS I need to get up," Emma said, bending over me to take a look at the alarm clock on my bedside table. Even disguised by the shapeless T-shirt of mine that covered her in a sea of grey cotton, her body couldn't be ignored. In an instant, my libido woke up. Emma wasn't going anywhere if I could stop it.

When she tried to lean away from me, I gripped her forearms and pinned her down, rolling so that I was on top of her.

"Hey!" She squealed, wriggling uselessly beneath me and giggling. "No fair. I've got to get up."

"Why?" I questioned, kissing her neck and counting the tiny freckles that dotted her skin.

"I was going to go get the oil changed on my stupid car before the line gets long," she said. "I'm overdue. I don't want my car to explode." Although she was talking a good game, her resistance was already fading. She'd wrapped her legs around my hips and was arching her soft tits up into my chest.

"That's just silly," I told her, pulling up the hem of the T-shirt to get a better look at her. Her skin was so pale it nearly glowed in the bright morning light coming through the windows. She looked like an angel. "I'll teach you how to change the oil yourself. You should never have to pay somebody to do it for you." I *wanted* to tell her that I'd just change it for her, but she'd interpret that as charity, which I'd learned that she despised.

"Okay," she said, although I probably could have just suggested that we go base jumping at that point. I'd taken her right nipple between my lips and was lavishing attention on it, something that I'd learned she absolutely loved. I loved it too, especially when it made her rock her hips against me like she was and turned her eyes glassy and vacant.

The jaded, cynical version of me that lived for one-night stands was astonished. That Ward had believed that spending too much time with the same woman would make her reactions become boring. Emma had silenced that voice in my head without ever even knowing it existed. How could I ever grow tired of watching her bite into her full bottom lip while I licked and sucked on her chest? Or the way she made little noises that seemed to be totally beyond her control when I stroked her inner thighs? It was impossible.

By the time we were shedding our final layers of clothing, I was forced again to admit to myself that Emma was the sexiest woman I'd ever had the pleasure of making love to. And also the most innocent. She approached sex like she did everything else, with an eagerness and curiosity. I'd turned on my side to pull off my boxers, and she pressed a soft little palm into my chest to push my back against the mattress.

"You get to be on top too much," she whispered in my ear, biting my earlobe and making me shiver. "My turn."

Anything you want. Especially that.

She took me inside herself on a slow, gentle descent, her mouth getting a little wider as she went down. I pressed my hands to her creamy white thighs, trying not to rush her but also squeezed so tight that I felt like I had to move or die. When she finally began to move it was a grinding, teasing movement, placing her hands atop mine while she did.

"You're beautiful," I told her. The awe in my voice was obvious. She smiled down at me, maybe, for once, believing me.

Her shell-pink nipples swayed with her movements, hypnotizing me as she worked. Her eyes had gone glassy again, and she rode me with that same, slow grinding until I could barely stand it. I'm not sure how long she danced like that on my cock, but it was beautiful torture. It felt like forever.

"Emma, fuck," I groaned, pushing my hips up into her as hard as I could, but she kept that grinding rhythm slow and steady.

I'd discovered she didn't need direct stimulation on her clit to make her come when she was on top, but I gave it to her anyway, rubbing her sweet little spot until she moaned and threw her head back. Her back arched, pointing her chest to the ceiling and showing the outlines of her ribs through her pale skin. Her orgasm clenched around me in pulsating waves. When her eyes cleared, and her noises slowed, I wrapped my hands around her ass to try and urge her on—to make her movements faster and more up and down—and thank god, she obliged.

Now bouncing energetically, the delicate muscles inside her were pushing me toward climax as quickly as her mouth could have done. I pushed back into her from below more forcefully as well, pulling at her hair with one hand and pushing down from her waist with the other.

"Yes, harder," she was saying, over and over, urging me on. I did.

Her second climax pulled me right over the edge with her, and I came with enough force to barely hear her screaming my name in a high, breathy voice. My neighbors probably heard it though. They'd left me a nasty note about it actually, taping it to my door and telling us to 'keep our ridiculous porno noises to ourselves,' but I hadn't told Emma about it and had no intention of doing so. They could get some earplugs, or better yet, move. I loved how damn loud Emma was when she came; it was genuine. She was too embarrassed about how loud she was to be faking it. I loved how easily she got embarrassed. I loved everything about her.

I loved her.

Now I just had to figure out how to tell her, before I lost her forever.

34

EMMA

"So, you and Ward, huh?" Lucas asked. He was one of the daytime laptop regulars, in addition to being Ward's buddy. Sometimes he stuck around into the evenings, too.

I raised an eyebrow as I set his beer down in front of him. "It's not serious." I honestly didn't know how to talk to Lucas. He was a customer, but he was also sort of my friend at this point and definitely one of Ward's. It felt like we shouldn't be having this conversation.

"Ward doesn't do serious," Lucas answered, sipping his usual (Live Oak Brewery's hefeweizen *with two orange slices*). "But he also doesn't do month-long one-night stands."

I tried to keep my face and body casual and relaxed. "Well, it's only been a couple of weeks," I answered. Three weeks and four days. It had been exactly three weeks and four days. Not that I was counting.

"Hmm," was Lucas's only reply. He was clearly keen to continue our little uncomfortable conversation about my sexual activities with his friend, but I smiled and walked away as fast as I could. I wished he hadn't stuck around tonight. His curiosity about Ward and me was making me nervous.

Was a month-long casual hookup too long? Was Ward going to announce in three days that we'd reached the limit of what he considered to be casual and that things were getting decidedly too real? I had a roommate once who had a friends-with-benefits situation that went on for about six months at one point. But they met *only* for sex. She said she wasn't even sure he spoke English for the first few weeks (he did, apparently). Ward and I hung out and got coffee. We'd been to see movies together. He even taught me how to change my oil.

I was so far out of my comfort zone that I couldn't even see the edge of it anymore. It was all uncharted territory as far as the eye could see. And I had no map, no compass, and no guiding star. I was totally just winging it.

"I actually asked for Miller Lite, not Guinness," my customer told me when I set her drink down a few minutes later.

"I'm so sorry!" I told her. I'd totally zoned out there for a second. I didn't even remember getting the beer. "That isn't even close, is it? I'll go get you the right one. Do you want to keep this too, or should I take it away?"

She looked at her date and he slid it toward himself with a sly grin. She shrugged and smiled at me. "I guess we'll keep it."

My mind was not in the game tonight. One wrong order wasn't a big deal, and hardly anyone ever complains about a free beer, but I needed to concentrate on the here and now. My tips depended on it. But all I seemed to be able to think about was Ward.

It didn't help that Ward was behind the bar looking perpetually sexy and cute. I put my head down, fixed my wrong order, and tried to concentrate. Just when I started to feel like I was getting back into my waitressing groove, Adam walked in and took a seat in my section. He was staring straight at me.

Fuck.

He must have gotten my message, carefully composed with Ward's help, telling him politely to fuck off.

Ward hadn't noticed Adam yet. He was chatting with Lucas now, who had moseyed up to the bar (presumably to grab more orange slices—he was a bit strange). I took a deep breath to steady myself and made my way over to Adam's table. Whatever he wanted, it was better to get it over with. He clearly hadn't come to drink. This wasn't his kind of place. He preferred the type of establishment where one was served drinks by a sommelier, not a cocktail waitress.

"Hello, Adam," I said politely. "Would you like something to drink?" Perhaps if I just seemed extremely professional and disinterested, he would get the idea and go the hell away.

"Hello, Emma," Adam replied. "Do you have wine here?" He'd rolled up the cuffs of his white shirt, which was the Adam equivalent of a casual look, but I noticed that his shirt was fairly ruffled. His hair, too, was even messier than usual. He also had dark circles under his eyes. In short, he looked absolutely miserable.

"We have a house red and a house white," I told him with a shake of my head. "You aren't going to like either of them."

He smirked. "You're probably right. I'll take the white."

I nodded politely. "I'll be right back."

Walking back to the bar where Ward was staring at me, knowing that Adam was also staring at me, was the longest twenty-five steps of my life. At least I didn't trip or spontaneously combust. I made it back to the bar and went to pour the drink myself. We didn't serve the wine very often, so it was easier just to do it myself than to interrupt Ward or Willie. I should have known I wouldn't get away, however, because Ward was at my elbow immediately.

"Are you okay?" he asked, his voice low but containing just the right amount of protectiveness to trick me into thinking he really cared. I tried to remind myself that he didn't.

"Yeah, fine." My reply was short, but I didn't think I could handle anything else. I grabbed the wine and a water pitcher and took off. The sooner Adam said his piece, the sooner he'd leave. Hopefully.

I refilled the water glasses of the other customers on the way to Adam's table, and dropped the wine in front of him. He didn't touch it.

"Emma, I really think we should talk," he said. "Could you just sit down for five minutes?" He gestured to the empty chair in front of him.

At the moment I had eight customers total. Three of them had already paid and were getting ready to leave. Four of them had drinks and wouldn't need anything in the next five minutes. The other one was a designated driver whose water I'd just refilled. This was a bizarre lull and as good a chance to talk as I was going to get all night. I sunk into the chair directly across from Adam and waited. I could practically feel Ward's eyes on us. I knew without having to look that he was riveted to the scene.

Adam smiled at me like he'd won something, and then he picked up the wine, sniffed it, and put it back down. He grimaced like he'd just sniffed drain cleaner.

"You didn't tell me it was *chardonnay*."

I shrugged. "I don't know what it is. It's white. I did tell you that you wouldn't like it."

His mouth twisted like he wanted to smile again, but then he settled back into a frown.

"Emma, I got your email. I started typing up a response, but then I wrote and rewrote it so many times it just became a huge mess. So, I decided to come over here and talk to you instead."

"Okay." I was keeping my voice level. It sounded reasonable. I was doing good on the outside. Inside my heart was pounding, but Adam didn't need to know that.

"Listen, I know we had an inauspicious start. I know that I did a bad thing by seducing you when you were my student. I *know* that. And I know I shouldn't have done it when I was engaged to someone else, obviously. But I didn't love her. I never did. I was in love with you. I still am."

I had no idea what to say. Adam was in love with me? He'd said that before and still crushed my heart to bits. It had been five years.

"You don't even know me anymore," I managed to say. "You can't be in love with me anymore."

Adam shook his head. "I don't think that's true. When I read your piece, I knew that we were meant to be together. It was like I was seeing inside your mind again, like I used to when you were in my class. I felt like I could see your soul in your writing."

"You gave me an A- in your class. Clearly, my mind wasn't that compelling." I was still irked about that fucking A-. I'd had a goddamned 4.0 before that.

"I did that because I *wanted* to make you angry. I was trying to drive you away. Look, I know this isn't going to make much sense to you, and you probably think I'm a total moron, but I had an addiction to you that I knew was inappropriate and I needed *you to be the one* to keep me from coming back. Making you angry, being cold and indifferent, that was my whole plan."

It made sense, in a twisted way, but it wasn't an excuse for the way he'd treated me. There was no excuse for what he'd done. No amount of justification was going to change that.

"Why are you telling me this?" I needed to wrap this up. My heart could only handle so much in a single evening.

"Why do you think? I'm in love with you. Ever since we were together, I've been trying to get back to you. I left Rhiannon. I left Yale. *I'm here because of you.*" Rhiannon was the woman he'd been engaged to. I'd hated her, briefly, before I realized I should pity her. I pitied her even more now.

"That's ridiculous. Despite what you told me, I wasn't the first coed you slept with."

"You were the first one and the only one that I fell in love with."

I shook my head. "I'm sorry, Adam. I'm sorry that you feel this way, and I'm sorry it's screwed up your life. But that's not my fault, and I don't reciprocate your feelings."

Adam's eyes flashed over toward the bar. "Is it because

of *him*?" He looked jealous, but only slightly. Mostly he looked sad.

"No, Adam, it has nothing to do with Ward."

"After he kissed you, I asked around in the department. You two are dating, though, aren't you?"

"Yes." We weren't, obviously, but I knew Ward wouldn't mind me lying about it to Adam.

"Do you love him? Does he love you?" Adam had placed both his palms flat on the table and his voice was pained. He looked like a man possessed. I was starting to believe him that he was in love with me, which was terrifying. No one had ever been in love with me before.

"I owe you no explanations."

He nodded, accepting my answer. He wasn't giving up though.

"You and I were meant to be together," Adam said, moving on. "I told Lieu about us when I interviewed, you know. Not that I was in love with you, but that we'd had a relationship in the past. He told me that he would love to have me on staff, my credentials were clearly more than adequate for a second-tier school like this, but he told me it was professional suicide to come here just to chase a PhD student. I told him we were F. Scott and Zelda Fitzgerald."

"You're an alcoholic who will drink himself to death and I'm a nutcase who'll die in an asylum fire? Fantastic."

I rolled my eyes and he grinned. He liked arguing with me, just like Ward did.

"No. We're star-crossed lovers. We're artists who bring out the best—and the worst—in each other. The poem that almost made me Poet Laureate? I wrote that when I was with you."

"You tried to trick me into sex by offering to help me with my work. It's exactly what you did when I was at Yale, only worse, because this time I don't want it."

He paused. "I shouldn't have written you that email. I just really wanted to see you."

"So, you admit you were trying to manipulate me?"

"*Yes*. Does that make you happy?" He frowned. "I admit I was wrong. I admit everything. Will you just entertain the idea that maybe I might really love you?"

I'd truly had enough. Love didn't matter. Not with Adam.

"No. Because it doesn't matter if you love me. Look, you can't talk me into loving you. I was in love with you once, but I'm not anymore. I've grown up. Maybe you should too."

I stood up to leave. This was beyond ridiculous. I couldn't continue to entertain Adam's crazy theory that we belonged together. Even if any of what he was saying was true—and that was a big if because he was *a known liar*—it didn't matter. I knew that I wasn't in love with him. I had grown up and out of my innocence, thanks to him. And because of that, I'd grown out of my childish infatuation too.

"If that's the way you feel, I won't bother you again. I just had to come here to tell you." He shook his head at me, laid a twenty on the table and stood. "Remember that I loved you. I screwed up my shot with you because I was stupid, impulsive, irrational, and proud. You deserve somebody to love you, Emma, even if it's not me. Don't make my mistakes. Don't ever waste your time with someone who won't do what it takes to be with you again. If there's one thing I learned from the past few years, from you and Rhiannon and everything, it's this: *don't ever be with someone who doesn't really, truly love you, because it erodes your talent and wastes your time. You deserve something real.*"

He left then, and my mind was reeling. Had he ever really loved me? Was this all some kind of fucked up mind trick? My heart hurt from the weight of his confession and his final speech. Even if he was flawed, he wasn't completely wrong. The truth of what he told me echoed in my brain, over and over, until it was a mantra. Until it was the only thing I could hear.

Don't ever be with someone who doesn't really, truly love you, because it erodes your talent and wastes your time. You deserve something real.

Adam was an asshole, but he was right. I did deserve something real. It was time to say goodbye to Ward.

35

EMMA

MY SHIFT PASSED by in a painful blur. I know that I served drinks, made small talk, cleaned tables, smiled and giggled at the lame jokes my customers made... I just didn't remember any of it in detail. By the time last call rolled around I had a pocket full of money, very tired feet, and five missing hours. I felt numb.

"Emma, do you have a second?" Ward asked, putting a hand on my shoulder and looking into my eyes like he'd been trying to get my attention for a while.

I nodded at him and made myself smile. "Sure. Let me just go drop this last glass of water, finish wiping down the tables, and then I'm done."

"Meet me in the office?" His voice was soft and the hand on my shoulder felt warm and comforting. He kissed me on the forehead. I wished I could rewind time to the beginning of my shift. Unlearn what I'd learned from Adam. But it was too late.

"Okay. Five minutes and I'll be there." I used the time to rehearse what I had to say to him. I wasn't sure I could do it, but it was time to find out.

When I wandered into the office, Ward was sitting on the edge of his desk, leafing through some papers.

"What happened with Adam?" he asked. "After he left, you were on total autopilot. You barely said two words to me and Willie for the rest of the night. Are you okay?"

Was I okay? No, not really. Not remotely. Not at all. My heart was breaking.

"He came to confess his love for me." I said it sarcastically, although he had sounded perfectly sincere. But it still sounded sort of ridiculous when I said it out loud. But the way he looked had shaken me to my core. Despite the pain that Adam had caused me, I had loved him once. There was a time when I would have done anything to get Adam to come and tell me exactly what he told me tonight. But now that he loved me, I no longer loved him. Life was really fucked up sometimes.

Ward's lips parted in surprise. "He did what?" The papers in his hands slid to the ground, forgotten.

I shook my head. "It was totally surreal. He came to confess his undying love for me, tell me that he would do anything for me, and beg me to take him back."

Ward looked like he had no idea what to say to that. He didn't get struck speechless very often. Silence stretched between us until he cleared his throat uncomfortably.

"Are you okay?" He asked again.

"Yeah," I lied, even though I felt paper-thin and so fragile that I might blow away. "I'm fine. I told him to go sit on a cactus."

The term 'sit on a cactus' was something that Ward had taught me. I liked it a lot. It was Texas-y. One day I would work it into a story somewhere and think of him. The stray thought made me frown.

Ward smiled when he heard that I'd rebuffed Adam, but he still looked concerned. Maybe on some level he could feel my anxiety radiating off me in waves. I've heard that humans have the ability to detect subtle pheromone changes, especially in those to whom they were physically and emotionally close. I was probably pumping out more stress hormones than I ever had before in my entire life. I couldn't even remember another time in my life that could come close.

Apparently, this is why they say that breaking up is hard to do. Except we weren't even together.

"Then why do you look so worried?" Ward asked, proving that even if he couldn't smell my hormones, he could at least read my face.

"Because I realized something important." I swallowed

hard. Took a deep breath. Broke my own heart. "I don't think we should see each other anymore."

In the quiet of the tiny office, I could hear my heart beating. Was it bleeding, too? It was definitely in two pieces now. It hurt so much that I could barely breathe.

"Because you're in love with *Adam*?" Ward's voice was confused, and that made my heart ache even worse. His face was completely unreadable to me now, like he'd raised up a wall behind his eyes that hid his feelings. I wished I could shut down my emotions like him. Maybe one day I'd learn how.

"No," I said softly. "No, it's not because I'm in love with Adam. I don't love him."

"Then why?" I hadn't really expected him not to ask. Part of me thought he might just nod and laugh, but he didn't. Even Ward, who didn't believe in relationships, apparently wanted an explanation for my sudden change of heart. On some level, even if it was tiny, he did care. And he also deserved to know why I was ending things. So, I would tell him the truth.

"Because I need to focus on myself right now." These were the words that I'd been rehearsing. "The last few weeks with you have been so wonderful. Beyond anything I hoped for. I hope you had a good time with me, too. I think you're amazing. But I need to focus on my writing. I need to cut out distractions and focus on what's real and lasting to me. I need to focus on what I love."

Ward looked at me with wide eyes. Even after staring into them over and over, the color of his eyes would always amaze me. Such a clear, bright, crystalline blue made brighter by the contrast with his dark hair and long eyelashes. And right now, Ward's incredible eyes looked utterly confused. Lost. I hated that it was my fault he looked unhappy. I never wanted to make him sad. I just couldn't continue to delay my own inevitable heartbreak. It was better to get it over with.

"Alright, Emma. I understand." Ward's voice was even and soft. Gentle. He swallowed, and his Adam's apple bobbed up and down in his throat. "I appreciate you being honest with me."

There was no anger in his voice or aggressiveness to his body language. He was simply listening to what I had to say and accepting my right to leave. Like a gentleman. Once upon a time I thought that Ward was a chauvinistic asshole, but he'd proved me wrong time and time again. The way he was handling this conversation was just more evidence that he had a hell of a lot more class than Adam, even if he didn't have a PhD and a vocabulary the size of Texas.

I nodded. "Of course."

In the time I'd known Ward, I had come to realize that he was not the type to share what he was feeling. So, even if he was saddened that I'd ended things, it wasn't showing on his face. But more likely, he simply didn't care that much. I was done. It happened. I was just another hookup in a long line of women that had graced Ward's bed. I hadn't missed the fact that he kept a box of extra toothbrushes and women's toiletries under his sink. He had the whole one-night stand thing figured out.

"I also think I need to quit the bar," I told him next. I'd saved this bit for last since I figured it was the most likely piece of news to provoke a negative reaction. "It would be too weird for me to keep working here."

Ward looked at me. His gaze was unsurprised. "Okay. If that's what you want to do, I get it."

"I'm sorry to quit without giving notice."

"It's not a big deal."

I shifted uncomfortably from foot to foot. "Can you just mail my last check to me?"

"Of course, I can."

"Alright."

"Okay."

Ward was staring at his feet. He wasn't saying anything. No jokes. No comments. Nothing. Just staring at his feet like they provided some answers that I couldn't.

Ward was a good guy. Someday maybe he'd realize that. Maybe, someday he'd let somebody love him again. But it wouldn't be me.

While I'd been obsessively rehearsing my lines to myself as I wiped down tables, I'd entertained a brief, hysterical fantasy where Ward refused to let me go. In the fantasy, he'd tell me that he loved me, sweep me up in his arms and kiss me. We'd ride off into the sunset and live happily ever after. God, I was such an idiot sometimes.

Rationally, I knew that the likelihood that two men would confess their undying love for me in one night was ridiculous. Especially if one of them was Ward. Ward famously didn't do relationships. He'd made that clear from the very beginning. It was unfair of me to even imagine that he would change his mind just because I wasn't going to be his fuckbuddy anymore.

I knew it was time for me to go, but I couldn't seem to move my body. Once I walked out the door, I'd probably never see this office again. Once I walked out of the bar, I'd probably never see Ward again. Or Willie. Or Kate. I hadn't realized until this moment how much it would hurt to say goodbye. I got attached to this place so easily, and so quickly. I hadn't even realized it was happening. And now it was over.

"I hope you aren't angry with me, Ward," I whispered. My hands were starting to shake uncontrollably, and my voice was wavering. "I just can't do this."

Something in me broke—snapped—and I suddenly couldn't stand to stay in the same room with Ward another moment. His gaze snapped up to my face, but before I could see him become disgusted with me and *my stupid feelings for him*, I ran away. I fled, out of the room, out the back door, and down the alleyway to where my car was parked. As I went, I passed Kate in the alley. She was sneaking a cigarette. She looked at me in surprise, noted the tears that were already running down my face, and said nothing.

Just like her brother did, Kate let me go.

36

WARD

EMMA WAS GONE, and it felt like all the air had left with her, leaving me suffocating in the tiny office. I hadn't felt this way since... well, now that I thought about it, I'd never felt like this. Losing Emma was officially feeling like a new low, and there had been some pretty deep lows in my life. If someone had asked me five minutes earlier, I would have certainly said that the one-two punch of losing my career and fiancée in the same week could have never been rivaled.

The piece that Emma had published lay at my feet. I'd ordered my own copy of the magazine, so I wouldn't have to steal hers. I'd made lots of little notes in the margins and been excited to talk about it with her. For the first time since middle school, I'd actually attempted to analyze and appreciate a piece of writing as art; I'd looked for themes

and metaphors and stuff and highlighted them. I'd probably done a terrible job at it, but I wanted to show Emma
that I cared.

My lame attempt was too late. Emma, who had never
been mine, not really, had realized that she didn't want to
waste her time with me anymore. I could hardly blame her,
but I thought we'd have more time.

If Emma had been anyone else, I would have been
relieved. Even my most casual fuckbuddies never lasted
three weeks. Usually because one of us found someone else
they wanted to play with, but sometimes because things
just got old. But Emma wasn't anyone else; she was different. Special.

While I was staring despondently at the ground, Kate
wandered into my office. Even her footsteps sounded smug.
I looked up at her expecting the 'I told you so,' but her face
shifted from knowing to confused.

"Ward? Are you alright?" Her voice was concerned. She
moved forward and pressed the back of her hand to my
forehead to check for a temperature. She thought I was ill?
I probably looked as shitty as I felt.

"I'm fine," I lied. "What's up?"

Kate's brow was furrowed. She looked like I'd knocked
her off her game. I was still waiting for her to comment
on how she was right, as usual. Instead, she shook her
head. "I just saw Emma running to her car. She was
crying."

Emma was crying? Was that my fault? I felt like I'd been punched in the gut.

"Oh. Yeah. She quit." My voice sounded casual. That was an achievement. "You were right."

Usually Kate loved being right, but she wasn't gloating. She bit her bottom lip and examined me closely. "Ward, you don't look good."

I think I have massive internal damage. Can't you see? Doesn't it show?

"I'm not feeling very good, either." I grabbed my wallet and car keys out of the desk drawer I kept them in while working. "I think I'm gonna go ahead and go home. I think I need to rest or something. It's been a long night. Can you finish locking up with Willie?"

Kate nodded. "Okay. Yeah."

There was obviously a lot that Kate wanted to ask, I could see the questions on her face, but she didn't push. For once, she let me walk out the door without her snippy comments. Usually, Kate was *very* observant when it came to me. Too observant. This time, however, I was glad that she wasn't telling me what she saw. I wasn't ready to deal with it.

My condo, which I usually loved because of the panoramic views of downtown, didn't feel like home. It was incredibly depressing to see the few little things that Emma had left behind. She had been very respectful of my space and careful not to put any of herself where it didn't belong.

But a few little things had slipped in: a few hair ties, a pair of silver hoop earrings, a toothbrush, and a little blue, see-through nightgown that she never wore (she always ended up in one of my T-shirts, or naked). I gathered up her things and put them in a paper bag, making a vague plan to drop them by her apartment when she wasn't there.

I wondered if she was doing the same thing right now at her own apartment. I couldn't remember leaving anything over there, but there were probably a few things there by now. Maybe a T-shirt or two. Would she call so we could arrange a trade? I wasn't going to call her. That would be weird. This all felt a lot more like a breakup than it probably should.

I tried to think back to what things had been like when Jessie left and found that the memory didn't sting nearly as bad as I thought it would. It was just a dull ache now. Jessie had moved all her things out of my place before I left the hospital. I'd returned home to a space that had been carefully cleaned of any female influence. The silver frame that had held our engagement photo had been moved to the kitchen counter. The photo was gone, replaced with the world's briefest 'Dear John' letter. I could still remember exactly what it said: *Ward, I'm sorry but this isn't what I signed up for. I can't do this. Forgive me. Jessie.*

At the time I thought I would never walk again without a cane. When I saw the note, I remember whacking the countertop as hard as I could with that cane; shattering the frame's glass and breaking the cane in two. We'd already broken up. Jessie wasn't such a coward that she wouldn't do it to my face, but the note just felt like a slap. Not as much of a slap as the fact that she kept her engagement ring, maxed out my credit cards, and cleaned out my bank accounts before she went, but still.

As bad as that time in my life had been, it was the betrayal that hurt the most. Maybe because Jessie had gone on a shopping spree with my money just to reveal how truly materialistic and shallow she actually was, but on some level I knew I was lucky to be rid of her. Jessie and I had never really loved each other; we were just playing house. I thought I loved her, but the person I loved really never even existed. It was all an illusion she sold me. Jessie was only with me to feed her ego and need for luxury. Emma wouldn't even let me buy her coffee most of the time. She truly didn't care about money. She'd shown no interest in my net worth, which was substantially more than she probably realized. I'd recovered well, although it had taken years to do it. Recovering my self-esteem had taken just as long.

As I lay down on my empty bed, I wondered how long it would take for me to recover from Emma. I wasn't even sure I wanted to. If this was all I got to have of her, I drifted off to sleep thinking that it was still a lot better than nothing.

37

EMMA

THE MORNING AFTER, I woke up crying. I'd cried myself to sleep at some point, and I guess my body didn't get the memo because my cheeks were still wet when I woke up. As soon as I remembered everything, fresh tears started all over again.

When I finally stopped crying, I made myself go take a shower. The crying started again inside the shower, but it's the best place to cry because you don't have to worry about drying your tears or wiping your nose. You can just stand there until the hot water runs out, bawling. At least, that's what I did.

I put on clothes, blow dried my hair, and tried to feel human. I still looked like shit. In fact, I looked like I'd had a bad allergic reaction. I accidentally swallowed a bee once when I was a kid, and I looked sort of like that. I was puffy, swollen, blotchy, and pink all over from rubbing my face. My nose was raw and red. I grabbed the concealer, the powder, and Rae's expensive de-puffing cream and went to work. Fifteen minutes later, the now-presentable Emma in the mirror looked at me with a mixture of pity and recrimination.

My one consolation, if it can even be called that, was knowing that at least Ward was okay. He would be grateful that I'd handled things like a grownup. I hadn't gotten all weird and attached to him. I hadn't begged him to love me. I just cut ties and got out of his way. Although it hurt my heart to tell him goodbye, I knew that he was better off without some silly girl falling in love with him.

Adam's words were still ringing in my ears.

Don't ever be with someone who doesn't really, truly love you, because it erodes your talent and wastes your time.

Now that I had cut distractions from my life, I could focus on my writing and finishing my PhD. I could focus on my future without getting mired in the present. Thankfully, I'd earned just enough at the bar to cover my rent for the next month or two if I also used my emergency credit card and cut my expenses down to instant noodles and gas. It would be okay. I had enough time to get another job.

"Good morning, Em—" Rae started to say when I emerged into the living room to grab my laptop charger. She took one look at me and fell silent. The spoon that had been delivering cereal into her mouth clinked back down into the bowl.

"Don't say anything." I replied. My voice sounded as beaten down and sad as I felt. "I know I look bad. Just let me go hide in my room, okay?"

"I'm going to kill him," Rae announced, ignoring me. She put her cereal bowl down and put both of her hands on her hips like Superman. "He's a dead man. What did he do?"

"Nothing," I said, shaking my head. I couldn't talk about this with her. Not yet. "I ended things, okay?"

Rae blinked. "Why?" Her voice was shocked, but her wide green eyes, much more vivid than my own, still looked furious.

I shrugged. "Because the casual thing isn't for me." I snatched the charger out of the outlet behind the couch and retreated to the hallway.

"Emma?" Rae clearly wanted to talk, but I just couldn't.

"Later, okay?"

"Okay. Do you need anything?" Her voice was unexpectedly soft, given the anger she'd been displaying a second ago. I knew that ice cream and booze was only a request away, but it was eight-thirty a.m. and I just couldn't do it.

"No thanks."

Back in the safety of my room, I opened up a new, blank document and... stared. I don't know what I expected to happen, but the magic, cleansing power of ending things with Ward didn't somehow transform me into a fount of ideas. In fact, I didn't even have one idea. I didn't even have half of an idea.

After a few hours of starting and then deleting the same sentence over and over, I put the laptop down. It clearly wasn't happening. Feeling empty, I reread my favorite poem for inspiration, *An Arundel Tomb* by Philip Larkin. I'd always loved it, thinking that it was beautiful to imagine romantic love even when it was fleeting or false. Today, however, the final stanza—telling of two long-dead aristocrats who, perhaps, never loved each other—rang much too true:

> *Time has transfigured them into*
> *Untruth. The stone fidelity*
> *They hardly meant has come to be*
> *Their final blazon, and to prove*
> *Our almost-instinct almost true:*
> *What will survive of us is love.*

On my phone, I pulled out the photo that Ward had taken of us on our fishing trip a few weeks earlier. Right before we became lovers, back when we were just barely even friends. I'd started the day furious with him. It was a masochistic thing to do, but looking at the photo made me feel closer to Ward. I could imagine that in ten years I might be able to look at the photo without pain. Maybe one day I'd look at it and remember the good memories, the fun times. Perhaps what would survive of us—Ward and me—was love. Even if it was one-sided.

The rest of the day was spent rolling around restlessly in my bed, occasionally venturing out to forage for food before deciding it was too difficult, and then retreating back to my bed. Getting ready and dressed had been unnecessary because I never even left the apartment. I barely spent an hour outside of my bed. When Rae returned that evening, she came armed with the intention to cheer me up and what she termed 'special comfort pizza.' It was just regular cheese, but I was hungry enough to take the bait. It was even from the one place in town that met Rae's high New York standards.

She lured me out of my room with it and we sat on the couch, not talking. Rae hauled out her laptop and put Kate on a Skype call with us. Soon, all three of us were sitting there not talking. Kate's little face on the screen was solemn.

"Today, I went by Dr. Lieu's office," Rae said after a while.

Rae went to Dr. Lieu's office almost every day. She worked there. I made a noncommittal grunt. Not very lady-like but it was the best I could do at the moment. Rae kept talking like I hadn't just made an animal noise. She was clearly trying to make some type of point.

"Dr. Barnstead was just leaving," she continued. Her eyes felt like they were boring holes into my skull.

"Hmm?" It was better than the grunt, but not by much. I took another bite of pizza and stared at the ground.

"Leaving, and also *leaving*, as I found out," she said. I raised an eyebrow at her. That didn't make sense and it must have shown on my face. "He resigned," she clarified. "Dr. Lieu told me all about it. He was really quite cheesed off."

"Oh." Monosyllabic answers were apparently becoming my thing. In truth, I couldn't think of something else to say. Adam wasn't lying to me. He did come here for me. Either that or he was playing a different sort of academic game with Dr. Lieu. That could be possible as well. Maybe he'd taken the position at UT in order to negotiate a higher offer elsewhere. He was scheming enough to run two cons at once.

"Emma, what happened yesterday?" Kate's voice was soft and sympathetic over the tinny speakers of the laptop.

I took a deep breath to tell them but couldn't seem to speak. My whole plan had been to remove the unnecessary and fake to focus on the necessary and real. But now I couldn't even talk. Rae and Kate waited patiently until I found the words.

"Adam came by the bar. He told me that he loved me. I told him that I didn't love him back—not anymore. I think he understands now that I want nothing to do with him. But he told me something that I think is true, too. He said that I should focus on the things that are important to me and seek love and happiness. That's why I ended things with Ward. He doesn't love me. He doesn't want a girl-friend, just someone to sleep with. I can't do that."

When I fell silent, I felt like I'd just run a marathon. All my energy had been expended to tell that one, short story. I didn't even have the energy to continue eating my 'special comfort pizza.' I pushed my plate away from me on the little coffee table Rae and I were eating at.

Kate and Rae digested my words for a moment.

It was Rae who eventually breached the silence. "Emma, I'm proud of you."

I pushed back into the couch and then drew my knees up to my chest. "For breaking up with Ward?"

"For making a hard decision." Rae set her head on my shoulder in a little half-hug. "I'm not going to say that I'm glad that you and Ward are done, even though I am, because I can tell it's hurting you right now. But you did it for the right reasons. Unlike Adam and unlike Ward, you're a rational adult. You make the best choices you can with the information you have."

Kate nodded on the monitor, clearly agreeing. "Rae's right," she said eventually. "You made the choice you needed to make for yourself."

"Then why do I feel so shitty?" My head was buried in my knees, so my voice was somewhat muffled.

Now it was Kate's turn to answer. "Because you cared about my stupid brother. He's lovable in his way, even I know that. But you knew from the start that you didn't like casual relationships and you entered into one with Ward anyway. It wasn't a great decision, but I get it. But when it got to be too much for you, when you knew you were getting in too deep, you were smart enough to end it."

I swallowed hard, blinking away tears. Having my decision validated by my friends felt good, but it was cold comfort.

"I think I want to go lie down now," I whispered, unfolding myself and grabbing my plate to wash it off. Rae touched my wrist.

"Leave it," she said. "I'll clean up. Go do what you need to do. Take care of yourself. It's all going to be better soon. I promise."

I sunk back down to the couch and hugged her. Rae and Kate were good friends to me. "Thanks for taking care of me," I told Rae. Kate looked somewhat guilty, but Rae just smirked at me before answering.

"You've done the same for me more than once. What are friends for?"

I was lucky to have them. They were on my side and reminded me why I was right to end things with Ward. If it wasn't for Kate and Rae, I probably would have put on just a trench coat and gone down to the bar to seduce Ward back or something similarly ridiculous. As it was, I curled back up under my sheets and tried to believe their promise.

It's all going to be better soon.

38

WARD

KATE FOUND a new waitress the very next day. Her name was Cameron and she seemed pleasant, professional, and motivated. According to Kate, Cameron was going to be moving to Dallas in a few weeks and we needed to find a more permanent fix, but it hardly mattered. It could be Cameron or anyone else serving the tables in the main room. Emma was gone but business went on.

Cameron came by the bar to grab her latest batch of beers, and I had to pull them really quickly because I'd been zoned out and talking sports with a regular. She flashed me a friendly, disinterested smile as she scooped them up and headed back off. Kate had told me that Cameron was married to a woman. Apparently, my sister wasn't taking any chances from here on out.

"Where's Emma? Is she sick or something?" Lucas asked me a moment later. He'd come up to the bar to get orange slices because obviously Cameron didn't yet know his unique need for citrus in his beer. I had a bad feeling that what he ate in the bar was his only source of fresh fruit, so I humored him. I tossed him an entire orange, hoping it would shut him up and make him go away. Instead, he brightened and sat down on a barstool to peel it.

"She quit." I pretended to be intensely focused on wiping the condensation off the taps.

Lucas sat up straight. His voice was several decibels softer when he spoke. "Are you okay, man? Did you two break up or something?"

Lucas and I had been friends since college. Actually, he did most of my coursework for me when we lived together. I didn't even ask him to, he wanted to do it. He was one of those super-genius type guys that interpreted it as an opportunity to learn. The guy was a triple major, extra honors in everything, classic overachiever. Lucas would gather up the papers I brought back on the rare occasions I went to class, and just do all my homework. Which was, coincidentally, why I graduated with a decent GPA when most athletes make the obligatory minimum to graduate (professors are not allowed to fail us, but they won't give us A's, either).

Lucas had known me for a long time. Long enough to see through my bullshit. He could tell I was not okay.

I sighed. "We weren't dating. You know I don't date." That didn't answer his question though. "I don't think I'll see her again." Technically that didn't answer it either, but I couldn't do any better.

Although his face was calm, I could almost see the wheels turning in Lucas's gigantic fucking brain. Lucas was smart enough to develop an app that had set him up for a good five years and allowed him to focus all his energy on his next big project—one so big that he wouldn't even tell me about. He knew I wasn't huge on talking about feelings. Very few men, including him, are. But I knew he wanted to help. He was trying very hard to find the right thing to say that didn't violate the standards of manliness and distance we'd always maintained. It was a delicate conversation.

"That's too bad. I liked her." Lucas went back to casually peeling his orange. I felt like he was peeling me instead. I'd been feeling raw and exposed all day. It had made me distracted and overly sensitive.

In an ordinary hookup situation, I would offer to give him her number. I'd done as much before, and he'd done the same for me. But this wasn't that, and we both knew it. He'd opened a door and now I had to walk through it. We were going to talk feelings, at least as much as we could. Neither one of us was exactly expert in this.

"I liked her, too."

A few feet away, Willie was eavesdropping as always. He'd been observing me curiously all evening but had clearly decided not to intervene or ask. Now Lucas was doing the hard work for him.

"Why'd she split?" He pushed his glasses up the bridge of his nose. He didn't actually need them for orange peeling. They were strictly to reduce strain on his eyes from staring at a screen all day. But he liked them. He thought they made him look smart.

"I think she wanted something I couldn't give her."

"Ah. She moved on," Lucas said knowingly, although he looked like he didn't believe it.

"I don't think that's it. I think it's more that she wanted something else. Something not with me." She'd told me that she needed to focus on her writing. What sort of a jerk gets between a woman like Emma and the thing she's been working her whole life toward? Certainly not me.

"With her creepy old professor?" He looked grossed out. Lucas listened to the idle chatter at the bar more than I'd like. He had hearing like a goddamned bat.

"Nah. Not him. She got rid of him for good." If there was one good thing about Adam stopping by the bar last night, it was that. I'd never met Adam, and I never wanted to, but on some level, I could empathize with him. He and I wanted the same woman, although I hadn't done anything nearly as creepy to her. He still deserved to be fired, but something told me that failing to make Emma love him was punishment enough.

"Sounds like she got rid of you both for good." Lucas kept on peeling his orange. He was almost done. I knew he'd leave once he reached the end. This conversation was taking a lot out of the both of us.

"Yeah." She certainly did.

"Do you think she might have had feelings for you and left because of that?" Lucas asked, discarding the peels in the garbage. He raised an eyebrow at me. Behind his fake glasses, his hazel eyes were direct.

I blinked and felt my mouth working uselessly before I finally spoke. "I, um, I don't know."

"Hmm. Well, thanks for the orange." He wandered back to his laptop and his table like our conversation had been no big deal.

Possibly no conversation that I'd had with Lucas had been a bigger deal in the history of our friendship. My mind whirled around the question he left me with. Would it change things? Could she be in love with me? Lucas bringing it up had made it true for me. I hadn't been willing to go there. If Emma left because she cared about me, then what? Did I just let her go? What did I want?

Could I let Emma go if I knew there was a chance of more with her? I didn't know my own thoughts. I couldn't trust my own mind. It had led me wrong once before, and it had taken me a debt restructure and a lawsuit in small claims court to be free of Jessie.

I needed to talk to Kate. If anyone knew what I was feeling, it was her. I only prayed that I was strong enough to hear it.

39

WARD

I WAS EXTREMELY surprised to find Rae and Kate sitting together on the patio late in the evening. Rae got up and walked away before she saw me coming, but the look on her face was unhappy. I watched her shake her head in apparent frustration as she walked off into the night, and then moved to take her recently vacated chair in front of my sister.

"I didn't know that you and Rae were friends," I told Kate, suddenly irritated. My voice was sharp.

"We go to spin class together," she replied, surprised. "How did you think Emma heard about this job? How did you think we got that private party? Through Rae."

That actually... made sense. I still didn't like it. "I didn't know." If I sounded a bit sullen, it was because I was.

"There are lots of things you don't know." Kate smiled

at me like I was an idiot. At the moment, I was ready to admit it. Especially if there was some way Kate could fix me.

"Enlighten me, then. What do I do now?" I cracked open a bottle of water, and she leaned forward to steal it from me. She took a long sip before answering me.

"You're seriously asking me?"

"I'm seriously asking you, yeah." It sounded ridiculous to me, too.

She savored the moment. "Okay. Here's what you should do. Go back into the main room and continue to tend bar until we close. Then you and me are gonna' go to Kerby Lane, get some pancakes and talk this through. Neither of us has time to do this right now."

Frustratingly, she was probably right. It was only eleven forty-five. "Fine."

Willie shot me a 'where the hell have you been?' look when I returned. We'd suddenly gotten slammed with a big group of thirsty college kids. Cameron was running around like a chicken with her head cut off. Her first night was trial by fire. The remaining few hours of the night had never felt longer. However, I think my glaring at the customers helped them clear out a bit faster. We managed to lock the doors a full thirty minutes early.

"Pancakes?" I asked Kate again as we walked to the cars. "Are you sure you want that at this hour?"

"I've never been surer of anything in my life. Pancakes are the proper food for your relationship troubles."

I was about to tell Kate that I didn't have relationships and, therefore, couldn't have relationship troubles, but at this point I didn't think it was true. I sighed instead. "Fine. Let's get pancakes."

The pancakes at the Kerby Lane Café—one of the few twenty-four-hour restaurants in town that didn't suck—were legendary. I got the apple spice. Kate got the banana nut. Both were delivered with more butter than could ever be healthy, powdered sugar, and maple syrup. I shoveled the tender, fluffy carbs into my mouth, willing to admit that Kate was correct about them being perfect for the way I was feeling.

"Okay, let's discuss," Kate said, staring across the top of her coffee cup at me. "We can start with the conversation I had tonight with Rae if you want."

"Okay... what did she say?" The fact that Emma's scary roommate and my sister were connected still gave me the creeps. Why didn't either one of them ever say anything? I felt like the world was conspiring against me.

Kate was frowning. She looked just like our mom when she did, even though both of us mostly looked like our absent, asshole father. "She was telling me about Emma. Apparently, she's really down in the dumps."

"Emma's upset?"

"Ward, she's heartbroken." My sister continued to look

at me like I was truly a moron.

"Oh." I hated the idea of Emma being sad. When she'd run away last night, her face had been teary, but I chalked it up to hating the awkwardness of the situation. Now, however, after I'd spoken to Lucas and given it additional thought... "She has feelings for me."

Kate nodded. "Yes. She does."

"And she left *because* she has feelings for me."

"Yes." Kate's face indicated that she was impressed that I'd gotten this far on my own. I decided not to tell her that it was actually Lucas who had led me to this realization. She didn't need that information. "She doesn't want to feel like she's disposable."

I frowned. "Disposable?" Trash was disposable. Had I treated Emma badly? I never meant to do that. "We were happy, and then she left. *I didn't do anything!*"

"Exactly. *You didn't do anything to keep her.* She's got feelings for you. She wants more than you've said you're willing to give her. Don't you get that?" Kate's face was frustrated. "Why is that always so hard for men to understand?"

"Which part?"

"Any of it." Kate pushed her pancake bite around in the syrup on her plate. "I've been in Emma's shoes before. Trust me, it doesn't feel great to know that a guy just saw you as a good time."

"But—"

"I know! I know you thought that was the deal. You're

honest at least, I'll give you that. The women you usually hook up with, they're cool with it, too. But Emma's different and deals change."

That seemed very unfair. When I didn't have anything else to add to the conversation, Kate ate more pancakes and watched me. I felt like I needed to be the one answering questions, not asking them, but she clearly wasn't going to make it easy.

"What if I go talk to her and she asks me how I feel about her? What do I do?" I finally asked Kate. She frowned.

"Then you just tell her." My sister looked unimpressed that this wouldn't come naturally to me. But I'd been burned before, and besides...

"I don't know what I feel."

She made a dismissive noise before saying, "That's bull-shit, and you know it, Ward."

"What? Why do you think I'm here?"

"You want me to tell you what to do. You want me to tell you what you feel."

"Exactly!" Thank God, she'd finally figured it out.

"But I'm not going to do that. It's enabling behavior. You know exactly what you need to do. *You know how you feel.* You just want me to spell it out, because if it comes from me, you'll try to talk yourself out of it."

"You really won't tell me what to do? You usually love to do that." In fact, I believed that ordering me around was one of my sister's greatest joys in life. She gave me more advice and instruction on a daily basis than I knew what to do with. But now, when I needed it, she was withholding her advice? It made no sense to me. Apparently, I was just a way to get free pancakes.

"I love you, Ward. You're my brother. But sometimes I don't like you. You act like you're clueless when you aren't." Kate shook her head at me again. "Do you have feelings for Emma beyond the usual temporary lust kind?"

I swallowed. "I might." Even admitting the *possibility* seemed like it was opening me up for pain.

"Do you think she has feelings for you?"

"I already told you... yes, probably." I still wasn't one hundred percent sure, but there was definitely a chance.

"Do you think there's a chance that if you went and told her how you felt, she'd take you back? And do you want that?"

"I don't know. Maybe. I think that I'm miserable right now, and there's only one way to fix it: get Emma back. I don't know what that will take, or if it will end up hurting me more in the end, but I don't know what else to do."

"Well then shit, you've just solved your own problem. You're freakin' welcome." She reached across the table to snag one of *my pancakes* onto her plate. I let her do it. Or rather, I was too stunned to stop her.

My lips had parted as I stared at her. She was right. It was simple.

40

EMMA

THE WORLD DIDN'T END because I was a sad, weepy mess. It felt like it should, but it didn't. The world still turned, the sun came up, and the next day dawned just like it always did. The apocalypse was only in my mind.

Day two post-Ward required me to do more than sulk, and I reluctantly dragged myself up to the library to return a few books. Technically, I could have gone online and extended my check-out period, but the tiny rational part of my brain that still functioned knew that the longer I stayed locked in the apartment, the harder it would be to leave. I still had a life to live, even if it was a lonely, troubled one.

Many of the best writers had been troubled, I told myself as I walked across campus. Very few artists managed to have functional relationships with anything, actually. If they weren't in toxic love affairs with other people (Arthur

Miller, Tennessee Williams, Leo Tolstoy, T.S. Eliot), they had toxic relationships with substances (William Faulkner, Truman Capote, Edgar Allen Poe) or, worse, their own minds (Emily Dickinson, Sylvia Plath, poor Zelda Fitzgerald). Some, like Hemingway, had toxic relationships with all three. A perverse little piece of my heart thought perhaps being broken would fuel my writing if it didn't consume me whole.

My introspection was interrupted by an unwelcome, semi-familiar voice calling my name. I spun and found myself face to face with Simon. I hadn't seen him since the gallery opening a month ago. At least Ivy and Jannie weren't with him this time. He really wasn't a bad guy, he just hung around with questionable friends.

"Hey, I'm really glad I ran into you," he said, pushing his asymmetrical, dyed-black hair back off his face. The man seemed to live in black. He was also sporting a new lip piercing today, and it looked painful. "I heard from Jannie that Ivy went into full-bitch mode at that gallery show. I just wanted you to know that I'm sorry that happened."

The gallery show felt like forever ago to me. Any irritation or hurt was nothing compared to what I was feeling now. It was water under the bridge at this point. "Don't worry about it. You don't need to apologize for Ivy." Karma would find her eventually. Or not. I really didn't care.

He shook his head at me, and his expression was amused. "Emma, you're too nice. She didn't have any right to talk to you like that. If someone had said that shit to me, I'd have slapped them into next week."

I shrugged. "I'm not much of a slapper. I've never slapped anyone in my life."

"I can teach you if you want." He grinned. "I'm something of an expert."

I believed it. Somehow, I managed to smile. The one good thing about waitressing was that it had taught me how to wear a smile at all times. "I appreciate the offer, but it's just not really my style. I prefer my violence to be emotional."

He giggled. "I suppose I can respect that. Hey, do you want to grab some lunch? I was just on my way to meet Jannie."

I paused. If it was just Simon, I probably could have managed. But Jannie could be a bit...

"Don't worry," Simon said, anticipating my refusal. "Jannie is a lot nicer when she doesn't have Ivy egging her on. We've both realized we don't need that drama anymore. She's an energy vampire. I know Jannie wants to see you, too. I feel like none of us have seen you in months."

He wasn't wrong. I'd seriously withdrawn from the department's grad student community this semester. Since Ward. I found myself nodding.

"Okay. Let me go drop off these books and I'll meet you."

Simon grinned. "Cool. We'll be in the union, facing Guadalupe Street."

When I met up with the two of them fifteen minutes later with my lunch in hand, I was glad I'd agreed. They were both funny and smart people when they weren't under Ivy's control. Catching up on the department gossip felt pretty good.

"So, are you still seeing that guy you were with the last time we saw you?" Jannie asked me eventually.

Oh no, she wants to talk about Ward.

I shook my head. "I haven't seen him lately."

"He was super hot. I'm not even into dudes and I thought he was super hot." Jannie's wife, Cameron, had just finished up her nursing degree. The two of them were due to move in a few months when Jannie graduated with her master's.

I wasn't sure how long I could talk about Ward without getting emotional. I shrugged casually. "He is, but we weren't really seeing each other."

"You know that's why Ivy was such a capital letter B, right?" Jannie asked. "She had a huge lady boner for your man. It was all she talked about for like the next three weeks."

"He isn't my man." Not now, not then, not ever.

"I'm just saying." Jannie shrugged. "She was jealous is all."

I shook my head. "She's welcome to give him a call. It's not like I own him."

"Yeah, don't tell her that unless you want to share STD's with her."

"We don't exactly talk on the phone every night." My voice was tart. "You seem to have really changed your mind about Ivy."

Jannie and Simon exchanged a glance before she answered. "I just got tired of feeling like I'd been in a fist-fight every time we hung out," Jannie sighed. "I feel like she just kept me around so she'd have an accomplice. I'm nobody's pet, and honestly, I don't enjoy tearing other people down all the time. It's fucked up."

I nodded. "I had a friend like that in middle school." *Fuck you, Becky.*

"Right?! But we're old now. We need to get past that petty shit." Jannie looked embarrassed. I decided I liked her. She reminded me a bit of Kate, only short and butch. "Anyway, I thought you should know about Ivy's thing for your guy. I'm working on being honest as part of my post-Ivy life plan."

Our conversation moved on after that, but the idea of someone else being with Ward stuck with me for the rest of the day. Like some sort of awful wound, the idea festered and grew. It turned gangrenous in my mind, rotting away at any competing thoughts. Soon it was all I could think of. Was he with someone right now? Who? What did she look like? Was she prettier than me? Smarter? It just wouldn't go away.

No matter what I seemed to do for the rest of the afternoon, jealously of Ward's next girl seemed to be the only feeling I was capable of. I had told myself that I was protecting myself by breaking things off with Ward, but now that I'd removed myself from the picture, he was free. He'd been free before, technically, but he was spending so much time with me that I knew there was no one else. But now... he could be on top of someone at that very moment. Touching her. Fucking her. Making her say his name while he pounded into her until she couldn't even speak. And it could have been me, instead. It would have been me, if I'd just kept my stupid mouth shut.

Rae was over at Ivan's for the night, so I was alone in the apartment. Being alone wasn't a good thing. I paced back and forth like a caged animal, imagining Ward with this fictional other woman. Hating her. In my fantasies, the woman looked an awful lot like Jessie, his former fiancée.

I'd found her Instagram after a little digging. She was *gorgeous,* even more beautiful than I'd imagined. She had tan skin, legs for miles, inky black eyes, long eyelashes, and the full, puffy lips of a Kardashian. She dressed like money was no object and seemed to subsist entirely on a diet of beautiful, expensive food served in exotic, luxurious locations. In comparison I felt like a tiny little freak living a tiny little life. Ward had said I reminded him of Tinkerbell when we first met. I was really more of a Keebler elf.

Self-loathing, regret, and jealousy were swimming around my gut like sharks circling. They were going to eat my heart. The realization that I was in love with Ward had prompted me to end things, but the thought that he could be with someone else made me wonder if I'd been wrong to do so. Maybe I should have just prolonged things as long as possible and pushed back the inevitable, even though it would hurt me more when he got sick of me. I flopped down heavily on the couch, exhausted from pacing, only to jump in surprise when someone knocked on the door. I had to look through the peephole three times before I believed my eyes.

Ward was at my front door.

41

WARD

I came over with a really great plan, but when Emma opened the door, I forgot what it was. She looked at me like she was expecting bad news. Her shining eyes were huge in her face and she had her arms wrapped around herself protectively. She was wearing a pale blue set of pajamas and it made her look even sweeter and more innocent than usual, although I knew the body under the fabric was perfectly designed for sin. Desire and fear fought inside me without a clear winner. I was either making a huge mistake or the most brilliant decision of my entire life. I guessed it was time to find out.

"Hi," I managed to stutter out. She blinked up at me and her soft, pink lips parted in surprise.

"Ward?" Her voice was soft, but I got the feeling that what she wanted to say was 'Ward, what are you doing here?' I took a deep breath to steady myself. There was a reason I'd come here. It had taken me hours and hours plus two shots of espresso to work up the courage to drive over. Then I'd sat outside for a good twenty minutes like the coward I was. Now that I was finally here, finally in front of Emma, I wasn't going to chicken out.

"Can I come in for a minute?" My voice came out steady, but my heart was pounding.

She deliberated for a second before opening the door and retreating into the space to let me in.

Translation: Please make it quick.

Her apartment looked the same as it always had, but it felt foreign to me now. My brain noted all the little changes, a few bed pillows on the ground, glasses and plates piled next to the sink, a full trashcan, a backpack on the counter, and books strewn across the coffee table. It wasn't nearly as neat as usual. Seeing the clutter made me feel slightly better. My apartment was a disaster zone at the moment. I also hadn't shaved lately or combed my hair, and I could only assume I looked homeless. I also hadn't slept properly in two days and was essentially running on caffeine and desperation. So, I probably looked homeless and crazy.

"I'm sorry about the mess," Emma said. "I haven't had a chance to clean up lately." Her voice was empty. Almost monotone.

Translation: I didn't expect you here.

I shrugged. "I didn't tell you I was coming over. Plus, you never need to clean for me."

Emma nodded, sitting down on one of the tall kitchen stools. "What's up, Ward?"

Translation: Get to the point, Ward.

"I brought over the stuff that was at my apartment." The paper bag was in my hand, and I placed it next to Emma on the counter before retreating three feet in the opposite direction.

Emma raised a manicured, golden eyebrow.

Translation: That's it?

"Thanks." She didn't sound that excited about it. I could hardly blame her. It would have been easier for me to simply leave it for her when she wasn't home.

"I also wanted to talk to you," I said. I shook my head in frustration. I had no idea what I was doing. I guess I just had to wing it. "Emma, are you in love with me?"

That got her attention in a hurry. Her eyes widened until there was no way they could possibly get any bigger. There was white showing all the way around her pupils. She looked like one of those Japanese cartoons where the women have the eyes that take up half their faces. Since she didn't look capable of replying yet, I kept talking.

"I need to know, Emma. Please." I'd never needed anything as much as I needed Emma to tell me if I was out of my mind coming here to confess my love to her. I wasn't sure that I was capable of doing it without knowing what she felt.

"Ward, why would you come here and ask me that?" She looked frightened or angry. Or maybe it was both. I wasn't sure. Her voice was small and unsure. Perhaps she thought I was playing games with her or just trying to get her back into bed. Her little hands had balled up into little fists.

"Can you answer the question first?" I seemed suddenly incapable of simply getting to the point. I wanted to tell her what I'd come here to say, but something was keeping me from just doing it.

Emma shook her head, realized that her hair was sticking out at weird angles and then tried to aggressively pat it down. "No. Because it doesn't matter." She paused and then repeated her question in a stronger voice. "Why are you here?" She was getting irritated with me, and that was making her more confident. I needed to get to the point before she threw me out.

"I know you said that you wanted to focus on the things that were important to you, the things you loved, and you thought that I wasn't serious about you. I mean, I know that I said that I wasn't. Serious, that is. We both did. Except I am...once you left, I realized..."

Christ, I was just rambling like a crazy person.

This was so not what I'd planned. I really was smooth most of the time, except when I needed it most, apparently.

Maybe if I could touch her, I'd work up the courage to tell her the truth. I stepped closer to her, and when she didn't flinch or run, closer again. I placed my hand over hers on the dated, mustard linoleum countertop of her kitchen. Her little hand felt warm beneath mine, but only for a moment, because she pulled her hand out from beneath mine and hid it in her lap. She didn't want to touch me.

"What did you realize, Ward?" Her voice was steady now. She looked at me like she was on the verge of figuring something out.

"I made a mistake." I swallowed hard. "I let you leave. I didn't tell you the truth about what I wanted from you."

She looked down at her hands. "What do you want from me?"

I wanted to admit it, but I couldn't quite spit it out. I wanted to, but my throat wouldn't let me. I shifted uncomfortably in my shoes. "Can I show you something really quick?"

She frowned, making a little line appear between her eyes. "Sure. I guess so." She was obviously confused by the sudden change of subject.

I pulled the literary magazine out of my back pocket and laid it on the counter in front of her. The one I'd *annotated*. Yeah, I'd looked up the definition of annotated. I wasn't ashamed to say the entire exercise had taken me hours.

Emma looked at it, then up at me. She pulled it closer

to her and read through it, silently. While she did, I watched on anxiously, feeling the seconds tick by like they were hours. When she finally looked up, she was smiling a confused little smile.

"Did you like it?" she asked me. Her head was cocked to the side like she was trying to decode me.

I nodded. "Yes. Not the annotation part so much. But I tried, and I liked reading your work. It was like I was talking to you, even though you weren't there. It made me feel closer to you."

She smiled at that, too. The quick slip of white teeth gave me hope.

"Why did you bring this over to show me?" Her voice was still guarded.

"I wanted you to know that I care about you." I frowned. "When you left, you said that you needed to focus on the things that were real and important to you. I got the feeling that you thought I didn't think you were important to me. I just wanted you to know that you are important to me. Very important."

She smiled again, but close-lipped. Her smile was smaller this time and didn't reach her eyes. That wasn't enough of an answer. Why couldn't I just spit it out? I was trying, but my self-preservation seemed to have kicked in and pressed the mute button. Once again, the situation was spinning out of control.

"That was very sweet, Ward. It means a lot to me.

Thank you for bringing this over. And the things I forgot."
She sounded tired now. She pushed her hair back from her
forehead and glanced at the clock on the kitchen wall.

Translation: Okay, you can go now. We're done.

"I'm not doing a good job with this conversation," I
confessed. "I had this whole thing planned out that I was
going to say to you." I shook my head in frustration. This
was all going completely, ridiculously wrong.

She shrugged. "Don't worry. You did just fine. It was
bound to be a bit weird after the last time we saw each
other. I'm glad you came by."

Translation: I forgive you. Time to leave.

"I'm saying everything all wrong. I should have led with
this: I love you." It all came out in one continuous word-
stream, leaving me feeling cold and frightened.

Finally. Thank you, Jesus. But I hope it's not too late.

Emma's eyes, which I thought were at their max size,
somehow got even wider. They were two sea-green pools in
the suddenly very pale backdrop of her face. She took a
deep, unsteady breath.

"What?" Her voice was a tiny whisper. I reclaimed her
hand from her lap, holding it tightly in both of mine.

"Emma, I'm in love with you."

What I was not expecting, and had not even imagined
as a possibility, was that Emma would start crying when I
told her that I loved her.

42

EMMA

HE LOVED ME? The tears were running down my face within one breath, and I was pouncing on him a bare second later. He made a little 'oomph' of surprise, stumbling backwards two steps before laughing in obvious confusion and holding me to him. I wrapped my arms tightly around his neck, holding him as close to me as I could, and wishing I could keep this moment forever.

"You love me?" I repeated, staring up into his eyes when I broke away enough to see him. I was still crying, but it was a pure catharsis. I felt like I was finally releasing the tension of the past few days. Every tear felt like it was healing the void that had been growing inside me like a cancer.

He nodded, but his expression was anxious. Those

stunning sapphire eyes that I adored looked pained—afraid I would reject him. "Are you going to say it back?"

"That I love you? Of course, I love you!" Like he didn't already know. What a stubborn man. He really was ridiculous sometimes. Lucky for both of us, he was also ridiculously sexy. And ridiculously kind. And ridiculously good. And now... ridiculously mine.

I held onto him for dear life, and he stroked my back while I sobbed like a baby. When my tears gave no sign of stopping, he stooped down to put an arm under my knees and scooped me up. He sat us both down on the couch and cradled me against his chest. I burrowed into his neck and soaked in his smell, his warmth, and his comfort. He felt like home.

"Emma, why are you crying?" he finally asked me. His beautiful eyes were so confused, and although I'd told Simon earlier in the day that I was not the slapping type, he could honestly use a good slapping at the moment.

"I'm happy!" I told him petulantly.

"This is you being happy?" His voice was skeptical.

I nodded. He still looked confused, but less than he had before. "Okay."

"Ward, why didn't you just tell me you wanted me from the start of this conversation?" I finally whispered against his ear. "Why did you let me go in the first place?"

He shook his head. The hands that were holding me

close shook slightly. "I don't know. I'm an idiot. I was afraid to admit what I wanted."

I sighed. He really did seem to be convinced that he wasn't very smart. At the moment, I was inclined to agree. But the way he was stroking the exposed slice of skin between the waistband of my pants and where my shirt had been hitched up was so... distracting. I wriggled in closer to him, enjoying the feeling of his body next to mine again. At the moment, I didn't want to talk. I just wanted to feel.

He seemed to be on the same wavelength. The hand that had been holding my upper back fisted my hair at the nape of my neck and pulled my head back. He kissed me. His mouth sought mine like he was trying to tell me that he owned me.

Our tongues fought for dominance, and it lit a fire inside me that I knew only he could quench. I shifted atop him, moving to straddle him, and was rewarded with a smile against my lips. He lifted his T-shirt over his head and went right to work on the buttons of my top, peeling it off my shoulders and looking at my bared chest like he'd been years without seeing a woman.

"I missed you," he said, and I got the feeling he was just talking to my boobs.

"My eyes are up here," I grumped. He squeezed my ass in response, hard enough that I squealed, and then gave me a swat for good measure. "Hey!"

"Do you have any idea what you did to me when you left?" He told me, grabbing my right hand and guiding it down to the bulge in his jeans. I stroked him happily over the thick fabric, rubbing him in time with the thrusts of my hips.

"Made you recruit another waitress on short notice?"

He swatted my behind again. "Technically yes, but that's not what I meant." Another swat.

"It can't have been worse than what I did to me," I answered. "I missed you too."

Ward shook his head at me and kissed me senseless. He seemed determined to tease me, although really he was the one that deserved teasing. He should have just told me the truth.

But thoughts were getting difficult to form, especially as he twisted me around again to pull off my pajama bottoms. Before I realized what was going on, I was sitting on his lap facing the opposite direction, now naked. *Huh?*

"Bend down and put your hands on the ground," he told me. His voice was a low, sexy rumble against my ears. I didn't know where this was going, but he seemed like he did. I was happy to comply. Once I was down there, it made more sense. From this angle, my ass and pussy were on full display to him. It was a sort of leaning forward reverse-cowgirl position. I could do this.

He scooted far forward, and I heard the familiar sound of his zipper. I was hypersensitive since I couldn't see much

TAYLOR HOLLOWAY

besides his feet this way unless I craned my neck. A moment later, he rubbed the thick, hot head of his cock over my wet entrance. I was so ready I could hardly stand any more teasing. I pushed backwards as much as I could, but I didn't have to wait for long. Ward joined our bodies with one quick thrust, filling me completely and sending my upper body toward the ground. With my head angled toward the ground at forty-five degrees, I was at Ward's mercy as he pulled my hips back down onto him over and over.

My body reacted to his urgency, becoming totally pliant. It felt so good like this, totally spread open and yielding to him. He was so much more possessive now that all the cards were on the table, and I adored it. His hands were everywhere on me as we moved together, and my climax took me by surprise, leaving me loose-limbed and still pushing senselessly down on his cock. He didn't slow for my orgasm, either. He kept pounding into me heavily from behind, making my pussy start to ache again immediately for a second round of pleasure.

He pushed me forward even farther, until I was fully on my hands and knees, off the edge of the couch with him kneeling behind me. I had more leverage this way and ground back into him with an increased eagerness. His hand slipped around my thigh to pet me, and I could hear his breathing coming faster. I rubbed my ass hips back up against him as hard as I could while he worked my excitement right back up to the edge. When I glanced back at him, his gaze was glassy and vacant; he needed this as much as I did.

I came again, staring into his eyes at an awkward angle, moaning his name and collapsing down onto my forearms while he continued his thrusts into me from behind. When he came a few slick, hot strokes later, it was with a low, satisfied moan of my name. We curled up together, sweaty and happy. Although relieved and deeply satisfied, I was mentally and physically exhausted, too. We lay there on the floor, naked and panting, for a long time.

"I feel better," I managed to say eventually. Ward, who had wrapped himself around me from behind, chuckled. It came through more as a feeling than a noise against my back.

"Me too. Does this mean you'll take me back?" Ward's voice was tired but happy-sounding.

"I don't think I ever really gave you up. At least in my heart." Admitting it seemed only fair.

"Good, because you're mine." His voice was surprisingly possessive.

I smiled. This morning I would never have imagined we'd end up like this on the living room floor. But I was as happy as I'd ever been. "You're mine right back."

"That's the idea."

"I'm not coming back to the bar, though," I told him, stretching and turning to look at him. "I really don't think we should work together, plus I'd just have to quit in another month and a half anyway."

He shrugged. "You were a great waitress, but I'd rather have you as my girlfriend than my employee any day." Then he looked sheepish. "Also, and don't get mad, but Kate already replaced you."

EPILOGUE

EMMA

"A little bit farther, keep your eyes closed," Ward coaxed, urging me forward through the condo. I fumbled along towards the sound of his voice, carefully shuffling my feet forward and wondering why we were heading toward the guest room. When I came home to Ward when he was this excited, we usually ended up in our *bedroom*.

"This had better not be another small kitchen appliance," I joked. Ward's last surprise, a crockpot, was perfectly welcome but not particularly romantic. He'd gotten into cooking lately, and while I very much appreciated being fed tasty food, the reveal of the actual crockpot had been a bit underwhelming.

Ward laughed. "Just keep your eyes closed for one more

second," he said. "And I promise, *this toaster is going to absolutely blow your mind.*" His voice was sarcastic enough that I knew he was joking. Which was good. We didn't need another freaking toaster. There was already one on our wedding registry. He turned me by the shoulders and then made a pleased noise. "Okay, yes. Perfect. You can look now."

I opened my eyes. The guest room was no longer a guest room. The guest room was... an office right out of my dreams?

"Is this for me?" I asked, turning around to look at Ward. He looked surprisingly anxious.

"Do you like it?"

He must have been reading my mind. The room was no longer military green and had been painted a tasteful light mocha brown. Crown moldings and a chair rail had been installed and painted ivory. Plush, heavy cream and pale pink velvet drapes had replaced the dated vertical blinds. In front of me, a huge, long wooden desk in a simple style already had my computer set up on it, along with a framed copy of our engagement photo. A plush, blush pink velvet swivel chair sat in front of it. In the corner, another cushy tufted ivory armchair sat beneath a cozy reading lamp. My books had been carefully arranged on the bookcase nearby, and there was a brass vase containing pink and ivory roses sitting next to the chair on a little table. 'A Room of One's Own' by Virginia Woolf sat prominently displayed next to the roses. It was almost too perfect.

"*I love it.*" My voice was properly astounded. "Did you decorate this?" I tried to picture Ward carefully choosing the lacy pillows, and just... couldn't. He was fundamentally not a decorative pillow kind of guy. Picking out our wedding registry had been the longest afternoon of either of our lives. The poor people of Crate and Barrel probably despised us both.

Ward shook his head and chuckled. "God no. I can't really take credit for anything here but the idea. Kate and Rae did pretty much all the design. And something called Pinterest?"

Oh, that explained it. Rae and Kate had access to my Pinterest pages for the wedding planning. They must have taken a look at the one called 'dream office.'

"Ward... It's so perfect!" I blinked a few times, just trying to make sure I was really seeing *my office.* I touched the little throw blanket that sat draped over the back of the reading chair. It was super-soft plush ivory fake fur. "Everything here is so... me."

He grinned. "Thank God. I was afraid it was too over-the-top girly," he admitted. "Rae and Kate promised it was right, but when they brought in the chandelier..." he trailed off and then added, "but as long as you like it, I'm happy." He grinned, obviously genuinely pleased.

Chandelier? I looked up. A little gold and crystal chandelier had taken the place of the horrifically ugly green ceiling fan that had been there before. Ward's condo—our condo—had once been owned by a small family that apparently housed their young son in this room. He'd been into green. I was into, well, girly stuff. And now everything was exactly like I wanted.

"You didn't have to do this, Ward." I honestly still couldn't believe he had. "You didn't have to give up the guest room." We technically had another room that could be used as a guest room, but it was where Ward's trophies lived.

"We can just shove a futon in the trophy room." He shrugged. "You needed a proper office... *Professor Williams.*"

"That's Dr. Williams to you," I said, wrapping my arms around him in a hug. He kissed the top of my head. I was still technically Professor Greene until I graduated with my PhD in a few years. Many name changes were coming. I'd already taken a job teaching part-time at a community college in town, and I was looking forward to teaching far more than I ever thought I would. And now, I'd have the perfect place to write when I got home.

Ward grinned broadly. "Dr. Williams," he shook his head. "That's going to take some serious getting used to."

"Well, if it makes you feel better, I'll technically be Professor Williams for several years first."

He made a comically annoyed face. "That makes it

more complicated, not less. Why does this have to be so tricky? Can't you just stay Emma?"

"Well, back in the day when a woman married, she stopped being under the authority and protection of her father and started being the property of her husband. It was a legal term called coverture. The term 'Mrs' actually used to be the possessive 'Mr's'."

Ward gave me a funny look. "That's fascinating. I wasn't actually asking that question literally, *professor dear*."

I stuck my tongue out at him. "Well, look on the sunny side, you get to stay Ward Williams."

"Thank God for that. It took me long enough to learn how to spell my name the first time around. Just ask Kate."

Ward was still convinced that he wasn't particularly bright. I rolled my eyes at him.

"Kate was a toddler when you were in kindergarten."

"Yeah, but I didn't learn to spell until high school."

I patted him on the arm. Kate had *actually* told me Ward was an honor roll student until he started playing football and was too busy to keep his grades up. Ward's self-deprecating tendency was just part of his personality.

"Speaking of illitcracy, is Cole going to make our party tonight?" I asked.

Ward winced. "Hey now. That's not nice, Honey," he chided. "Cole isn't that dumb. Definitely not any dumber than me."

I giggled at him. "*That's not what I meant.* I was talking about your financial literacy thing."

"Oh!" Ward looked vaguely chagrined that he assumed I'd just been casually insulting his friend. "Yeah. He came in this afternoon."

Ward and Cole were teaming up to talk to other young players in the NFL and excelling at college football about making smart investments and protecting themselves. It was just an informal drink here and there right now, but it helped Ward feel like he was doing his part. Cole had the idea to incorporate the conversation into a larger discussion about head injuries. The fact that more players were retiring earlier meant it was even more important to be careful with finances during the years when the players were high earners. Although it was a world I had no place in—and helping millionaires stay millionaires wasn't exactly rescuing war orphans—I knew that it meant a lot to Ward.

"Do we have time to take a shower before the party?" I asked Ward. As much as I wanted to spend some time in *my new office,* I wanted some sudsy time with Ward more.

"We've got two hours," he said, glancing at a little brass clock I hadn't noticed yet on the desk.

"It'll be a bit tight, but I think we can make it work."

Ward winked. "That's what she said."

· · ·

THE PARTY WAS at the bar, of course. I wouldn't have it any other way. Ward wasn't bartending though, and neither were Willie or Kate. We'd hired a catering company to do the hard work tonight.

"Emma! You already look like a bride," Kate cried. I was wearing an off-white bodysuit and a tea length off-white and blue ombre tulle skirt. My heels were silver to match my jewelry. The whole look did look vaguely bridal-ballerina. Of course, that was the idea. Her idea. My future sister-in-law had a serious knack for design. I did a little twirl at her instruction and she squealed in delight when the skirt flew out in a satisfying poof.

"Ward showed me the office," I told her. "I can't believe you and Rae kept that from me!"

Rae and Ivan had moved to New York a while back. It was hard to lose her, and I was worried that their relationship was not as happy as it used to be. They'd been fighting a lot more than they used to. We'd exchanged promises to visit and Skype date regularly, but I knew that Rae's future was in big business and she needed to spread her wings.

"You could have gone in there at literally any second," Kate said, laughing. "I was so scared you'd go and ruin the surprise, but if we told you not to go in there, it only would have tipped you off. It was all very nerve-wracking."

I shook my head at her. "You poor thing."

"So, do you love it?"

"Oh my God, yes!"

We both made the high-pitched noise that I thought only cheerleaders and teenagers made. It turns out a really, really beautiful office can bring out the cheerleader in me. Ward, who was standing a short distance away, looked over in horror.

"What's going on over there?" he said, coming to sweep me away from his sister. "That noise was straight out of my nightmares."

"Oh, it's because Emma's pregnant," Kate said matter-of-factly, and then laughed when Ward turned a color that could not have been healthy. His eyes went the size of saucers and I feared that he might faint. "Congratulations!"

"Stop that! Stop that! You'll give him a heart attack!" I scolded, hugging my future husband protectively and covering his ears. "Don't worry, baby, that's why we use protection," I whispered when I pulled back. He hugged me to him again and glared daggers at his sister.

"You're evil, you know that?" he scolded.

She shrugged. "It runs in the family."

"Kate," I said, touching her arm to reclaim her attention, "I have something really important to ask you."

She looked suddenly nervous. "Oh no, what did I do?"

Ward grinned, and I elbowed him. This was a solemn moment.

"Will you be my maid of honor?" I asked, watching eagerly as her nervousness melted into joy.

She made the noise again that Ward had cringed at and

threw her arms around my neck in answer. Her towering height forced me to stagger back a few steps, laughing.

"Is that a yes?" I asked to confirm.

"Of course, it's a yes!" she replied, and then added, "Oh my God, does that mean I get to go dress shopping with you?"

I nodded, and she gasped and giggled with such glee that I actually became a bit nervous. Shopping with Kate usually meant that I got turned into a living fashion doll. According to her, all clothes were made for tiny people like me. If I had legs for days like her, however, I would not be complaining about having to hunt for pants.

I could already see the dress-hunting wheels turning behind her eyes, but her smug smile slid off her face, and she turned the same purple-puce combination that Ward had been wearing a moment before.

"Kate?" I asked, following her gaze. Cole had just arrived at the party and was standing in the doorway looking over at us, or more specifically, looking at Kate. "Are you okay?"

Ward and I stared between Kate and Cole in confusion.

"Yeah, fine," Kate said distractedly. "I'm going to go powder my nose. Be right back." She took off toward the ladies' room. Cole watched her go, frowning.

"Am I missing something?" I asked Ward. He looked just as confused as me.

"I think I need to go have a chat with Cole, I mean,

other than the whole best man thing," he said. His confusion had hardened into something conflicted but overall less pleasant. Ward was nothing if not protective of Kate, but he was close with only two of his friends: Lucas and Cole. The idea that either relationship might be at risk worried me.

"Be nice," I told him. "Don't assume anything." If there was something between those two, our meddling probably wouldn't help matters.

Ward frowned. "I'll try to keep an open mind, but he better not have ever hurt Kate."

I rolled my eyes at that. "Keep in mind the fact that Kate would have simply murdered him if he had. She's already proved that she's perfectly capable of *dousing the guy in freezing deer urine.* Maybe she went to go buy some just now." I truly believed that Kate could fight her own battles. If Cole had done something to deserve Kate's wrath, well then it was his funeral. Ward might be big enough to take him on in a fair fight, but Kate was the one that would ambush him in a dark alley, stage a mugging, and then fake an airtight alibi. Only a total idiot would mess with her, and Cole didn't seem like one to me.

Ward thought about it for a second and then smirked. "Okay. Good point. You know what? I'm not going to say anything. I'm just going to ignore it and enjoy our party. Let's let them figure it out on their own." He grabbed us a pair of champagne flutes and we toasted to it. Champagne tasted a lot better when I didn't have to serve it.

"Sounds good to me. It ought to be entertaining, at the very least."

"I'll drink to that."

EPILOGUE

KATE

EMMA LOOKED gorgeous in the outfit I picked out for her. The delicate tulle of the skirt could have easily looked too cutesy on somebody so petite, but when paired with the simple silk bodysuit, the studded, metallic heels, and matching clutch and jewelry, it totally worked. She was so pretty and delicate looking that she was easy to dress, but it still felt good to see the look for her engagement party come together.

"Emma! You already look like a bride," I told her proudly, turning my finger in a circle to direct her to spin. The skirt spun out like a goddamn Disney princess when she did. It was perfection.

"Ward showed me the office," she told me after I stopped admiring her, "I can't believe you and Rae kept that from me!"

I grinned at her astonished expression. Ward was supposed to take a video of her reaction, but I would bet good money he forgot. I could still barely believe we'd pulled off the surprise. There had been several close calls, including the time that she had come home early and Ward had just carried her to the bedroom to give me time to sneak out. But she didn't need to know about that.

"You could have gone in there at literally any second," I told her in between chuckles. "I was so scared you'd go and ruin the surprise, but if we told you not to go in there, it only would have tipped you off. It was all very nerve-wracking."

She smirked and shook her head at me. "You poor thing."

"So, do you love it?" I asked anxiously.

"Oh my God, yes!" Emma cried. Her porcelain skin was flushed with happiness. Seeing her happy made me happy. I couldn't have asked for a better sister-in-law.

Our little celebration noise caught Ward's attention. He looked at us like we'd just transformed into a pair of cackling goblins.

"What's going on over there?" He said, recapturing his future bride's hand. "That noise was straight out of my nightmares."

Emma frowned. Leave it to Ward to be a huge buzz kill.

"Oh, it's because Emma's pregnant," I told him with a big, shit-eating grin on my face. "Congratulations!"

His fear was instant and total. I laughed. For a man who claimed he would never marry, he'd readjusted his thinking within months when the right woman came along. I was sure he'd adapt to having kids just fine when the time came. Emma made no secret of her desire to populate the world with little towheaded babies. Hopefully they'd get her brain.

"Stop that! Stop that! You'll give him a heart attack!" Emma scolded me, covering my poor, gullible brother's ears. She whispered something in his ears to soothe him and he relaxed. He hugged her and glared at me.

"You're evil, you know that?" he scolded.

I shrugged. "It runs in the family."

"Kate," Emma said a second later, touching my arm and looking at me seriously, "I have something really important to ask you."

Did she already find the giant dildo I hid in her bookcase? Or that one of the pictures on her gallery wall was of Rick Astley?

"Oh no, what did I do?" I asked.

Ward grinned, and Emma elbowed him. I'm sure he enjoyed watching me squirm.

"Will you be my maid of honor?" she asked, watching me eagerly for a reaction.

I made an unintelligible happy noise and threw my arms around her neck in answer. Emma's tiny size meant it was like hugging a kid and she toddled backwards on her high heels.

"Is that a yes?" Emma asked to confirm.

"Of course, it's a yes!" I replied, and then added, "Oh my God, does that mean I get to go dress shopping with you?"

Visions of lace, tulle, satin, and silk charmeuse danced in my head. Emma needed to wear a slinky style. She was built for an old Hollywood dress. Something that Vivian Leigh would have worn to the Oscars in the 1940's. Not white either, antique ivory or maybe even a light champagne gold. I could already see it coming together in my mind's eye.

Staring dreamily off into the distance as I weighed the pros and cons of a corseted style, my eyes caught on a familiar face. Cole's face. *He was staring right at me.*

In a dizzy instant, my happiness drained out of me all at once. I felt empty and lightheaded from the sudden shift.

Oh god, why didn't somebody warn me he'd be here? My own mind answered back with a snide reply, *because nobody knows about your weird, fucked-up fascination with him.* Cole was still staring at me knowingly.

"Kate?" Emma asked, following my gaze. "Are you okay?"

Well, almost nobody.

"Yeah, fine," I said, shaking my head. I needed to get away before I lost it. "I'm going to go powder my nose. Be right back."

I scuttled off and splashed cold water on my face (who the hell powders their nose?). I looked at my cowardly reflection in the mirror until I couldn't stand the sight anymore. Although I was sure I'd just given away my carefully concealed secret to Ward and Emma with my bizarre reaction, at least I was able to breathe again in the dark hallway near the bathroom. I leaned against the wall, counting to ten, then twenty, and then thirty. By the time I got to one hundred and ten, I had to admit that the counting wasn't working.

"Hey there, stalker," a familiar, humor-filled voice called to me. Cole had found me. He approached down the shadowy hallway, causing my heartbeat to race with a suicide mixture of feelings I couldn't even try to identify. "If I didn't know better, I would have thought you weren't happy to see me again."

THANK you so much for reading 'Admit You Want Me'! Keep your sweet and sexy binge going with the next book in the Lone Star Lovers series, available now!

Find out what happens when Emma's best friend Kate gets involved in a hot, secret-filled relationship with Ward's best friend Cole in 'Kiss Me Like You Missed Me'.

HOW TO GET YOUR FREE EXTENDED EPILOGUES!

IF YOU'RE LOOKING for more **free** bonus content, including exclusive extended epilogues and check-ins with your favorite characters go to www.taylorholloway.com/email.html to sign up for My Mailing List! If you're already a subscriber check the last newsletter you received, the link is always at the bottom of the email.

XOXO
Taylor

ALSO BY TAYLOR HOLLOWAY

Lone Star Lovers

1. Admit You Want Me - Ward
2. Kiss Me Like You Missed Me - Cole
3. Lie with Me - Lucas
4. Run Away with Me - Jason
5. Hold On To Me - Ryan
6. A Bad Case of You - Eric
7. Touching Me, Touching You - Christopher
8. This one's For You - Ian
9. Bad For You - Brandon (Coming Soon)

For fans of exciting, romantic mysteries full of twists and turns, check out my Scions of Sin series!

Prequel: Never Say Never - Charlie

1. Bleeding Heart - Alexander
2. Kiss and Tell - Nathan
3. Down and Dirty - Nicholas
4. Lost and Found - David

71732964R00215

Made in the
USA
Middletown, DE